Family and Friends

Emma Page first began writing as a hobby, and after a number of her poems had been accepted by the BBC and her short stories began appearing in weekly magazines, she took to writing radio plays and crime novels. She was first published in the Crime Club, which later became Collins Crime.

An English graduate from Oxford, Emma Page taught in every kind of educational establishment both in the UK and abroad before she started writing full-time.

By Emma Page

Kelsey and Lambert series

Say it with Murder
Intent to Kill
Hard Evidence
Murder Comes Calling
In the Event of My Death
Mortal Remains
Deadlock
A Violent End
Final Moments
Scent of Death
Cold Light of Day
Last Walk Home
Every Second Thursday
Missing Woman

Standalone novels

A Fortnight by the Sea (also known as
Add a Pinch of Cyanide)
Element of Chance
In Loving Memory
Family and Friends

Family and Friends

Emma Page

HARPER

This novel is entirely a work of fiction.
The names, characters and incidents portrayed in it are the work of the author's imagination. Any resemblance to actual persons, living or dead, events or localities is entirely coincidental.

Harper
An imprint of HarperCollins*Publishers*
1 London Bridge Street
London SE1 9GF

www.harpercollins.co.uk

This paperback edition 2016
1

First published in Great Britain in 1972 by Collins Crime

A catalogue record for this book is available from the British Library

ISBN: 978-0-00-817598-6

Printed and bound in Great Britain

MIX
Paper from responsible sources
FSC™ C007454

FSC™ is a non-profit international organisation established to promote the responsible management of the world's forests. Products carrying the FSC label are independently certified to assure consumers that they come from forests that are managed to meet the social, economic and ecological needs of present and future generations, and other controlled sources.

Find out more about HarperCollins and the environment at
www.harpercollins.co.uk/green

CHAPTER I

A damp and desolate afternoon in Milbourne, a hangover day filmed with the melancholy of the old year's passing.

Little swirls and eddies of fog among the grey stone streets. The yellow lights of shops half-heartedly welcoming the straggle of dispirited housewives beginning the new year as they had finished the old, plugging the gaps in the family store-cupboard against yet another week-end, another succession of mountainous meals to be consumed in the name of festivity.

In the manufacturing quarter of the town, a mile or more away from the main shopping area, Owen Yorke sat at his desk in the small cramped office on the ground floor of Underwood's. He had built the factory in the years of restriction that followed the second war.

No thought of luxury then, no concern to provide himself—the managing director and joint owner—with impressive surroundings of pale wood and a wide sweep of window, only the urgent necessity to produce, to sell, to start the wheels turning and keep them turning.

Now, twenty-five years later, success and the eternal need for expansion had brought Underwood's to the point at which the old factory would no longer do. The plans for the new building had already been approved, work was to begin on the site in a matter of weeks, as soon as the fierce grip of frost showed signs of slackening.

Owen Yorke bent his head over the plans uncurled on his desk, considering the lay-out of the storage bays. The factory was silent now, the machines idle until Monday morning brought the workers streaming in again through the gates. Only a skeleton staff in today, the man who looked after the old-fashioned heating system, a handful of clerks catching up with the paperwork, cleaners busy with mops and buckets.

Owen tilted back his chair and stared thoughtfully at the opposite wall, not seeing its clutter of charts and graphs, the gay new calendar, the framed photograph of Ralph Underwood, his father-in-law, dead now for more than a quarter of a century but still looking out from the yellowing cardboard with his habitual half-smile of tentative goodwill.

Rather astonished, old Ralph would have been, at the way his modest gown and mantle shop in the High Street had given birth to this thriving garment factory. Even more astonished if he could have run his eye over the new plans and glimpsed the magnificent edifice his son-in-law was proposing to erect on the new manufacturing estate outside Milbourne.

Owen ran a finger along his nose. Everything was going well. I'm barely fifty, he thought, I have fifteen good years of work in me, twenty perhaps with luck. He looked after himself, didn't smoke, took a drink only when the social side of business demanded it; he paid attention to his diet, found time for a round of golf now and then.

And he was respected in the town, highly thought of both as an employer and a responsible citizen. He lent his name to good causes, wrote out dutifully philanthropic cheques, had long ago taken care to join the right clubs.

He gave a little smile of satisfaction. At the next meeting of the Independents' he would be nominated as President for the coming year, elected without a voice raised in opposition. An old and locally powerful organization, the Independents', reaching out an intrusive finger into every pie worth mentioning.

As a young lad going straight from school into Ralph Underwood's gown shop, glad of any steady job in that grimly depressed time, working as general dogsbody doing everything from sweeping out the store-room to taking annual stock, he used to walk past the Independents' Club on his way home every evening. He would glance at the broad stone steps, at the weighty front door with its large knob and heavy brass knocker, and wonder if he would ever manage to storm that citadel of status and prosperity . . . And now he was going to be president.

His eyes encountered the sepia gaze of his father-in-law. I made it, old man, Owen thought with an amused lift of his shoulders. In a week or two they'll raise their glasses to me at the Independents', they'll toast Owen Yorke with his tirelessly humming machines, his fat bankroll and his well-preserved waistline—and what else besides?

He put up a hand to his face with a moment's sudden surprising shaft of sorrow, a searing sense of loss, of something valuable beyond all reckoning that had eluded him. He pressed his fingers against his forehead, forcing away emotions he had learned long ago to suppress but which had sprung up lately more than once, astounding him with their continuing existence, their vitality and power, when he had thought them withered from disuse.

Behind his closed lids he had a startlingly clear vision of young Owen Yorke, the lad from Underwood's, staring up at the lighted windows of the Independents', reaching out to grasp at dreams. He had wanted money and success all right, but he had wanted something more besides. He had wanted love, marriage, children. He had wanted happiness.

Someone rapped at the office door. Owen came at once out of his thoughts; he called a brisk 'Come in.'

'I thought you'd like some tea.' One of the female clerks smiling down at him, proffering a cup, knowing his secretary had the day off.

'Thank you, yes, I was beginning to feel thirsty.' An easy interchange between them. He had never seen the necessity for undue formality towards employees. Underwood's had started out as a little family business and a family business it remained, in spite of all the changes in the busy years.

He glanced at his wrist-watch. 'I think you might all

get off home now. Would you look into Accounts on your way, see if Mr Pierson is still there? Tell him I'd like a word with him before he goes.' Might as well raise the matter now of the High Street shop, the original gown and mantle emporium. Monday would bring its rushing tide of work, it would be easy to overlook, and the question of the shop had to be settled sooner or later.

'He's still there.' The girl paused by the door. 'I saw his light on as I came by.' It hadn't crossed her mind to take Mr Pierson a cup of tea. One of the cleaners could do that—if indeed he was to get a cup of tea at all. Not exactly a man to inspire such little courtesies. Silent, self-contained, with a brooding, occupied air, hardly the type to set a junior clerk dreaming, to strive to make him notice her with skilful interruptions and gaily tinkling trays. 'I'll tell him you'd like to see him.' She closed the door and went off towards Accounts, rapped smartly on the door panel and put her head into the room without bothering to wait for a reply.

'Mr Yorke wants a word with you.'

Arnold Pierson raised his head from the comfortingly impersonal columns of figures in whose beautifully precise ranks he was able to lose himself eight hours a day. Nothing startled about the movement of his head; he looked like a man who would never entirely be taken by surprise.

'Thank you, I'll go along right away.' He stood up with a controlled flexing of his powerful muscles; a big man, broad and well-built, dressed in utterly unremarkable clothes. He walked without haste to the managing director's room.

Owen Yorke stood by the window, looking out at the hostile afternoon with its grey wreaths of mist. He felt fully alive and expansive again, a man only now on the brink of the real adventures of life, just beginning to scratch at the huge surface of possibilities opening up before him. He was back on the plane of living where all uncomfortable, intrusive emotions were firmly battened down, away out of sight and so out of existence.

'You saw the New Year in in style, I hope?' he said to Pierson as soon as the other man was inside the door, falling at once into the briskly cheerful manner he invariably wore like an armour in his business relations.

'Hardly that.' Pierson's tone held the faintest overlay of rebuke and Owen remembered with a thrust of embarrassment that Arnold's father, old Walter Pierson, was seriously ill with influenza.

'I'm sorry, I forgot for a moment. How is your father? On the mend, I hope?' But he knew old Walter might not be expected to weather the attack. Over seventy now. He'd served in the first war with Owen's father, green lads together in that terrible baptism of fire and mud.

They'd both been decorated for a joint act of youthful heroism, crawling out one bitter night to where their mate, another local lad named Cottrell, lay helpless in a pocket of gas with half a leg blown away. They'd managed to drag young Cottrell back to safety of sorts. He'd lived another half-dozen years after that night, long enough to marry the girl who waited for him at home, long enough to father a son.

Arnold shook his head. 'Dr Gethin isn't very hopeful.' He let the answer lie there, unqualified by any easy optimism. He stood with his hands hanging by his sides, waiting for Yorke to say what he wanted to see him about.

Owen dropped into his chair, indicating with a gesture that Pierson should sit down.

'It's about the shop.'

Arnold leaned back in his seat with a little movement of relaxation, as if he had expected Yorke to raise some other, trickier, matter. 'I imagine you've decided it will have to be closed.' His mouth twitched with a hint of amusement. 'And you're not too anxious to tell Sarah so.'

Sarah Pierson managed the shop; she was Arnold's stepsister, older than himself by ten or eleven years. Her father had been a first cousin of old Walter Pierson's. Walter's wife had died of pneumonia when Arnold was still a child in a push-chair, and Sarah's mother, herself widowed a couple of years, had naturally enough given Walter a hand with the rearing of his son. The two houses were in neighbouring streets; she had drifted into the habit of doing the washing, then the shopping and cooking, finally drifting into marrying Walter, moving her furniture and her daughter across the intervening couple of hundred yards.

Arnold had no memory whatever of his own mother but he remembered his father's second wife with the deep attachment of a son. It might have been nothing more romantic than convenience, habit and old acquaintance that had prompted Walter to slip a gold ring on the finger of Sarah's mother but there had been someone after all in the trim semi-detached house to offer her strong and unwavering love.

Arnold had been in a Japanese prison camp when he heard the news of her death. The war was already over, the prisoners waiting for repatriation, when the letter had come, six months out of date. The thought of her had kept him going, he had dreamed in the humid nights of walking up the narrow path to where she stood smiling in the doorway. And she had lain for more than six months in the cold earth of the municipal cemetery with a marble stone at her head and an urn of flowers at her feet.

None of it had mattered any more, the homecoming, the medal—for someone in authority had appeared to think that Arnold had earned a decoration at some moment in that incredible time—the piece in the Milbourne paper, his father's hand resting proudly on his shoulder.

The only thing that had come through to him in those phantom weeks had been the realization that however long he lived, in joy and happiness or in wretchedness and despair, he would never see her again. And as it hadn't much mattered what he did or where he went, he had stayed in

Milbourne, had taken a job in the new factory Owen Yorke was beginning to get under way.

'You know the shop isn't making much money these days,' Owen said now with a deprecating movement of his hands. 'You've seen the accounts. It hasn't done really well for the last few years. Ever since . . .' Ever since Zena Yorke had ceased to take an active interest in it.

Owen fell silent for a moment, thinking with recurring astonishment of the change that had come over Zena with the onset of middle age. The prettiness of youth—and she had been pretty, with curling blonde hair and lively blue eyes—had totally disappeared.

The blue eyes, faded now, veiled with chronic discontent, looked out at him these days from a pale and puffy face, the once-delicate skin heavily powdered, patterned with a fine hatching of lines. The slim curves of her figure had vanished beneath distorting layers of slackened flesh. And the self-indulgent years of over-eating, over-drinking, increasing idleness, had brought ill-health in their inexorable train.

But Owen hadn't the slightest intention of discussing his wife with Arnold Pierson. Some deep-lying part of his mind was aware that if he ever took it into his head to examine closely the exact nature of the relationship between Pierson and Zena, he might very well uncover matters that were better left concealed.

He set a high value on his own peace of mind and so he very firmly declined to probe, entrenching himself instead—as far as possible—behind a deliberate attitude of detached pity for the woman who had been the girl he had loved and married.

'Don't think I'm in any way criticizing your sister's management of the shop,' Owen said. 'But it doesn't fit in with the way the business has developed.' Owen had never had a passionate interest in retail selling; what he liked was manufacturing. He concentrated now entirely on the production of ladies' coats and suits; Sarah Pierson bought in dresses from the wholesalers, together with knitwear and lingerie, scarves, handbags and a host of other fashion accessories.

'You've definitely decided to close the shop then?' Arnold didn't much relish the prospect of breaking the news to Sarah. She had spent her entire working life behind the double glass doors, forty-four devoted years, beginning as an apprentice alteration hand in the days when Ralph Underwood managed the business himself and his daughter Zena was playing with coloured building blocks in her first year at kindergarten.

Owen nodded. 'Sarah still has a couple of years to go till the normal retirement age but there'd be no difficulty about that. Her pension will start as soon as the shop is closed down.' He allowed himself to contemplate for an instant the fact that it wasn't going to be a very magnificent pension. It was based on the salary Sarah received and as that salary had been fixed by Zena, it wasn't exactly princely.

Sarah had never complained and probably thought she was well enough paid when she remembered the wage she had started out with. Her living expenses can't be all that large, Owen thought, I imagine she lives rent-free with old Walter, probably doesn't even have to pay for her food, gets it all for nothing in return for looking after the two men. And if Walter Pierson shouldn't recover from his bout of influenza—well then, there'd be a little money coming to her there, no doubt, and a half-share in the house too, most likely.

He had been on the verge of adding that a lump sum of a year's salary would be paid over to Sarah in addition to the pension but he saw now quite clearly that she wouldn't in the least need such a sum.

'She'll be fifty-eight on the first of February,' Arnold said suddenly. It struck him all at once as a cheerless sort of age. 'Do you want me to break it to her about the shop or will you do it?'

'If you could have a word with her—I'm afraid it's going to be a bit of a blow to her, no getting away from that, but it might soften the blow, coming from you.'

'I don't know about that.' Arnold looked at Owen with a trace of amusement. 'But I'll speak to her, if that's what you want.'

Developers were already at work in Milbourne. A property in the High Street could be converted into a supermarket or simply torn down to make way for a new office building. Owen didn't much care what happened to old Ralph's emporium. It had served his purpose once but was now of no further use to him and so would be dismissed without a single pang of sentimental regret.

And the money it would fetch would be more than welcome. The expansion of Underwood's had brought with it a massive need for more capital and in these days of credit restriction many of the conventional sources of fresh capital had inconveniently dried up.

'She can retire on her birthday,' Owen said. 'That would seem to be convenient all round. She can make the January sale a closing-down sale now,' he added. 'Any stock that's left over can be jobbed off to some other dress shop in the town.' To Linda Fleming, for instance, he thought suddenly, seeing with a surprising leap of pleasure a clear picture of the young widow with her soft dark hair and gentle hazel eyes, kneeling in the window of her little shop, arranging a trail of artfully crumpled material at the foot of the display stands.

He would have been astounded to know that Arnold was also contemplating a mental vision of Mrs Fleming, only in Arnold's mind she was smiling up at him from the other side of the counter in her trim establishment, offering him advice about a purchase. I could call in on the way home, Arnold thought with an agreeable flash of inspiration, I could buy something for Sarah's birthday.

He stole a glance at his watch. He could clear off in a few minutes, as soon as he'd locked up in Accounts; Mrs

Fleming would be sure to stay open till half past five at least. She'd taken the shop over only a few weeks before, coming to Milbourne as a stranger, from some town on the east coast; she couldn't afford just yet to close early during holiday seasons.

'One other thing before you go,' Owen said. 'The date of the annual audit—' He broke off as the phone rang sharply on his desk, he reached out and picked up the receiver.

Arnold made a movement to go, leaving him to take the call in privacy but Yorke halted him with a raised hand. Arnold settled back again into his chair, expelling a little breath of resignation at the swift march of time towards the closing of Mrs Fleming's shop.

'Won't be a moment,' Yorke said softly above the shielded mouthpiece. 'It's Zena.' He withdrew his hand and stared down at his desk with an impassive face, listening to his wife's voice.

'I expected you home long before this, I've been waiting for the tonic, you promised to call in for it. You know I'm not at all well . . .' Owen closed his eyes for an instant, blocking off part of his mind against the familiar outpourings, recalling with guilty irritation that he had totally forgotten about the tonic.

He gave a barely perceptible sigh. If Zena would only take herself in hand and behave with some modicum of common sense, if she would for once in her life follow Dr Gethin's exasperated advice, cut down on the over-rich and fattening food, cut out the alcohol, stop dosing herself with useless patent medicines, make sure she got eight hours' sleep at night and sufficient fresh air and exercise by day, she might not be able to cure entirely her largely self-inflicted diabetes and its attendant train of disabilities, but she would at least be able to control it, to bring it down to manageable proportions, she might even be able to dispense with the insulin injections.

As it was, she was slipping further into invalidism. She

had already ended up twice in the Milbourne hospital in a diabetic coma, the second time only last September.

'You've had a pretty narrow escape this time,' Gethin had told her with angry bluntness when she was sufficiently well again to be lectured. 'You'll indulge yourself once too often, my girl. If you go on as you are doing, there'll be a coma one fine day that no one can pull you out of.' He had brought Zena into the world and he still treated her as the spoiled child she had been when her parents were alive. As indeed she still was, Owen had thought, standing behind Dr Gethin with an expressionless face, listening to the warnings they both knew would be blandly ignored.

'I could lie in my bed and die for all the notice you take of me,' Zena said now over the phone, well into her customary recital of grievances. Owen passed a hand over his face. Could be she feels she's no longer the focus of attention, Gethin had said to Owen more than once. A beautiful young woman like that, cherishing parents, a younger brother to trot about at her beck and call all through their sunny childhood. It isn't easy, Gethin's attitude implied, when the years take away youth and good looks. The parents go one by one . . . no children to absorb the energies, to engage the emotions . . . and Neil, the adoring young brother Zena had without effort dominated and overshadowed for so long, Neil had grown up in the end, had acquired a wife and daughter of his own to claim his affections.

Gethin had given Owen a direct look. Only a husband left to her, Gethin's glance had said. Can it be that she stage-manages this illness to throw a spotlight on herself once more, to give her back the centre of the well-loved boards? Might explain perhaps why she sometimes 'forgot' to take the injections, precipitating an occasional dramatic crisis, the need to be rushed into hospital.

Owen had given the doctor look for look. You've been acquainted with her since the day of her birth, his eyes had answered, but you don't know her. She doesn't love me, she has never loved me, I realized years ago that she didn't even love me when she stood beside me at the altar.

What she did love, what she married me for, was the depth and intensity of the love I felt for her. She basked in the warmth of its fires, she felt herself important and secure in the fierce glow of a passion she thought would last all her days—but it never once occurred to her that there was any need to return it. It had survived countless thrusts and wounds, he remembered now with a savage resentment that took him by surprise.

He gripped the receiver tightly, oblivious of Pierson motionless in his chair, no longer bothering to identify the substance of his wife's complaints, plunged into the bitter past, assailed by the stabs and hurts of memories he had fancied decently interred and forgotten.

It had been a long and painful time in dying, that old and powerful love, but it had died at last, completely and for ever, closing its eyes in the end against the renewal of intolerable suffering.

'You could have asked Emily Bond to go out and get the tonic,' he said suddenly into Zena's fluent stream of words. 'She's still with you, isn't she? You could send her out now if you're so anxious to have it.'

'Emily? She's behind enough in her work as it is, without breaking off to go running errands in the town.' Zena was deflected into an angry appraisal of the old charwoman's shortcomings.

She had worked for Zena right from the Yorkes' wedding-day. In all the difficult times when domestic help had grown scarce and then almost unobtainable she had turned up faithfully, week in and week out. She might not have been the most skilled of workers but she had always been there. She was turned seventy now and old age had done nothing to improve her efficiency—but she was still there, and that, Owen thought, defensive on Emily's behalf, was surely something.

'I'll be home shortly,' he said abruptly, abandoning suddenly all further resistance. 'I'll bring the tonic with me, I won't forget.' He replaced the receiver and sat looking down at it for a few moments, his face set in lines of anger and frustration.

'I'll be locking up, then,' Arnold said at last, confident that Yorke had forgotten all about the date of the audit which could surely now be left till Monday to discuss. He pushed back his chair and stood up. 'You'll be wanting to get off home yourself.' There was still time to call in at Mrs Fleming's shop; the encounter would cast a glow over the whole evening, would extend its gentle radiance across the entire week-end.

'Oh—yes. Right ho, then.' Owen got to his feet, pulled back to the present. 'If you let me know on Monday—about your sister, that you've briefed her.' He had some elusive notion that there was something else he'd intended to mention, but he couldn't recall it now. He raised his shoulders, letting it go till after the week-end. 'I hope you find your father improved,' he remembered to say as Pierson opened the door to make his escape.

When the door closed again Owen crossed to the row of hooks on the wall by the window and jerked down his overcoat.

He glanced at his watch—better get a move on, the shops would be closing soon and he didn't relish the thought of Zena's welcome if he arrived home without the precious tonic.

But he didn't immediately shrug his coat on. He stood looking out of the window at the descending twilight, at a couple of gaily chattering girls released from the typing pool to the pleasures of the week-end. To boy-friends and lovers, dates and parties, he thought with a startling wash of envy that held him motionless, his eyes fixed on the graceful girls with their lovely fluid movements.

He watched them out of sight in the uncertain dusk. I'm not old, he thought, I could marry again, and the words dropped one by one into the depths of his mind with the slowness and finality of a decision that has been a long and shadowy time in forming.

He turned and stared at his unsmiling features in the mirror above the mantelpiece, seeing the face of a man in his prime. I could marry again, he repeated silently, and the moment seemed to illumine his future with a great shaft of glittering light. I could have children. He had always wanted children; he had neither comprehended nor forgiven Zena's unwavering refusal even to countenance the idea. And now he saw that it was still not too late. A vast wave of joy swept through him, momentarily blinding him to the problem of Zena, who was scarcely likely to be reasonable about making way for a successor when she had been reasonable about little else.

He saw himself holding a child by the hand, he saw other children laughing and calling from a summer garden. And the face that he saw smiling out at him from that flowering doorway was the gentle, pretty face of Linda Fleming.

In the corridor outside his office a cleaner rattled a bucket down on to the floor and the sound brought him abruptly back to reality. He picked up a bunch of keys and moved swiftly round the room, locking up for the night. One or two calls to be made on the way home.

Zena, he thought, there's something I have to get for Zena . . . He stopped suddenly, frowning, remembering, looking down at his arrested hands for an endless moment. Then he straightened himself, raised his head and met his own intent gaze in the mirror.

CHAPTER II

Arnold Pierson strode between the last of the shoppers, his mind as usual engaged on the convolutions of his own inner life which seemed a good deal more vivid than the shadowy figures moving past on the edge of his vision.

In the middle of the High Street he was forced to step into the gutter with its crisp heaps of slatternly snow, to give passage to a couple of gossiping women pushing prams.

The momentary interruption to his progress broke through his preoccupation. He glanced about him as he stepped back on to the pavement and saw that he was outside Underwood's. He paused in front of the lighted windows. A couple of discreet stickers announced the sale due to begin on Monday morning. A girl knelt behind the plate glass with her back to him, pinning a ticket to the skilfully draped bodice of a dinner-gown in sage-green crêpe.

No sign of his stepsister of course; Sarah's exalted position as manageress had long ago removed her from any necessity to crouch before the public gaze and arrange in artistic folds the skirts of last season's models. But she wouldn't be barricaded away behind her office door, conducting the business by remote control; that was never Sarah's way. She would be moving along the carpeted aisles, keeping a sharp eye on the manners and attitudes of her assistants, or taking up her position behind one of the mahogany-topped counters, to serve a valued customer.

She would remain after the sign on the front door had been reversed to read *Closed*, dealing efficiently with the books, the orders, the monthly accounts; she would be the last person to leave the premises. Not even old Walter Pierson's illness would cause her to go home so much as ten minutes early.

For a good many years now she had employed a woman

for a few hours every day to clean the house, wash the breakfast dishes and in general perform the bulk of the chores that Sarah herself in her younger days had somehow managed to attend to in addition to a full-time job. Over the past couple of weeks she had simply arranged for the woman to stay all day, looking after Walter as well as the house.

Arnold put up a hand and ran a finger along his cheek, inclining his head and frowning down at the pavement, trying to visualize Sarah suddenly set free from the compulsion to open the front door at eight every morning, in fair weather and foul, and make her way to the warm, enclosed world of Underwood's.

She had worked hard all her life. Would she see retirement now as a long-yearned-for release? Or would she feel herself all at once grown old and useless, banished from the absorbing bustle of commerce to a suburban desert?

Arnold shook his head slowly in bafflement. He simply didn't know. Forty years since Sarah had followed her mother up the path into Walter Pierson's house and Arnold still could never guess with any certainty how Sarah would feel or think about anything important. She never quarrelled with him but neither did she ever laugh or joke with him. If the two of them sat together in a room without talking, it wouldn't be a companionable silence but the total deadness of a couple of switched-off radio sets.

The kneeling girl put out a hand and steadied herself against a display stand. She turned her head to glance out at the last of the afternoon and her eyes met those of Arnold, unwaveringly fixed on her without seeing her, looking back down the long slope of years at some childish memory of Sarah jerking him along to school in the grey of winter and the blue of summer, on her way to work.

The girl blinked, disconcerted and a little alarmed by the intent quality of that gaze, at once piercing and veiled. She drew her brows together in irritation at the queer fish staring in at her goldfish-bowl activities and then, suddenly recognizing the watcher in his dual identity of Miss Pierson's brother and accountant at Underwood's, did her best to transform her expression into one of professional friendliness.

A whirling eddy of icy air stung the blood into Arnold's cheeks, whisking him back from the gate of that far-off infant school to the yellow lights of the January evening, to the melancholy plateau of middle age and the abrupt recollection that if he was going to catch Mrs Fleming before closing-time, he had better get a move on. He turned from the window, totally unaware of the girl and her nod of recognition. His long strides took him in another minute or two to the top of the High Street, down a side turning, past another intersection, and into the quieter road that led to Linda Fleming's establishment.

It was still open, he saw as he approached. The lights shone out into the street and a woman who had been studying the window display walked without haste into the shop. Arnold halted in front of the polished panes adorned with a long streamer proclaiming a sale shortly to begin. Between the bright dresses and the trim coats he could see into the shop above the partition that reached only halfway up the back of the window.

Linda Fleming's pretty profile as she leaned forward, listening earnestly to her customer's requirements. Her soft dark hair was taken up in a casual swirl on top of her neat head; he could see the gleam of a large tortoiseshell slide that held the tresses in position. Behind the opposite counter a young girl reached up to a shelf, restoring boxes of knitwear to an orderly appearance.

Mrs Fleming pulled open a long drawer and took out a brilliant assortment of silk scarves, spreading them out before her one by one, lifting a corner to allow the shimmering material to drape into delicate folds. The customer assumed an expression of intense thoughtfulness. She'll be there for four or five minutes yet, Arnold thought with a vast sense of relief. No need to walk inside just yet.

He was seized with a powerful impulse to flee. That trim dark head with its puffs and curls, those finely-wrought features, that gentle smile, seemed all at once to represent danger, the terrifying possibility of intimate involvement on a deep and intolerably sensitive level with another human being. He glanced up the road, at the drifts of fog deepening about the street-lamps, and the path to safety seemed also to lead to a dull and deadly emptiness. He had a brief, bleak vision of the days ahead, with his father gone and Sarah sunk into apathetic retirement. He closed his eyes for an instant against that appalling picture, the two of them locked in a silent vacuum for ten, twenty, thirty years.

He stared in again at Mrs Fleming, smiling and chatting to her customer, at her hands moving lightly between the patterned silks, and he saw those hands now as holding not only the threat of danger but the impossible notion of happiness.

He drew a deep breath and began to search the window display with his eyes, looking for something he might buy for Sarah's birthday. He had bought her Christmas present from Mrs Fleming, nerving himself to enter the little shop and strengthen the slender connection with the pretty new proprietress—he had met her for the first time at the factory, when she had called in to view the sample garments and place a small order.

Owen Yorke had come across her at a social gathering of one of the trade federations of which he was a distinguished member. She had joined every organization that seemed to offer assistance; she was not very long widowed, inexperienced in business, a stranger to Milbourne, desperately anxious to make a success of her new venture. Owen Yorke had taken her under his wing, offered to advise her, invited her to take a look at his factory.

And the only thing Arnold Pierson had been able to think of, having no factory to show her round, had been to buy Sarah's Christmas present at Mrs Fleming's shop. There had been several customers at the time, Linda had been able to give him no more than a few minutes' half-abstracted attention. He had bought a handbag, careless of the fact that Sarah already had three or four handbags more than she would ever have occasion to use, and that her own shop held several drawers stuffed with handbags of every conceivable shape and material.

Not that Sarah had expressed either irritation or exasperated amusement at the gift; she had in fact expressed nothing at all beyond the ritual words of thanks with which she had received presents all her life.

In the whole of her existence no living soul had ever wrinkled an anxious brow over a Christmas or birthday offering for her. She had always been given—when she had been given anything at all—something chosen dutifully and swiftly, any pleasure or usefulness resulting from the occasion being entirely accidental. She invariably made her own annual purchases on the same obscure principles, having grown up with the conviction that this was the way the system operated between relatives and she had never had a sweetheart or indeed a close personal friend, male or female, to cause her to review the system in the fierce glow of love or affection.

Arnold swept his eye over the jersey suits, the fur-collared coats, the Shetland sweaters, rejecting them all. But he frowned in determination, resolved now to buy *something,* even, if all other inspiration deserted him, another expensive and useless handbag.

Inside the shop, Linda Fleming admired her customer's choice, wrapped it in gay paper and uttered a farewell comment on the harsh weather.

'You can lock up now, Iris,' she said to her assistant as soon as the door had pinged behind the departing customer. 'I don't think Mrs Bond can be coming. She ought to have been here ten minutes ago.' She sighed, tired from the long day and the unreliability of her charwoman. 'Not that she's all that much use when she does come.' She sighed again. 'I wish I could hear of somebody younger.' Old, erratic, no longer sufficiently competent, Mrs Bond did at least turn up from time to time. She was better than no one at all; it would be folly to dispense with her limited services before a more vigorous and willing replacement could be found.

Iris bustled about the shop, straightening it for the night. 'I'd stay myself and do a bit of cleaning for you,' she offered with the cheerfulness of one who knows this is out of the question. 'But you know how it is at home, with Mum in bed and the kids to see to.' Her mother had been laid low by the influenza that was beginning to sweep through Milbourne and there was a limit to how far neighbours could be called on when their own families were afflicted.

'Yes, I know, I wasn't dropping a hint, it was good of you to offer.' Linda hoped fervently that the influenza wouldn't claim Iris as its next victim, leaving her to struggle along without an assistant as well as a charwoman. 'Wrap up well, it's bitterly cold outside.'

Iris reversed the sign behind the glass panel of the door. 'Oh—there's another customer.' She glanced at Linda. 'Shall I let him in? It's past closing-time.'

The look of weariness dissolved from Linda's face and was at once replaced by a professional air of welcome.

'Open the door,' she said briskly. 'I'll serve him.' She was as yet in no position to turn away any customer, however late or dilatory. 'You get off for your bus.'

Iris flung open the door and Arnold found himself inside the shop with his heart thumping and Mrs Fleming smiling at him with friendly recognition.

'It's Mr Pierson, isn't it?' The card-index of her mind threw up the relevant details. Accountant at Underwood's, an expensive leather handbag bought just before Christmas —and the eyes, she had docketed the memory of those eyes, dark and brooding, a hint of some granite-like quality and yet at the same time a suggestion of powerful feeling restrained by iron control.

'I hope Miss Pierson liked the handbag?' Linda was longing for a cup of tea, fervently wishing he would get to the point so that she could serve him and lock up.

'Oh, yes, she was delighted with it.' Even as he spoke the words Arnold realized the incongruity of the word *delighted* in connection with Sarah. But actually giving tongue seemed to free some block in his paralysed brain. 'It's her birthday soon.' He glanced vaguely about the shelves and stands. 'I want to get her something.'

Iris had struggled into her coat and tied a scarf round her head. 'I'll be off then. See you in the morning.' She pulled on her gloves and picked up her bag. 'I hope Mrs Bond turns up after all.' She jerked the door open and let herself out into the icy air.

'Preferably something she hasn't got in her own shop,' Arnold said rapidly, realizing with a stab of panic that he was now alone with Mrs Fleming and anxious only to buy something, anything at all, and clear out.

Linda narrowed her eyes in thought, running over in her mind the contents of drawers and cupboards. It occurred to her that it would have been far more sensible for Mr Pierson to have visited an entirely different kind of shop for his sister's present, one that bore no resemblance whatsoever to Underwood's. Flowers, chocolates, books, there were a hundred and one gifts he might have chosen without any difficulty about picking something Miss Pierson might have in her own stock. It suddenly struck her that the birthday present might be merely an excuse, that he had some other reason for propelling himself through her door. A half-formed notion rose in her brain: could it conceivably be that he fancied her?

The idea startled her, flinging up all at once into her mind a vision of Pierson holding her in a fierce embrace, bending his head to hers. She had an almost physical sensation of his arms around her, of the warmth of his face against her cheek. She shook her head with a small, abrupt movement, with difficulty blinking away the disconcerting image.

'I see your point.' She tried to smile at him and found to her surprise that her lips were trembling slightly. He was looking at her so intently that she was seized with a feeling that he might at any moment stride round the counter and take hold of her. 'It would never do to buy her something like gloves or—' She broke off; she had been about to say, 'or a handbag' when she remembered that it was a handbag he had bought at Christmas. Miss Pierson's stock surely held dozens, hundreds of handbags. So his last visit had also, in all probability, been a pretext.

'Or a cardigan.' She finished her sentence, still contriving to maintain an air of casual ease. 'We must try to think of something a little different.' She was briefly aware that her tiredness had vanished; she felt alive, stimulated, no longer irked by the threat of the chores relentlessly awaiting her as soon as he had gone. She turned and surveyed the shelves. 'Now let me see—' It certainly wasn't Iris who had drawn him to this quiet street; he hadn't so much as glanced at the girl, had scarcely seemed aware of her existence.

Inspiration struck her. 'I know!' She raised a hand. 'I've just remembered.' She threw him a triumphant look. 'There's some pottery, hand-made, quite good pieces, ornaments, vases, book-ends. I took it over with the rest of the stock. It's in one of the store-rooms, at the back.' She jerked her head towards the curtained archway. 'Would you like to come through and take a look at it? I'm sure you'd find something your sister would like.'

Arnold saw the precipice yawn before him. Another step and he would be plunged into a void of rushing darkness. He tilted his head back, knowing the door behind him. He had only to smile and say, 'I'm afraid not, Sarah doesn't really care for pottery, I'm sorry to have wasted your time—' and he could be at the other side of the door, drawing a breath of relief, alone, unthreatened . . . and headed back towards the bleak and solitary wastes of freedom.

'Thank you, I'd like to see the pieces. If you're sure I'm not keeping you too late.' He was astounded to discover his heart had steadied itself. In place of the black chasm he had an impression of sunlight, birdsong, green and blue spaces, the cradling warmth of idle summer air.

'Not at all.' She smiled at him as if she really didn't mind, her voice seemed to hold a note of genuine pleasure. 'But I will just secure the door.' She came round the end of the counter. 'In case anyone else wants to come in.' She snicked the catch and the sense of alarm that always invaded him when a key turned or a bolt barred his way, faded almost as soon as he recognized its customary thrust. He was aware instead of a delicious feeling of being shut in with her in a pleasant and gentle world.

She led the way through the arch, along a narrow passage and into a store-room.

A couple of long rails holding dresses veiled in transparent covers; brown-paper bundles tied with string; cardboard boxes, bales of knitting-wool. 'I'm afraid it's not very tidy, I haven't had time to go through everything properly yet.' She opened a cupboard to disclose rows of vases, bowls, figurines. 'I haven't made up my mind what to do with all this. It dates back a good many years, to when it was a fancy-goods shop. I thought I might try a few pieces in the sale. If they don't go, I might sell the whole lot to one of the stores with a china department.' She began to lift out jars and dishes, setting them down on a table.

'Let me help you.' He came and stood beside her. She caught the damp moorland smell of his tweed overcoat; his sleeve brushed against her arm as he reached among the shelves. 'Yes, I like this. Good shapes and colours.' He ran a hand over the fine glaze of an oval platter decorated in soft greens and browns, touching it delicately and caressingly.

She watched the slow movement of his fingers and a strange sensation crept over her, an agreeable, dreamy feeling as if all her cares were being soothed away, as if she were being gently lulled to sleep by the touch of a hand stroking her shoulders, the back of her neck.

Somewhere in the town a church clock struck the quarters. She drew a little sighing breath, with an effort forcing away the insidious image. She took a couple of steps towards the door.

'If you'd like to look over the rest of the pottery, I'll make a cup of tea. It won't take long.' He was standing with his back to her; he said nothing, merely nodded to show he'd heard. 'But please don't feel in any way obliged to make a choice. If you don't find anything really suitable, just say so.' He nodded again and she walked briskly away to the kitchen, relieved to find an everyday normality return to her.

She put the kettle on to boil and went through into the little sitting-room to take cups and saucers of flowered china from the glass-fronted cabinet. On a side table her dead husband smiled at her from a holiday beach enclosed in a silver frame. She levelled a long look at the handsome face arrested in perpetual youth while the eroding years hurried her remorselessly forward to the desert of middle age.

She set the china on a tray and carried it back to the kitchen. Milk and sugar, teaspoons, a small plate of fancy biscuits. She dropped into a chair and sat with her elbows propped on the table, her chin resting on her clasped hands, staring at the row of green and white canisters on the dresser but seeing in the recesses of her brain Owen Yorke getting to his feet behind his desk as she came into his office at the factory. Holding out his hand, a look of pleasure on his face.

A successful man, clearly ambitious still of further success, by no means old, a position of some consequence in Milbourne, no son or daughter to be taken into account . . . though surely a man in Yorke's position, whether naturally fond of children or not, might wish now he had an heir to succeed to the business he had fostered with such unremitting toil.

And Zena Yorke . . . fat and faded, gone to seed . . . Linda had never clapped eyes on Zena but Emily Bond was as fond of gossip as the rest of her kind while growing yearly less fond of Mrs Yorke with her chronic ill-temper and nagging criticisms. 'Can't think why Mr Yorke puts up with her,' Emily had said, leaning on her mop in Linda Fleming's kitchen. 'He'll up and leave her one of these fine days, mark my words, and no one'd blame him.' She plunged the mop-head into the soapy water, frowning, pursing her lips. 'If she doesn't kill herself first, that is.'

'Kill herself?' Linda had turned in the doorway, startled.

'Digging her grave with her teeth.' Emily thrust the mop at the red-tiled floor. 'Eating and drinking all day long. And her with her complaint. Sugar in the water.' She lifted the mop and squeezed the cotton tufts with aged fierceness. 'Beats me why that Doctor Gethin don't make her see sense.' She slapped the mop into the bucket. 'Not that I'd have him for my doctor.'

'Why? Is he no good?' Gethin was no more than a name to Linda.

Mrs Bond raised her shoulders. 'Good enough in his day. But he's past it now. Don't know why he hangs on, ought to retire. Doesn't really care any more.'

The thought of Mrs Bond jerked Linda back to the present moment and the recollection of the cleaning still to be done. She got to her feet with a last lingering memory of Owen Yorke and the pressure of his fingers, a little longer, a little stronger than altogether necessary. 'Only too happy to advise you,' he'd said, his tone edged with implication. 'I'll look in on you when I'm passing.'

The kettle was still some way from boiling; Linda clicked her tongue in momentary irritation at the lowness of the gas-pressure. She went along to the store-room with rapid footsteps. Arnold was contemplating three items he had separated from the others.

'I like these best,' he said as she came in. 'I find it difficult to choose between them. Which do you prefer?'

'Oh, the dish,' she said at once, not wishing to prolong the discussion, already regretting her offer of tea, hoping he would say he couldn't wait any longer, would take himself off with his disturbing presence, allow her to forget that curious moment when she had stood beside him. 'It has beautiful lines.'

'Very well then, I'll take the dish.' He didn't pick it up so she was compelled to move forward and reach out for it. There was a long moment in which they stood side by side. 'There's a theatre in Milbourne,' Arnold said suddenly. 'I don't know if you've been to it yet, it's supposed to be rather good.' He had never set foot inside the Milbourne theatre. The last time he had seen any kind of stage performance had been in the dispersal camp at the end of the war.

He had sat in his misery and wretchedness under the glittering stars, islanded by guilt and bitter self-reproach, unable to join in the defiantly cheerful singing, to applaud the antics of a line of half-starved troopers decked out as chorus-girls with simulated bosoms and costumes fashioned from the rags and tatters of survival. He had never, until this moment, felt any desire to enter a theatre again.

'There's a comedy thriller on at present.' He mentioned the name of the play; he had no difficulty in recalling it, he passed the theatre every day. He was almost certain Linda would smile and accept his invitation. He had felt the current flow between them as they looked at the ranks of ornaments. 'I think it would be easy enough to get seats.'

For an instant he allowed himself to nurse the wild hope that it would be possible one day to lay his head in her lap and tell her the whole story of that searing time. Every last scarring detail, holding nothing back, purging himself totally and finally of the corrosive poison that ate away his peace of mind, prevented him from walking under the wide skies in easy acceptance of life and all that it might bring.

He clenched his fists and slackened them again, letting

the mad notion of absolving confession fall from him. Once and only once in the long silent years he had given way to the urge to speak, but that once had been more than enough; he had regretted it bitterly ever since.

It was not very long after he had begun to work for Owen Yorke in the new factory. He had felt for a brief period the shadowy possibility of a fresh start. And he had met Zena again. She had been the beautiful goddess of his boyhood, she had tolerated his youthful worship, allowing him to dance attendance on her till the third year of the war had swept him up and away from Milbourne. Owen Yorke had escaped military service; some minor physical incapacity that hadn't prevented him from working energetically for Ralph Underwood. Most of the eligible young men vanished from the town but Owen remained. Zena had married him—for what was more natural? Passionately in love with her, indispensable to her father and above all, always there.

By the time Arnold came back to Milbourne after the war she had grown a little bored, more than a little restless. Her cherishing parents were now dead, Owen was absorbed in his schemes for expansion, her brother had been conscripted for National Service. In the running of her home and management of the shop she was hedged about with the frustrating restrictions of austerity; the social life of Milbourne had dwindled almost to extinction.

And Arnold had changed. He had grown into a silent rock of a man with a suggestion of suppressed forces that she found immensely intriguing. It had amused her in those idle autumn days, gusty with spattered rain or melancholy with blue-grey smoke drifting from careful bonfires, to puff a delicate breath into embers that looked greyly dead.

Arnold, struggling to orientate himself in a post-war Milbourne at once reassuringly familiar and alien with bewildering change, like the landscape of home glimpsed in a nightmare, had felt the devouring heat of the flames. He had flung open his arms, his heart, his soul, to Zena, believing for a brief delusive season that he had broken out of the terrifying vacuum that had enveloped him for so long.

He had kept nothing back from her; the savage horrors of that inhuman questioning that had gone on and on, the torrid nights slipping unperceived into scorching days—even now the mere mention of the word *interrogation* had power to pierce his mind with terror. He had opened his mouth at last and told his captors what they wanted to know. He had no actual memory of the words he'd used; consciousness had come and gone in clouds of pain. But the beatings had ceased abruptly; he had been carried back to the hut and dumped among the others, to recover as best he might.

Two days later word had filtered through the camp, B Company taken by surprise at night, three-quarters of them wiped out. Men he had known, had joked with.

No one had connected the news with himself; there had never been a look, a word of accusation, spoken or unspoken. He had been his own judge and warder, serving ever since his unending sentence of isolation, knowledge, remorse and guilt.

Now he stared straight ahead with a fixed look, not seeing the crowded rails and high-stacked shelves of Linda Fleming's store-room, remembering with a bitter thrust of emotion how Zena had inclined her head, had listened, had put out her hand and taken his with a gentle touch that had seemed to offer both healing and a promise.

'I'm not all that fond of thrillers,' Linda said in a casual tone. She began to wrap the dish, swiftly, neatly. 'And I don't get a great deal of spare time at the moment, as I'm sure you'll understand.'

Arnold made no reply; he didn't appear to have heard her. The lines of his face were harshly set, his eyes maintained their rigid gaze. A faint ripple of apprehension moved across her consciousness.

'It's very kind of you to invite me.' She hesitated, undecided whether to add a conventionally polite reference to some other evening. Better not, instinct warned her; let things lie. 'I hope you enjoy the play,' she added lightly.

Arnold jerked his attention away from his mental picture of Zena. Some mechanism in his brain sprang into action, playing over at once its faithful recording of Linda's utterance, allowing him to register the fact that she had refused his invitation. He smiled at her without reproach.

'I quite understand.' He wasn't overwhelmingly disappointed, recognizing now with habitual acceptance that he had never really expected anything else.

Linda held the parcel out to him. In spite of the gentler look that still turned his mouth up in a half smile, he seemed to her a man capable of anything, violent action, a sudden release of pent-up forces—even heroism.

'I hope your sister likes the present.'

'Yes, I'm sure she will,' Arnold said abstractedly. He felt the walls of the room begin to advance upon him as they sometimes did in palpitating nightmares even now, more than a quarter of a century after he had turned his head and looked for the last time at those miserable ranks of prison huts.

'If you'd like to come into the shop—' Linda walked smoothly and swiftly into the passage and through the arch. 'The dish is three pounds,' she said with impersonal pleasantness.

He drew a five-pound note from his wallet and laid it on the polished wood, withdrawing his hand immediately. Another man, Linda thought suddenly, taking the note and ringing up the till, any other man who had just made a pass at her, would have seized the opportunity to touch her fingers. But this man no longer even looked at her.

A sense of his absolute loneliness struck at her, his acceptance of rejection as normal and customary; she was all at once aware of the effort it must have cost him to ask her out. She stood, briefly irresolute, washed over by a flood of compassion. And then she sighed and gave a tiny shake of her head. There was simply no place for him in the pattern of her life.

'But I'll take off ten per cent because of the sale,' she added.

'Thank you.' His voice was brisker now, he could breathe more easily in the wider spaces of the shop. He took the change and turned to go.

'I'll lock up after you.' Linda came round from behind the counter and followed him to the door. 'Good night. And a happy New Year to you.' Even as she uttered the words she thought he looked like a stranger to happiness or even the notion of it.

'Thank you,' he said again. He strode off into the icy evening without a backward glance. No hat, no scarf, his coat blowing back. He drew a long cold breath of freedom, savouring the misty solitude of the streets.

Linda looked after him with a flicker of regret. In the distance the church clock struck the hour, its tones muffled by the heavy air. Six o'clock—and no sign of the charwoman. She drew a long breath of exasperation, closed the door with a firm snap, turned the key and thrust home the bolts.

'That Mrs Bond!' she said aloud with irritation. 'I'd like to wring her neck!'

CHAPTER III

'Emily!' Zena Yorke flung a shout towards the door that stood open between her large bedroom and the long narrow bathroom constructed seventy years ago from a slice chopped off the end of the adjoining dressing-room and her husband's room beyond it.

'Yes?' Emily Bond screeched back. She no longer bothered to tack a deferential 'Madam' or even 'Mrs Yorke' on to her utterances and it was many a long day since she had troubled to interrupt a task in order to trot obediently at Zena's call and put her head round the door of whatever room the summons had issued from. If Mrs Yorke didn't like it, Mrs Yorke could blooming well lump it.

Plenty of women in Milbourne only too eager to find a charlady—and to pay better money than Mrs Yorke. Sweeter-tempered women, too. Emily rubbed vigorously at the mirrored front of the medicine cupboard, lost for a moment in a comforting fantasy of those other idealized housewives smiling gratefully at her, proffering steaming beakers of cream-laden coffee.

'I can see a huge cobweb over the wardrobe,' Zena yelled from the downy nest of her double bed with its richly-quilted coverlet of rose-pink satin. She ran her eyes over the rest of the room, alerted now for further evidence of slapdash work. She heaved herself up with an effort, scanning the crevices and corners, lighting with a glance of triumph on a curl of grey fluff under the washbasin.

'You'll have to do in here before you go. You were supposed to clean this room out yesterday.' Her voice cracked on a high note. She reached angrily over to the bedside cabinet and snatched a king-size cigarette from a carved wooden box, flicked impatiently at her lighter and flung herself back against the heaped-up pillows.

She closed her eyes, temporarily exhausted by the bellowing, tempted for the hundredth time in a month to give old Emily the sack, but recollecting for the hundredth time that it might be impossible to replace her. The domestic agency in Milbourne had adopted a very wary note in recent years when she had rung up to demand assistance.

There had been a time when they had willingly answered her appeals, supplying her with a stream of helpers, living-in maids, living-out maids, foreign girls, local dailies. None of them had stayed longer than a couple of months. And word had got about among the small band of daily women. Times were growing a good deal less hard and there was no longer any reason for a competent domestic to put up with bouts of bad temper—and wages that were less than handsome.

Throughout the long procession of female feet in and out of the Yorke household, only Emily Bond had remained a constant. Not, Zena reminded herself sharply, that it was any reason actually to spoil the woman.

'Do you hear me?' she cried, revived by the cigarette, bored again, in need of the stimulus of a heated exchange. 'This room's filthy!'

Mrs Bond insinuated a duster among the bottles and boxes in the cupboard. If your bedroom's filthy, she said in her mind, pleased with a certain lofty note in her imagined tone, that's on account of your spending half your days lying about in it pretending to be poorly when there's nothing wrong with you that a good dose of salts and a month's starvation wouldn't cure.

'It'll have to wait over,' she called. 'I should have been gone to Mrs Fleming's the best part of an hour ago. I'm off as soon as I've done in here.' She picked up a small brown bottle and studied the label. Sleeping-pills. Mr Yorke's sleeping-pills. Mrs Yorke bawled at her again but she closed her mind and let the sound bounce off her eardrums.

'I hear you,' she said calmly, not having the remotest idea what her highness was on about this time but adding from force of professional habit, 'I've only got one pair of hands,' a remark she had usefully employed thousands of times in the last fifty-five years.

She put the bottle back on the shelf and gave a final righteous flick of her cloth along the ranks of medicines, scattering the greater part of the dust she had removed a few minutes before. She clicked the cupboard shut.

'That'll have to do you for today,' she said firmly, making her way back into Mrs Yorke's bedroom and standing for a moment in the doorway like a general surveying the scene of a recent battle.

'I'm off now.' She unfastened her apron to show she meant business. 'Got to look in at Mrs Fleming's.'

Zena's restless attention, diverted from cobwebs and fluff, alighted on the notion of Linda Fleming. She had never met the woman, having no reason to go poking her nose into every little upstart draper's shop in Milbourne but it was in her nature to keep tabs on people, to docket and file away scraps of information.

Her self-indulgent habits had gradually trimmed away the keen edges of her once-active existence but her mind still darted about like a ferret, reduced now to nibbling at other more purposeful lives. And she had been connected with the trade since the day she was born; she could hardly escape a stir of curiosity about the newcomer.

'Quite young, I think you said?' She stubbed out her cigarette absent-mindedly; she had smoked barely a quarter of it.

'Who?' Emily halted, baffled, on her way to the door. 'Oh, you mean Mrs Fleming. Not much over thirty, I'd say. Pretty too.'

'Does she go out a lot? Has she got many friends? Men friends, that is,' Zena added in case Emily missed the point. 'Is the shop doing well?'

'It's early days yet, she hasn't been in the town but five minutes.' Emily considered Mrs Fleming's possibilities, a good-looking young widow building up a smart little business. 'Give her time. They'll be round her like flies round a honeypot.' She shook her head at the grasping ways of men, always looking out for a comfortable berth.

'Where did she come from?' Zena asked. 'And what happened to her husband?'

'I'm sure I don't know what happened to him,' Emily said crossly. 'He's dead, that's all I know. I'm off,' she added abruptly and banged her way out of the room. At the head of the stairs she paused for breath. I'm getting old, she told herself in ritual lamentation. All this rush and bustle is a bit too much for me these days. I'm going to have to slacken off a bit, start taking it easy.

She went heavy-footed down into the hall and along to the kitchen quarters to find her coat. Then she cocked a questioning ear towards the stairs. All serene. From the bread-bin she took, as she always did, the stale rolls and ends of loaves. 'Just a few crumbs for me birds,' she said aloud, righteously. A body had to love something and birds were a good deal more satisfactory than most human beings.

She eased open the door of the fridge and smiled with pleasure at the contents. One or two little odds and ends of food and drink left over from the festive season that would slip nicely into her hold-all and never a soul the wiser.

Outside the back door she heard a plaintive mew. 'All right, me beauty, Emily's coming,' she said soothingly. She poured a saucer of milk and took it out, setting it down by the step; the cat pushed its head against her fingers. 'Go on,' she said urgently, 'get that inside you, and quick about it.' The cat rubbed against her legs, so pleased at a friendly contact that in spite of its hunger it couldn't at once give attention to the milk. 'You'll lose me me job,' Emily said with affectionate fierceness. 'Get a move on.'

At last the cat crouched over the saucer, purring loudly. A lean black stray, an abandoned pet most likely; some people had no heart. Mrs Yorke had caught her feeding it only the other day, couldn't abide cats, Mrs Yorke, always a bad sign, Emily had observed that more than once in her long life. 'Don't encourage that filthy beast!' Mrs Yorke had cried, ever so nasty. 'If you want a cat, why don't you keep one yourself?' As if she hadn't explained a thousand times why she couldn't keep a cat. On account of her birds, it stood to reason. You could keep a cat or you could feed wild birds, you couldn't do both, any fool would know that.

'Finished, have you, me lovely?' She stooped and retrieved the saucer. 'Go on, scarper.' With her foot she gently pushed the stray back from the door, went inside and washed the saucer, put it away. 'Now then,' she said briskly.

'Better get going if I'm going to get me bus.'

As soon as Emily was safely out of the room Zena heaved herself half-way out of her nest and fumbled about under the bed like a sea-lion baffled by a new trick. Her fingers encountered the squared edges of a box. She smiled in triumph and hauled herself up again, clutching at her booty.

She tore away the Cellophane wrapping, snatched off the lid and sat upright with her hands clasped, gazing down with anticipation at the elegant rows of petit-fours. But there was no time to sit and gloat; at any moment her husband's car might sweep into the drive. She began to stuff the sweetmeats into her mouth, giving herself barely time to taste them, but experiencing all the same the intense pleasure of satisfying an overpowering greed.

In four minutes' flat she had put paid to most of the top layer. She raised her head and glanced at the clock on the mantelshelf. Not quite half past six. No sign of Owen yet. Surely now she had time for just one quick sip?

Yes! Of course she had! She stuffed the box back under the bed and tried to contort herself into a position in which she could wrench open the door of the bedside cabinet. She groaned and tugged but it was impossible; she was compelled at last actually to flop out from between the sheets on to the carpet and in a cross-legged posture she sank a tot of neat brandy. By the time she had drained her glass for the second time she had ceased to bother about Owen's car.

A terrible sense of sorrow and the harsh injustice of life welled up inside her. Some sentinel fragment of her brain insisted that it was never meant to be like this—how had Daddy's little golden-haired princess come to be slouched on the floor of Daddy and Mummy's bedroom, fat and ailing and unlovely, a little drunk and more than a little nauseated?

She silenced the disturbing voice in the only way she knew—she filled her glass again and lifted it to her lips.

But she couldn't finish the drink. After a few sips she began to feel so unwell that fright restored her temporarily to sobriety. She levered herself up and went over to the basin, where she emptied the glass into the sink and ran a tap to wash away the traces.

She splashed her face with cold water and dabbed it partly dry. Ah! That was better! She got back across the room and pushed the brandy bottle into a corner of the cabinet.

Twenty minutes to seven and Owen still not home. Brandy-inspired anger began to mount in her brain. I could die here all alone, she thought with savage resentment, and he wouldn't bat an eyelid. Resentment suddenly gave way to near-panic as this habitual expression of self-pity all at once translated itself into a terrifying possibility. I *could* actually die! The words leapt before her eyes in characters of fire. I *am* ill! Desperately ill! It isn't just a game I've been playing.

Up to this moment she'd always cherished the illusion that she could stop whenever she chose, pull herself together, like a child saying, 'I'm going to be good now, for ever and ever,' as if the debilitating years could be dissolved in a single flash of resolution and she could wake up next morning slender and beautiful, radiantly healthy and gloriously young again.

For one piercing moment she saw the skeleton face of reality rise up from the pit. She shut her eyes tight, forcing the image away, down, out of perception and consciousness. She slid back, lying full-length on the satin spread, and dropped at once into a doze that lasted barely a minute.

When she opened her eyes again she had the impression that she had been asleep for a long time. The brandy had resumed its interrupted work; she felt relaxed and dulled. The terror had vanished, leaving behind only a hazy notion that she ought to ring her doctor. She raised herself up and went with a kind of floating motion into the dressing-room that linked—or, more accurately, separated—her room from that of her husband's.

The phone stood on a small table at the other side of the room. She wove her way towards it, sat down and dialled the number. The engaged signal sounded in her ear. Not at all put out, she replaced the receiver and leaned back in her chair, ready to try again in a couple of minutes. It never occurred to her to wonder whether fifteen minutes before the start of evening surgery might not be an ideal time to phone a busy doctor.

Owen Yorke turned his large black saloon car into the narrow road—little more than a lane, really—that led to the secluded house where he lived with Zena. He had never been able to think of The Sycamores as home although he had inhabited it for half of his fifty years.

His speed dropped until he was barely keeping the car in motion. He hadn't consciously slackened the pressure of his foot on the accelerator, it was just that he was finding it more and more difficult every evening to propel himself towards the house at all.

A couple of weeks back his eye had fallen on a paragraph in the paper, some man who'd been missing from home for more than a month, a prosperous professional man with a family life that seemed ordinary enough; he'd turned up, unkempt, half-starving, in a bleak little mining town in the north, hundreds of miles away from his comfortable base. Discovered by a policeman late at night, sitting all alone on a stone bench outside the post office in the middle of a snowstorm. He hadn't been able to offer any explanation.

The item had stuck in Owen's mind. It was the kind of trivial news story which didn't merit a follow-up. One never knew how it ended or indeed, why it had begun. The thought of that man would spring into Owen's brain quite often now as he opened the door of his car in the evenings and a prickle of fear was beginning to accompany the thought.

All his life he had relied on the exercise of his will to channel his energies and discipline his emotions and desires so that the whole of his conscious effort kept him unswervingly directed towards the goal he saw so clearly.

Status, wealth, respectability; he could put not a pin-point between them in order of importance. He had never for a single moment questioned the validity of his ambitions and he still wasn't questioning them.

What troubled him now, what caused the tingle of apprehension to run across his mind in the middle of everyday routine activities was a horrid suspicion that his will was no longer absolute master of his personality. He felt as if he had for fifty years been damming behind a massive barrier deep and powerful forces of whose existence he had been totally unaware.

And now the barrier was beginning to crack; he sensed the underground currents seeping through. As he drove out of the car park at the end of each busy and purposeful day he would be seized for an instant by a nightmare panic that the whole structure of his identity might suddenly and uncontrollably topple, that he might vanish from the familiar environs of Milbourne, materializing inexplicably weeks later on a bench in an alien blizzard.

The long driveway of The Sycamores appeared before him. The car made its way over the gravel at little more than walking pace. I must take some decisive step, he thought, summoning to his aid his ancient ally of resolution. Two courses lay before him. He could either plough on along his chosen path, crushing down the minutest sign of internal conflict—or he could stand back and let the defences crumble, look calmly and courageously at what was left when the torrents subsided, begin to build all over again from scratch an edifice he could not at this moment even begin to imagine.

He was astonished to find, now that he actually dared to examine the notion of violent upheaval, that it was exhilaration and not terror that ran through him. He got out of the car and stood looking up at the house. Then he shook away his train of thought. Some other time, he told himself, when there is peace and leisure, I'll work it all out another day. He gave his determined attention to the matter of the rest of the evening.

The car—no need to put it away in the garage, he'd be running up to the Independents' again later on. He'd called in at the club once already after leaving the office, looking for a member with whom he had business dealings. But the man wasn't there, wouldn't be in for an hour or two.

He became aware that it was bitingly cold out here in the driveway but he still lingered under the arching trees. The house was well named; the sycamores had multiplied themselves in the hundred years since the grounds had first been laid out, great spreading branches reaching in places to a height of sixty or eighty feet.

He took a step or two backwards and stared up at the grey walls built of stone from a local quarry, the long windows with light escaping from between heavy curtains. Zena was never one to go round economically switching off lamps. He pictured her up there in the best bedroom, lying back against the embroidered pillows, looking up at the ceiling, waiting for him.

What a brooding, gloomy-looking place it was—and how imposing it had seemed to him when he had been despatched here on some errand from the shop in his apprentice days. He and Zena had begun their married life in a modern bungalow; they had moved to The Sycamores a year or two after Ralph Underwood's death, when the war was over and it became possible once more to think of heating and running a place of this size.

Something more cheerful, he thought suddenly. A new house perhaps—or if an old one, then something from a more elegant time, Georgian or Queen Anne. And a more open kind of garden without all these overpowering trees. He didn't allow his mind to circle round the question of who was going to share the Georgian mansion with him or if indeed he was going to share it with anyone at all.

A sharp gust of wind blew chilly air against his cheeks. I'd better get a move on if I don't want to stand out here all night, he told himself. The notion brought with it a nasty reminder of the post-office bench under the whirling snow, sending him rapidly up the steps and in through the front door, closing it behind him with a momentary sense of relief, a return to normality.

He hung up his coat, stamped his feet to restore the circulation. He could do with a holiday, that was all it was; a few days away somewhere pleasant and he'd be as right as rain. Something about the New Year, for all its frantic jollity, that inspired a feeling of depression and futility; he'd seen its effects in other men. Almost cheerful again, he mounted the stairs, already fixing a smile across his face. Zena was probably feeling much better now after her rest. They had spent last evening—and a considerable stretch of the early morning—at a dinner-dance in the largest hotel in Milbourne. Zena had overdone things a trifle, eating and drinking rather more than was strictly good for her. But it was only natural, really; she was after all entitled to deal with the midwinter glooms in her own way.

He flung open the bedroom door and levelled his smile at the bed; his face had by now assumed a certain mask-like quality which might have appeared quite startling if there had been anyone to see it.

The bed was empty, the covers flung back in a disorderly heap. Through the open door of the dressing-room he heard Zena's voice, high-pitched, argumentative. His smile abandoned him but he kept on, round the foot of the bed, through the door, pausing on the threshold.

Zena was sitting hunched in a chair, talking fiercely into the phone; she was wrapped in a fleecy dressing-gown of pale blue wool. Her eyes flicked over him without a sign of recognition.

'I'm back,' he said. She made no reply. He felt disembodied, unreal, a figment of his own imagination—the real man perhaps even now looking up from a stone seat into the questioning face of a policeman.

He turned and caught sight of his face, pale and ghostly, dark hollows where there should have been eyes, in the mirror on the opposite wall. He dropped his gaze, appalled at the sight of such blank futility, bafflingly at odds with his habitual image of himself as a jovial, successful man.

He saw the bright flash of a pair of scissors lying on the shelf below the mirror; he was seized suddenly with a wild and powerful impulse to stride forward and pick them up, raise them aloft and drive them down with force into that flaccid flesh under the pale blue wool.

He closed his eyes in terror that he might actually take a step forward; he felt the barriers begin to slip and crumble in his mind; he exerted all his strength and beat back at the invading tide. It began to recede, it slipped away, a little more and it was gone. He drew a long sighing breath and opened his eyes. Quite himself again now. Stupid to stay up so late. Not enough sleep, that was his trouble. But he kept his eyes well away from the steely brilliance of the scissors.

'I'll just have a quick wash,' he said lightly. Zena gave no indication that she had heard. He went back into the bedroom and through the bathroom door. As he ran the taps he became aware of a weight in his jacket pocket. Ah—the tonic. Zena would be wanting that. He turned off the taps and stood looking down at the bottle in its neat white wrapping.

'If you could just say exactly what it is that's the matter with you, Mrs Yorke,' the receptionist said yet again, striving for the right tone of professional firmness. New to the job, acting as a temporary relief, the regular girl being away with flu. 'Then I'll slip in and have a word with Dr Gethin.'

'You're not by any chance a qualified doctor?' Zena threw in acidly. 'No? Then I can't see how describing my symptoms to you can be of the slightest use.' Quite enjoying herself now; nothing she found more enlivening than a good brisk exchange. She felt energetic, free from the effects of the brandy.

'You go along and tell Dr Gethin I want to speak to him. I'm very ill, I suffer from diabetes. Dr Gethin knows all about my case, he knows how serious it is, he's been my doctor ever since I was born. He'll want to come out and see me.'

She doesn't sound very ill, the girl thought uncertainly, she sounds full of life. But one never knew—

'Oh, very well, then,' she said abruptly as Mrs Yorke embarked on a fresh onslaught. 'Hold the line, please.' She left her desk and went across the passage to Dr Gethin's door.

'I'm terribly sorry to disturb you.' She put her face a few apologetic inches into the room. 'But it's a Mrs Yorke. She insists on speaking to you. I can't make her see reason.'

Gethin looked up from the paperwork he was trying to deal with before the first wave of patients engulfed him.

'Mrs Yorke?' He took off his reading-glasses and rubbed his eyes. He looked unutterably weary—and the rest of the evening still to be got through. 'If you can make Zena Yorke see reason, you'll be the first person who's ever succeeded.' He let out an irritable breath. 'New Year's Day. I have a very good notion what's wrong with her. Over-indulgence. Simply won't make any attempt to diet.'

He sighed again, loudly. Disease and natural disasters, he thought—with the accumulated anger of a lifetime spent in combating the follies of mankind—the only things we ought to have to battle with; all the rest is wished upon us by ourselves or our fellows.

'What shall I tell her?' the girl asked timidly. 'She's blocking the phone for other calls.'

'Tell her to go to hell.' He saw the girl's anxious look.

'No, wait a minute.' He'd have to do something about the woman. She was after all the wife of Owen Yorke, shortly to be made president of Gethin's club. And Gethin had served in the first war with Owen's father, they'd lied about their ages, both of them, been through two years of fire and mud before the Armistice. One didn't forget those things, old and soured though one had become. He stood up.

'I'll speak to her.' He went out of the room, tall and spare, a little stooped now, his hair silvery white.

'Ah! Dr Gethin!' Zena said in triumph as soon as he spoke. 'I told that silly girl—'

'I employ no silly girls,' he said. 'Though I have some remarkably silly patients. Have you had your injections regularly? Yes or no? Don't bother to play games.'

'Yes. Well, most of the time. But I'm sure they don't do me any good. I feel so dreadful—'

'You'll feel even more dreadful if you keep on as you're doing. Where's Owen? Is he in? Let me speak to him. Go on,' he added as she broke in. 'Get him. I've got patients waiting to see me.' He drummed his fingers on the table, glanced at his watch, did his best to control the irritation which had become habitual with him. 'Oh, there you are, Owen. Anything really wrong with Zena? Or just looking for notice as usual?'

'I'm sorry she bothered you,' Owen said. 'It isn't really anything. She overdid things last night, New Year's Eve, you know how it is.'

'Make sure she keeps on with the insulin. I'll try to look in on her tomorrow, talk some sense into her. You'll be burying her one of these fine days if she doesn't mend her ways.' He rang off abruptly, nodded to the girl and went back to his room.

Happily married himself until his wife had died twenty years ago, he hated to see a decent fellow like Yorke caught up in the destructive toils of a wretched union like that.

Balance and discipline, he repeated in his mind, the twin essentials for the control of diabetes. Zena was conspicuously lacking in both qualities. It wasn't medical assistance she required, it was miracles.

Self-pity, self-dramatization, boredom—what drugs could be prescribed for those? A woman at a kind of malicious loose end in life, he found it impossible to feel a shred of sympathy for her. He stretched out a hand and pressed a bell on his desk. When the door opened to admit his first patient he saw with a feeling of relief and pleasure that it was one of his elderly arthritics, someone suffering from an identifiable complaint that could be eased and made tolerable.

'Good evening,' he said gently. 'And how are we today?'

'There's plenty of cold stuff in the fridge.' Zena settled herself back in bed. 'You can open a tin of soup if you want something hot. I think I'll go down later and watch television.' She picked up the glass Owen had set down on the table. 'Do you know what's on?'

'I haven't the remotest idea.' He stood watching her take a long drink. 'I'm going down to the club. I'll get a bite to eat there.'

She pulled a face. 'Oh—this is bitter. They must have changed the formula. I'm sure it didn't taste like this last time.' But she drained the glass, feeling the tonic doing her good, much better than old Gethin's mixtures. Her mind registered what Owen had said. 'You mean you're going out again, leaving me here all by myself?'

She gave him a searching glance, actually seeing him for the first time that evening. Something decidedly odd about his expression, a fixed, strained look. She had a sense of a good deal going on in his mind, things she couldn't get at and drag out into the open. I do believe he's up to something, she thought, experiencing in successive flashes anger, resentment, curiosity and finally a sharp pleasure at having a whole new area of interest to poke about and pry into. She almost smiled at him.

'You won't be by yourself,' Owen said. He was pleased

to find he could look at her now without emotion of any sort. A couple of seconds more and he succeeded into shifting his mind into the correct gear, achieving the mood of detached pity that allowed him to live with her at all. 'You said this morning that your brother would be coming in.'

'That won't be till later on. In the meantime—'

'There's plenty to occupy you.' He jerked his head at the radio, the pile of magazines and novels. 'Or you could get some sleep before Neil comes. Will Ruth be coming too?' No point in asking if Jane would also be tagging along; a pretty girl of seventeen would have better things to do on New Year's Day than trot dutifully beside her father to visit an egotistic aunt.

Zena pouted. 'I don't suppose so. Ruth's never liked me.' Her brother's second wife, many years younger than Zena, slender, well-dressed, strikingly beautiful, conducting a successful career in addition to running a comfortable home.

Ruth Underwood had been prepared on her marriage, almost a year ago, to make a genuine effort to get on with her difficult sister-in-law. But it was scarcely to be expected that Zena could welcome into the family a newcomer whose entire mode of life threw her own shortcomings into even greater prominence. And Owen whole-heartedly liked and admired Ruth, which was enough in itself to make Zena detest her.

'I'll be off then.' It did cross Owen's mind that he ought to tell Zena about his decision to close the High Street shop. She would have to be told sooner or later—she was joint owner with him of the whole business enterprise that still traded under her father's name of Underwood. And she could be relied on to make a fuss about the closure whether she secretly considered it wise or not, simply in order to demonstrate that she still legally controlled half the purse-strings.

'Leave the front door on the latch for Neil,' Zena said.

I could mention the shop now, Owen thought, then I

could cut and run for it; give her time to come off the boil before I get back.

'This room is like a pigsty,' Zena said suddenly, realizing how it would appear to her brother with his liking for more orderly ways. 'Emily Bond is the limit these days. I told her to clean up in here, but would she? Oh no, she had to go running off to her Mrs Fleming's.'

A warm glow of pleasure spread through Owen's frame. I'll call in on Linda Fleming after I've been to the club, he decided, I can speak to her about jobbing off the left-over stock.

No wish now to embark on the tedious chore of breaking the news about the shop. He felt again the exhilarating sense that in a very short time everything might be entirely different. He went from the room at a rush, only just remembering in the doorway to turn and raise a hand in a gesture of farewell.

Zena threw back the bedclothes. There was nothing for it, she'd have to make some show of tidying the room herself. She still cared what Neil thought about her. He had worshipped her all during their carefree childhood, given her admiring affection throughout their youth. She felt that he still loved her, that he was probably the only person alive who could look at her and see the lovely Zena Underwood; his image of her had been too deeply engraved too long ago to be altered by anything as trivial as the passage of time.

She shuffled her feet into fluffy mules. As she straightened herself to begin her task she frowned, recalling the strangeness of Owen's manner, his preoccupation, his casual attitude towards her health. She moved slowly about the room, picking up garments, closing drawers and cupboards. It was only in the last few weeks that she'd really noticed the change in him. Had anything happened to spark off that change? Had any new factor appeared in his life? She was by now quite certain that he was up to something.

Abstractedly she re-arranged the heap of magazines and

books. I could do a great deal worse than have him followed, she thought. A nice little job for Arnold Pierson. She drew a long breath, savouring the notion. It was so exactly the kind of thing she most keenly relished, killing, as it undoubtedly would, half a dozen birds with one skilfully-aimed stone.

It would arm her with information about Owen's carryings-on, allow her to jerk the string that bound Arnold to her, gratify her taste for deviousness and intrigue, keep boredom at bay—and all without the necessity so much as to set foot outside her own bedroom.

Yes, she would do it, her mind was made up. She glanced at the clock. Seven-fifteen. Arnold would be home from work by now, he would probably be eating his supper. Phone him, say, in twenty or thirty minutes, catch him before he had a chance to go out again, he would be here and gone long before Neil's arrival. And he would just be in nice time to get down to the Independents' to keep an unobtrusive eye on Owen's car.

What especially delighted her about the scheme was the deep revulsion she knew it would inspire in Arnold—and his total inability to do anything but fall in with her commands.

Her movements grew quite brisk; she finished tidying the room in another few minutes. Then she spent a little time on improving her own appearance, discarding the woollen dressing-gown for an elaborate affair of silk and tulle, a flattering shade of turquoise that did what it could for her and drew a discreet veil or two over the rest.

She switched on the radio as she made up her face and attended to her hair. Gay, inspiriting music burst into the room; she smiled at her face in the glass, feeling well and lively, better than she'd felt for quite some time.

A few liberal sprayings of expensive perfume and she was ready for the fray. A little remaking of the bed, a plumping-up of the pillows. And that was about it. She looked at the clock and decided to give it a few more minutes. Just enough time for some slight refreshment.

She knelt down and plunged a hand under the quilted drapes. Still the whole of the second layer of petit-fours. Before she climbed back into bed she opened the cabinet and took out the brandy bottle. One—or perhaps two—plenty of time before Arnold actually got here.

She poured out a generous measure, settled herself comfortably into her nest and lifted the lid from the box of confectionery. The radio began to play a tune from the old days, carrying her back twenty or thirty years to the golden time before everything turned sour.

'A-ah!' she said aloud on a long note of satisfaction. All in all, it promised to be a very agreeable evening.

Owen drove slowly through the misty streets towards the club. Not many folk about on this dismal evening. He let his mind slip back to its current preoccupation, trying to look at his total situation with the dispassionate eyes of an intelligent outsider. One of the many shrewd businessmen down at the club, for instance. He imagined himself confiding in such a man—not that he would be fool enough ever to indulge such an insane impulse. What would this sensible adviser suggest?

Can't quite see your problem, he might say with a lift of his eyebrows. Divorce your wife, marry again, start a family. Plenty of time left to you. Other men have done it; why can't you? We live in less rigidly puritanical times, old boy; no one expects a fellow to live in misery these days; the laws are more humane, public opinion more enlightened.

Owen halted his car at the traffic lights. It isn't quite as simple as that, he told his shadowy listener. Zena would never agree to a divorce. She's a vain woman, and vanity, injured pride, do more than anything else to keep one partner in a dying marriage clinging fiercely to an unwilling mate. If I left Zena, it would be five years before I would be free to marry again.

Five years! He set the car in motion again. A pretty

young woman like Linda Fleming was scarcely likely to be unmarried in five years' time.

There are other women in the world besides Mrs Fleming, said that insistent voice. Owen shook his head. He didn't want the other women, he wanted Linda.

And simply setting up house with her, living together without benefit of legal ceremony, was totally out of the question. It might be all right in London or some other great city but not in a place like Milbourne with its narrower, more censorious views. He couldn't visualize himself even opening his mouth to mention such a scheme to Mrs Fleming.

And I can't uproot myself and move away, he thought with finality. My business is here, the new factory—it's not possible to contemplate such a step.

The factory—there you are! he said to the imaginary adviser. The new laws may be a fraction more humane, but they're a good deal more stringent about the division of property. Everything I possess would be split down the middle, Zena would be entitled to half. And she would take a vicious pleasure in insisting on that half in cash. It would be the end of Underwood's. He'd have to sell up in order to pay her.

No possibility these days of raising such a massive loan; he'd been hard put to it to find enough borrowed capital for the new factory. And he could never repay the additional loan even if it could be raised. The interest alone would probably bankrupt him.

He turned the car into the park beside the Independents'. Grossly unfair, this new ruling on property division, he thought with a surge of anger.

Old Ralph Underwood had bequeathed his daughter the High Street business and half of his fairly substantial savings; the other half had gone to Neil. But it was Owen who had slaved night and day to develop the really quite modest business, who'd built the old factory after the war and would shortly see the new factory begin to take shape.

What had Zena to do with all that expansion? She'd run the gown shop until she'd grown too idle even to go down there once a month. Left to herself, she would by now have been merely the owner of a failing, out-of-date business and she'd have frittered away her capital. True, she'd agreed years ago to let Owen raise a mortgage on the shop. And she'd put her money into the postwar factory readily enough in those friendlier years when their marriage was young.

He switched off the car engine, not caring at this hostile moment to contemplate that happier time. She knew I was an ambitious and enterprising man, he told himself, dismissing sentimentality; she knew I'd put her money to good use, she was well aware when she was on to a good thing.

For a harshly cynical moment he allowed himself to believe that that was why she'd married him, then he shook his head slowly, compelled in justice to admit it wasn't true. But he refused to dwell on the complex motives that had led her to say Yes. It was all a long time ago; it no longer mattered very much. Whatever she had done for him in the past didn't give her a moral claim now to half his assets, in spite of anything the law might say.

He squared his shoulders and set his mouth in a grim line. Divorce might be a non-starter but there were surely other ways of resolving his difficulties; there must be other ways.

He opened the car door and stepped out on to the asphalt. He stood looking up at the solid face of the club. In a short time he would be president, he would stand even higher in the opinion of Milbourne.

He locked the car door and thrust the keys into his pocket. Perhaps after all it might be wiser to hang on to what he had got, consolidate his position, be thankful for what life had handed him instead of imperilling it all, put away fanciful notions as many another man had done.

With a firm tread he walked towards the wide stone steps. A question of discipline, after all, control of the inner mind. And if the mutinous dog beneath would not always be quelled, if he stirred sometimes in the late evenings, raised his head in the bleak watches of the nights, there was always a remedy, there were always sleeping-pills.

He smiled briefly to himself, raised his hand and pressed a forceful thumb on the doorbell.

Twenty-five minutes past seven. Zena studied the face of the clock, reluctant to leave her satin bower and make her way towards the phone in the dressing-room. A little yawn escaped her. If she left it much longer, Arnold might have gone off somewhere for the evening.

Her gaze travelled a few inches and came to rest on the brandy bottle. Another five minutes. Seven-thirty was a nice round figure. She yawned again, more widely this time, leaned out and grasped the bottle by its neck.

CHAPTER IV

Supper was over in the Pierson household. Sarah sat upright in a straight-backed chair at one side of the sitting-room fire, knitting assiduously a square of bright red wool. All over Africa sick natives huddled themselves under the comfort of patchwork blankets stitched together by Sarah over more than forty years. Or so she liked to think.

At the other end of the little room, as far away as possible from the fireplace, her stepbrother lowered his newspaper an inch or two and stole a glance at her. He had told her at supper about the closing of the shop. She had said nothing, merely raising her eyes to give him a single veiled look and then continuing to serve the food while he did his best to soften the blow. He explained the wisdom of the decision, enlarged on the certainty of an earlier pension, pointed out the new leisure to be enjoyed.

To all this she had made no reply. When his voice had finally ceased she flicked him a glance that seemed to hold sardonic amusement. Or a trace of quiet pleasure at the prospect before her? It was gone before he could read it. She had begun to talk about his father lying upstairs.

'He doesn't seem to be picking up. I'll get the doctor to look in on him again.' Of course, worried as she was—as they both were—about old Walter, she might not think retiring a year or two earlier a matter of any particular consequence. But he would just like to be sure. He shifted in his chair, nerving himself to raise the subject again.

'You could take a holiday,' he ventured. 'A good long holiday.' He couldn't remember when she had last been away from the house for a single night. Arrangements could surely be made for himself and his father. 'You'd enjoy that.' He tried to picture her on her own in a seaside resort; all he could see was an image of her sitting straight-backed in a hotel lounge, fashioning rainbow coverlets for ailing Africans. Hardly a scene of compelling gaiety.

She raised her head and held it in a listening attitude. A sound came from the room above. Arnold got to his feet.

'I'll go up and sit with Father.' He abandoned all attempt to talk to Sarah and went slowly upstairs into the front bedroom.

Walter was struggling to lift himself against the pillows. His face was flushed, his look restless and bewildered. He frowned as Arnold bent over to assist him; trying to place him, to come out of his clutching dream.

'Oh—it's you.' He passed a trembling hand over his face. 'I thought I was back in France.' Relief now in his voice. 'A bit of a nightmare.' He sank back for a moment into that grim memory. 'We were going out after Cottrell. Yorke and myself. There was a bright moon.' He let out a long shuddering breath. 'We could hear him screaming.'

'It's all right, Father,' Arnold said soothingly. He straightened the bedclothes. 'It was only a dream.' But he knew himself the clammy horror of such dreams when the present dropped away and there were only the helpless cries of men long dead.

He crossed to the washbasin, moistened a flannel with cool water, came back to the bed and passed the cloth gently over his father's face and hands.

'You'll feel better in a moment.' He picked up a towel. 'Would you like something to drink? I won't leave you, I can give Sarah a shout, she'll get something hot.'

Walter shook his head. 'Don't bother Sarah. I'll just have some of that.' He gestured at the tray holding a glass and a tall jug of orange squash covered with a beaded muslin drape. He watched Arnold pour the drink.

'Do you ever see anything of Cottrell's son these days? David. He grew up a good lad. His father would have been proud of him.'

'I see him now and again.' Arnold held the glass while his father drank from it. 'In the street sometimes. Just to nod to.' He'd been at school with David Cottrell, they'd been called up together in the middle of the war, served in the same county regiment; they'd been taken prisoner together, had endured the scarring years in the same Japanese camp. And now they merely nodded to each other in the streets, at once linked and held apart by the long chain of shared experience.

'You should ask him round some evening when he's off duty,' Walter said. 'I'd like a chat with him.' Cottrell had gone into the police after the war, a detective-sergeant now, well thought of in the town.

Arnold replaced the glass on the tray. 'I'll see if I can catch him one of these days.' He hadn't the slightest intention of asking Cottrell to the house. And by tomorrow Walter would have forgotten the request.

Downstairs in the hall the phone rang sharply. 'Sarah will take it.' Walter put out a detaining hand as Arnold turned to go. 'You stay and talk to me.'

But Arnold eluded his grasp. As he reached the door he heard the receiver lifted and Sarah's brisk voice.

'Good evening, Mrs Yorke. I hope you're feeling better?' He drew his brows together, listening.

'Who is it?' Walter asked impatiently. 'Sarah can deal with it.'

'It's Mrs Yorke.' Arnold came slowly back towards the bed.

'Then it'll only be some business about the shop. Pull up a chair and sit down.'

Arnold looked about for a chair, trying without success to catch at fragments of the conversation below.

'I must confess I was a little surprised at the news about the shop,' Sarah said into the phone. After her long years of service she might surely have expected to be told the decision with due ceremony by either Mr or Mrs Yorke instead of in this secondhand fashion through her step-brother.

'What news?' Zena asked sharply.

'That the shop is to close down, of course.' Sarah maintained the deferential courtesy of her tone in spite of a thrust of impatience. She wished Mrs Yorke wouldn't play her devious games.

'It's news to me,' Zena said. 'I'm certainly not thinking of closing the shop. Where did you get hold of such an idea?'

'I don't think there can be any doubt about it. Arnold told me this evening. Mr Yorke spoke to him this afternoon.' She heard the intake of Zena's breath.

There was a brief silence at the other end of the line and then Zena spoke again in a lighter, more casual tone. 'I'll have a word with Owen about it later. Actually, I rang up to speak to your brother. Is he in?'

'Yes, I'll get him, he won't be a moment.' Sarah laid down the receiver.

So I wasn't mistaken, Zena thought, biting her lip. There is something going on. *My* shop—Owen has the nerve to talk about closing down my shop—and without a word to me. I have to learn about it from an underling! He stood there as calm as you like this evening, never uttered a syllable about it. She drummed her fingers on the table. Where was Arnold? He was certainly taking his time.

'Mrs Yorke wants to speak to you.' Sarah came into the bedroom, ready to take Arnold's place while he was gone. Her tone was drily neutral, her eyes expressed nothing.

For years she had been aware that Zena had some kind of hold over Arnold. She had speculated about it, resented it, failed to understand it. He had been sweet on Zena when he was a lad, of course, and there had been some kind of fusion between them for a short time after the war; she'd have had to be blind not to have seen it. But it certainly wasn't affection that linked them now, she was sure of that. She had caught his look when her name was mentioned, the uneager way he moved whenever Zena's imperious command summoned him to the phone.

Arnold went reluctantly downstairs. In the hall he stared at the receiver with distaste before picking it up. Whatever Zena wanted of him, it wasn't likely to add to his peace of mind.

'Yes?' He threw a great deal of meaning into that single word.

'I want you to come over here.' No question whether it might be agreeable or convenient. 'Owen's out. I'm by myself.'

'I'm busy this evening.' He always gave this initial jerk of resistance.

'How is your father?' she asked. 'I thought I might look in on him one of these days. Have a little chat.'

He closed his eyes, accepting the inevitable. 'All right. I'll come over later on.' Zena had it in her power to darken old Walter's last days. And Arnold knew with absolute certainty that she wouldn't scruple to speak if it suited her.

'No, not later on. Now, right away.'

'Very well.' He replaced the receiver without another word. At his sides his hands clenched and unclenched themselves. There was the laughing, dazzlingly pretty Zena of his youth, and there was this sour, dangerous woman with touched-up hair and a puffy face. At what point of time had one image overlaid the other? Even now they seemed to him totally distinct, as if she had been two separate women, the one who had gone away and the one who had bafflingly taken her place.

'I'm going out,' he called up the stairs. 'I don't think I'll be very long.' He snatched his coat from the stand and shrugged it on, flung open the door and let himself out into the misty lamplight of the empty street.

A surge of melancholy rose inside him. He was forty-seven years old, no wife, no child, no house of his own, not even a spectacular success at his job. His mediocre qualifications had been laboriously acquired by sweating his way through an accountancy course at evening classes; it was highly unlikely that he could ever hope for a really good post.

He pondered again the possibility of clearing out, making a fresh start in some other town. It seemed for a hopeful moment that it might be the answer. At one stroke he could turn his back on the past, stepping down from the train in that far-off place a completely different man. Outgoing, at ease, in command of his life.

But there was never really a fresh start. Among the inescapable luggage one carried the burden of personality. And in that other town he would start without any kind of contact, he would be even more alone. He saw the bleak lodgings, himself confined every evening to a single room or wandering about streets that didn't even call up, as the streets of Milbourne sometimes did, memories of a cherished childhood.

He shook his head, relinquishing the notion of escape. As he turned into the narrow road leading to The Sycamores he fell back into an old habit of mind he employed whenever depression threatened to overwhelm him. It was a trick he had begun to practise in the prison camp; it had kept him sane then and it had served him during all the years that followed. Sometimes it worked, sometimes it didn't, but even when it failed, the effort involved at least took his attention for a brief spell from his blackest imaginings.

What he did was to switch his brain into another gear, trying to alter the whole climate of his mind, looking back into his boyhood, attempting to think himself into the same attitude of carefree gaiety to life.

He would look at the sky, the trees, the buildings, striving to see them as they had appeared to him then; he would watch a child skipping by and grasp at the notion that the time and place and weather that seemed so carelessly joyful to the child existed also at that very moment for himself.

And click! sometimes the brief miracle happened and he could glance about him with hope and pleasure, feeling the bright air as inviting, the roads as beckoning, as forty years ago. As if he were constantly practising the memory of happiness so that if he were ever fortunate enough to encounter it again in reality he would remember and recognize it, clutch it to him before it slipped away for ever.

By the time he turned the knob on the front door of The Sycamores he felt composed, almost cheerful.

'Hello there!' He sent an enquiring call soaring from the hallway. A moment later he heard Zena's answering voice, and he went briskly, confidently up the stairs.

In the comfortable sitting-room of his small detached house in a quiet area of Milbourne, Neil Underwood sat at his bureau, shuffling a little pile of bills into a tidy square. He sighed; his face wore a baffled look. The exuberance of Christmas had faded now, leaving behind a wash of regret for the rash generosity that had sent him out so blithely to the silver-glittered shops.

Rates, electricity, gas, coal; the record-player for his daughter. Once again he flicked through the accounts as if they might magically have diminished in the last three minutes. His glance came inescapably to rest on the biggest body-blow of the lot, the one he had so far managed to thrust into some merciful recess in his mind—the appalling, horrifying bill for Ruth's fur coat.

Four hundred and fifty pounds! For an instant he felt almost proud of the figures, magnificent, princely. A noble gesture of a man towards his new wife on her first Christmas in the bosom of his family.

A week ago, with pine needles scattering the carpet and sprigs of holly peering out from the tops of pictures and mirrors, it had seemed worth every penny. Ruth had slipped the coat on with delight, sinking her fingers into the silky pelt. He had felt himself a maharajah, an emperor. And there had been the lunatic notion that Santa Claus might suddenly remember his duties, there might be a windfall, a legacy—a gold necklace from the Iron Age might spring up in his back garden.

He jabbed a pen down on the papers, considering the possibility of an overdraft, shaking his head even as he pondered the word. Some little time now since his bank manager had smiled at him; his eyes these days took on a wary, calculating look as soon as he saw Neil. Bank managers weren't notoriously helpful to men who ran through their patrimony, actually spending capital instead of doing what every natural law commanded, sending it out to increase and multiply.

And not only to live up to the hilt of his less than princely salary from the local council but to take a new wife in addition! None of your homely stew-and-semolina-pudding wives either but an elegant, sophisticated young woman whom any bank manager would at once associate with a regrettable taste for fillet steaks and smoked salmon.

Ah well! Jabbing at the bills didn't seem to have helped much, so he swept them all away into a pigeon-hole, slammed the desk shut and stood up. He'd done his bit for the time being; he'd taken the damned things out and looked at them, about all any civilized creature could be expected to do on New Year's Day. It would be a few weeks yet before the final notices shrieked out their red-ink warnings. All kinds of things might happen in that time. He crossed over to the television set and switched it on.

Ruth came in from the kitchen ten minutes later. She dropped into an easy chair.

'I've made a sketchy kind of risotto with the very last final farewell remains of the turkey.' She pulled a face. 'I don't wish to clap eyes on another fowl for a considerable length of time.' Her face was flushed. A coil of her very long, very thick, very blonde hair—and naturally blonde at that—had detached itself from the pins that kept the rest of the mass piled on top of her head; she suddenly discovered the fact and skewered it back into position with a forceful gesture. She wore a nylon overall, her feet were thrust into sheepskin slippers. And with it all she contrived to look breathtakingly beautiful.

'Do you know what time Jane's coming in?' she asked.

Neil tore his eyes away from her and glanced at his watch. 'She'll be here in a few minutes.' Friday was a late night at the library. He let his gaze rest again on his wife; he thought she was the most lovely creature he had ever seen. Fine, high cheekbones, sea-green eyes, a honey-coloured skin. She smiled at him suddenly, put out a finger and flicked it at his cheek, then she let herself slip back into the cushioned embrace of the chair.

'Oh—this is nice. I'm so sleepy after last night.' Up till all hours dining and dancing. 'I'll be glad to get to bed early.'

He frowned. 'I'm going over to see Zena after supper. I thought you might come with me.' Tension crept into the air.

Ruth sat up. 'We saw Zena last night. And Owen.' And pretty maddening Zena had been too, drinking more than was good for her, growing quarrelsome as the relentless jollity ground on. Ruth had got well and truly tired of Madame Zena, would be happy not to see her again till next New Year's Eve.

'I ran into Owen in the town at lunch-time,' Neil explained. 'He said Zena wasn't very well, she's in bed.'

Ruth gave a little laugh. 'I'm not surprised.'

Neil felt irritation begin to prickle along his nerves. 'You know she suffers from diabetes.'

'She suffers from self-indulgence.'

He decided to ignore that, being unable to think of an adequate reply. 'So I gave her a ring, I told her I'd be over later on. I know she's hoping you'll come too.'

Ruth laughed out loud. 'Really, Neil! She can't stand the sight of me.' She considered for a moment whether she could be bothered to put a good face on it and go along with Neil, if he thought it so important. But she was tired and she couldn't see much point in making the effort. She couldn't go on making an effort for another twenty or thirty years so she might as well cease now. 'I don't think I will go, if you don't mind,' she said with easy affection. 'You can have a good natter with her, all about the old days and dear Dad and everything. I'd only be in the way.'

'Very well, just as you please.' The injured tone that he always employed when he felt her slipping beyond his control. He passionately desired her to be two entirely opposite human beings, the lovely, independent creature she was, followed by the eye of every male in her vicinity, and the mild, unremarkable, acquiescent person his first wife had been, unnoticed by any man unless he fell over her feet.

'Don't sulk,' she said teasingly, smiling at him, trying to restore lightness to the atmosphere.

He set his jaw. 'I'm not sulking.' He shifted in his chair and turned his eyes to the television set. The demon that had been sneaking up on him had him now by the throat, taking him as usual totally by surprise. When Muriel was alive he had never known the meaning of jealousy. He had been unable to comprehend such emotion, regarding it with contempt as a childish weakness carried over into adult life.

And now, painfully and humiliatingly, scarcely a day

passed without at some time plunging him into the same dark pit. When the black mood was on him he was powerless to resist its obsessional broodings. Every word and glance of Ruth's seemed to carry a second meaning beneath the innocent overlay. Sometimes the misery would mercifully last only a few minutes, sometimes it persisted for two or three days, vanishing always apparently of its own accord, like sunlight piercing a storm-cloud.

And all the time some rational observer in his brain would be saying, 'You could throw all this off in a single moment, now and forever, you could just let go, relax, love her, you could be ecstatically happy.' He would struggle to obey, to force himself up from the pit, he would almost succeed. And then memory would stab at him again; he would recall the tone of her voice, the casual way she had greeted him or the warmth of some remark she had let fall about a male colleague. He would slip back at once into a despair that held a kind of resentful triumph. You see! he would cry out silently from the pit, she doesn't love me! I mean nothing to her! Has she not just proved it?

Oh lord! Ruth thought now, seeing the way he hunched his shoulders, here we go again! It was possible that he fancied these ridiculous displays might precipitate her into rushing across the room to fling her arms round his neck in wild penitence at some imaginary offence, beg his pardon, receive his forgiving kisses, dab away her tears. And probably fetch his slippers into the bargain like a well-trained dog, she added to herself with a twitch of her lips. Whereas in reality what she felt prompted to do was stride over and punch him on the jaw.

She's actually smiling! Neil thought with savage anger, having briefly turned his head to note her expression. She's laughing at my torments! Enjoying herself! He leaned forward and frowned with fierce concentration at the screen.

Ruth sprang to her feet. 'I'll go and dish up,' she said lightly. 'I'll put Jane's supper in the oven to keep warm. Come along when you hear me shout.' Don't come if you don't want to, she added to herself. Congealed risotto will probably suit your state of mind.

As she went into the hall the front door burst open and Jane came in, blowing an icy breath of air in with her.

'Oh, hello!' Ruth said, smiling at her step-daughter. 'You're just in time, I am about to present the turkey's last goodbye.'

Jane didn't smile back. Her eyes didn't quite meet Ruth's. 'I'm going out again as soon as I've eaten and changed.' She addressed her words to a point a few inches to one side of Ruth's face. Ruth took a fractional step sideways, playing a little game she had evolved over the last ten months, trying to shift herself swiftly and unobtrusively into a position in which their glances would inescapably interlock. But Jane was as always just a little too quick for her.

'There's a party on. One of the girls from the library. It should be quite decent.'

Not that she always evaded Ruth's gaze or treated her with this show of cool detachment. She was quite often spontaneous and open, even friendly. It was simply that she was only seventeen and hadn't yet been able to accept this beautiful stranger in the place of her very ordinary and beloved mother.

Ruth didn't usually mind her withdrawals though there were times, such as the present moment, when it would be pleasant to be able to speak to at least one person in the house and be certain of a normal response. She'd been prepared for difficulties with a step-daughter and she liked the girl, welcomed any little advances she made and was quite happy to wait for time to do its work.

'Anyone special at the party?' she asked lightly.

Jane's face remained closed. 'No, just the usual gang.' She turned to go upstairs. She hadn't forgotten the time a couple of months back when she'd brought a rather promising youth in for a cup of coffee after the theatre and the wretched lad had sat and gawped at Ruth with goggling eyes for the best part of an hour. Until Jane had smartly kicked his shin when no one was looking, unsubtly indicating that his time was up, he'd better take himself off. She hadn't clapped eyes on him again and she had no wish to do so.

She frowned as she went slowly into her bedroom. It was going to be rather a problem. Any boy she really fancied would have to be brought home in the end, would slide his eyes from her own perfectly wholesome and reasonably pretty face to the quite staggering countenance of her stepmother.

She jerked open the wardrobe door and ran an impatient hand along the rail, considering the merits of various dresses.

It was horribly unfair. All the other girls she knew had plump and unassuming mothers or mothers who were bony and scraggy rather than slimly rounded. Mothers with frankly greying hair or corrugated waves touched into improbable tints by the heavy hands of provincial hairdressers. Not huge masses of the most wonderful pale gold, thick and shining.

She pulled out a newish dress, a sort of orangey-brown, carried it over to the dressing-table and held it up against herself. M'm, not bad. It made her somewhat indeterminate colouring look more interesting, brought out coppery lights in her hair, emphasized the delicacy of her skin. Creamy, she decided, my skin looks creamy. The word pleased her, she began to feel a little more cheerful.

She threw the dress on the bed and bounced along to the bathroom. Perhaps she could run away and get married when the time came, make sure the bridegroom never set eyes on Ruth till he was safely bound hand and foot. She ran the taps and splashed about quite gaily, humming a tune and looking forward to the evening.

And then it struck her that the stupid loon—her imaginary new husband that is, a creature she was by now beginning to be heartily sick of—might go and fall in love with Ruth *after* they were married. That would be a fine how-d'ye-do. She groped about for a towel, gritting her teeth in exasperation.

Either she was going to have to keep away from Milbourne for the whole of her married life or she was doomed to remain a spinster. She let out a long sigh. I suppose I could emigrate, she thought hopelessly, searching for the toothpaste. Canada or Australia.

She saw herself tilling the soil in some primitive station in the outback. Dressed in a washed-out cotton frock, her hair faded by relentless suns. Her man—for the stupid loon now reappeared as an earthy, monosyllabic hulk—hacking down mighty trees for some obscure purpose of his own.

'Supper's ready!' Ruth's cheerful voice from the hall.

Jane picked up the towel from the floor, realizing suddenly that she was extremely hungry. She stuck her head out of the door and yelled, 'I'll be down in a minute.'

Actually Ruth wasn't so bad; she was obviously trying to be kind and helpful. And there was nothing so very wrong with her own looks. Only the other day one of the girls at the library—and they were a highly critical bunch, heaven only knew—had said she wished she had legs as long and slender as Jane's.

By the time she got back to her room she was singing again, very loudly.

Downstairs in the hall Ruth stood looking fixedly at the door of the sitting-room. No sound of movement from within. Neil hadn't answered her summons. He was going to sit there then in front of the television set with unseeing eyes, until it was time for him to go off to The Sycamores. What a waste of time—when they could be so happy together. She clicked her tongue impatiently, then came to a decision and threw open the door.

'Come on, Neil,' she said coaxingly, regretting the necessity to treat a man ten years older than herself as if he were a toddler in a tantrum or someone a little soft in the head. 'Come and eat your supper while it's hot. It isn't too bad. The turkey was a noble bird, we'll speed his passing with a glass of wine.'

Neil moved ever so slightly in his chair. 'Please, Neil.' A soothing, gentle tone, suitable for the elderly or ailing. 'I put some peppers and mushrooms in the risotto, especially for you.' Oh, do put a sock in it, she thought, beginning to run out of sweetness and light.

He turned his head and looked at her. She closed her eyes for an instant in relief; any movement was a hopeful sign. She smiled at him, went over and sat on the arm of his chair, put a hand on his shoulder and gave a little squeeze.

'I do love you, Neil. I wish you wouldn't—' Wiser perhaps not to finish the sentence.

All at once he felt remarkably better. He leaned his head against her warm soft body. 'I'm sorry, Ruth, it was all those bills.'

As soon as he uttered the words he regretted them. In the ten months they had been married he had unswervingly maintained the position of being the open-handed head of the household, the true breadwinner. This had enabled him —most of the time—to feel in command of things, and allowed Ruth's salary to be looked on as the little woman's pin-money.

In fact she earned now two-thirds of what he earned. And as he was only number two in the local housing department, the head of which was a vigorous man still under fifty, and Ruth—as a junior executive in a large firm of food processers with branches scattered throughout the country —could expect early and continuing promotion, there was a very good chance that in a few years she would be getting two or three times as much as Neil. To these hard facts he deliberately closed his mind.

Unable altogether to credit his astounding good fortune in actually marrying this bird of paradise, uncertain that he would be able for very long to hold her, he had relied on money as his most powerful ally.

An unnecessarily lavish honeymoon, the extravagant replacement of perfectly serviceable furnishings, presents of clothes, perfumes, jewellery, had put paid in quick time to what remained of his inheritance. He was either going to have to count pennies from now on, producing a rapid and inescapable alteration in his whole attitude towards his wife —and indeed, towards his image of himself—or he was going to have to find some more money. Rather a lot of money. A continuing supply of money. Or else a massive sum that would produce a hefty annual return.

Ruth gave his shoulders another squeeze. 'Is that all you're worried about?' she asked lightly. 'I'll help with the bills. Tell me how much you want.' She was under the impression that they were talking about some minor difficulty, the need perhaps to sell some shares when the stock market was sluggish. She believed Neil was quite rich. He had given her every reason to believe it.

'Oh, there's no need for that,' he said, managing a gay laugh. Once he started laying hands on her bank account, that would be the beginning of the end between them. She wouldn't stand for it very long when she realized the true situation. And why should she? he asked himself with a sense of justice. Why on earth should a beautiful and intelligent young woman supply her husband with the cash to pay for her own Christmas present?

'It's perfectly all right, really.' His tone easy and casual now. 'It was just the way they all come in a bunch at this time of year.' He put up a hand and gave a little yawn. 'Makes them seem a lot bigger than they are.' He felt a strong impulse to change the subject. 'Well now, might as well see what this famous risotto's like.' Not that he was in the least hungry; the bills and the demon between them had destroyed what little appetite was left from the New Year feasting.

She stood up and pulled him to his feet.

'Don't stay too long at Zena's, will you?' She smiled up at him. 'Then we can have an early night.'

'If you go now,' Zena said, glancing at the clock, 'you'll

be in good time. He'll still be at the club.' Anger took hold of her again at the notion of Owen taking decisions behind her back, slipping away from her, escaping. Where? To what? There was an unpleasant sense of change in the air and she was at an age when all change seemed disturbing.

Arnold remained seated. He often found when it came to the point that he was more relaxed with Zena than with anyone else. No need to be on guard with her, he thought with a trace of wry amusement, she knew all there was to be known about him. Or nearly all.

'What am I supposed to do if he drives off somewhere in his car? I can hardly keep after him on foot.' He hadn't the remotest intention of taking part in such an insane procedure but there was no harm in appearing to fall in with her fantastic commands.

Easy enough to string her along. All he had to do was report from time to time that he had dogged Owen's footsteps—he almost laughed aloud at the ludicrously theatrical notion, typical of a woman who spent half her time lounging in bed—and that Owen's behaviour was a model of innocence.

He looked at Zena with a moment's deep compassion for the garish muddle of her life. She had started out with so many advantages. If she had had a little more common sense, a little more insight, a little less egotism. But she hadn't dictated her temperament or arranged her upbringing. And his own hamstrung existence hardly gave him the right to criticize anyone else's.

'You can get a taxi,' Zena said impatiently. 'There are always taxis coming and going round there. Go on, get a move on.'

'All right then.' Arnold levered himself out of his chair. 'But I don't think you've got anything to worry about. You do rather imagine things.' To her surprise he stooped and patted her hand.

The action didn't please her; it didn't square with her

feeling of manipulating people, exerting power over events. For a long time now her relationship with her husband had lacked the bite, the edge that provided her with the needling stimulus she absolutely had to have if the days were not to wash over her in savage grey monotony. Owen had somehow sidled out of her reach into a position from which he seemed able to survey her with acquired calm. She had come to rely instead on her exchanges with Arnold, on the curious blend of old intimacy and present hostility that gave a sharp lift to her spirits.

But if Arnold in turn were to wriggle free—she frowned and pulled her hand away.

'I have no need to imagine things.' She threw significance and force into her look. 'I have enough hard facts to be going on with.' And saw with a return of pleasure and reassurance that his face hardened again.

'Be sure to leave the front door on the latch.' She picked up a book and opened it, no longer bothering to look at him, levelling the command with a casual authority that tightened his nerves. 'I'm expecting my brother shortly.' Her shoulders moved luxuriously against the pillows; her mouth opened in a wide and pleasurable yawn.

Arnold went rapidly from the room and down the stairs, trying to release by swift movement the angry tensions that twisted inside him again. He let himself out of the house, plunged down the steps and into the drive.

It might not be very much longer now that he would have to dance—or maintain a ridiculous show of dancing—to Zena's tune. His father was seventy-two; old age had gathered its forces in the last year or two, had struck more than one shrewd blow; he seemed no longer able to rally with the remains of his youthful vigour.

Arnold halted for a moment, appalled at the direction of his thoughts, jerking them away with a violent shake of his head. He loved his father, he certainly couldn't wish him dead simply to snap the bond that kept him dangling at Zena's call. He resumed his quick step beneath the arching trees, forcing his mind away from the memory of his father lying with flushed cheeks, confused by fevered dreams, in the old double bed at home.

His thoughts circled briefly round the foolish errand on which Zena believed she had despatched him. Was it after all possible that she was right, that Yorke had allowed his eyes to stray? Not so very unlikely perhaps. Yorke was in the prime of life. His carefully-laid plans were all bearing fruit; he might feel now the need for something warmer, gentler, in the busy pattern of successful days.

His mind threw up a sharp image of Linda Fleming walking gracefully along the corridors of the factory, and Owen Yorke attentive and smiling beside her, putting a hand under her elbow to pilot her through a doorway. I wonder, he thought, frowning at the notion . . . Linda Fleming . . . I suppose it is conceivable. He was startled at the fierce thrust of jealousy that struck at him; he halted again, closing his eyes for an instant, willing away disturbing emotions.

He opened his eyes and glanced about him, sighing at the rest of the chill evening in front of him. He had reached the main road. Where to now? Back to the neat semi-detached and Sarah's busy silence? Or wander without objective through the Milbourne streets, killing a couple of the pointless hours that advanced towards him one by one until the last hour of all and total oblivion.

A car came round the bend of the road, cruising smoothly and without haste. He glanced at the number-plate, at the sleek outline, placing it immediately, one of the local police cars. The driver turned his head, raised a hand in greeting. David Cottrell, patrolling the New Year streets, idly watchful. Arnold nodded briefly in reply.

'Who's that?' In the passenger seat young Detective-Constable Quigley half-swivelled round to look back at the solitary figure wreathed in mist.

'Pierson. Accountant. Underwood's.' Cottrell supplied the staccato information, accustomed to filling gaps in local knowledge for newcomers to the force. Only a month or two in Milbourne, young Quigley, but shaping well, anxious to learn.

'Not the most pleasant evening for a stroll,' the constable said.

'Wouldn't be just a stroll. That lane he was coming out of leads to The Sycamores, nothing beyond, except fields. His boss lives in The Sycamores. Owen Yorke.' Up to the house on business of some sort; Cottrell automatically filed away the information. Pierson was hardly likely to have been engaged in a purely social activity. 'Not exactly the life and soul of the party, Arnold Pierson,' he said aloud, remembering all at once a different Arnold in the days when they were lads together. 'He was sweet on Zena Yorke once. Zena Underwood she was then.'

Quigley tilted his head back. 'Perhaps he is still.' Married barely six months himself, he inhabited a world in which everyone was—or ought to be—in love.

'Not he,' Cottrell said with finality. 'He was just a kid then.' He stared back at the past. 'We were in the army together. Taken prisoner by the Japs.' He pondered briefly on the way it had affected some men, changed them permanently, while other men, himself among them, had been able to put it behind them. 'He's always been a bit odd since then, a loner, takes him all his time to speak to me if I stop in the street.' He sighed; whatever he and young Pierson had expected on that long-ago morning when they'd burst through the door of the recruiting-office, they'd surely never imagined it would end like this, the cool nods of total strangers thirty years later.

'I've never really been able to make out why it took him like that.' Of all men he would have expected Pierson to have been able to come to terms with life in a Japanese camp, to have cast it off later without crippling bitterness. 'He just withdrew, right into his shell, pretty well from the moment we were taken prisoner, and he's stayed like that, locked up inside himself, ever since.'

Quigley made no reply. Not even born until the war was well and truly over, he had grown out of his childhood passion for hearing old campaigns refought, merely bored now by tales of what old So-and-So had been through in those stirring times. He allowed his mind to slip into another gear where it was pleasantly occupied by thoughts of Sharon, his Sharon, actually his very own wife Sharon, at this moment without doubt cooking supper for him with her beautiful delicate hands.

Cottrell slid a glance at him, recognizing that glazed and dreaming expression as of one who hears far off the music of the spheres. Give him time, Cottrell thought, well-used to these symptoms in newly-wedded constables; the dreaming days don't last for long. Two or three years of irregular hours, night duty, haphazard social life and the dust would begin to drift over the gilding, Quigley would start to frown like other men, young Mrs Quigley's voice would take on a higher, more acid note. Seen it so many times, had Cottrell—which was why, being in spite of everything a romantic man who liked his giltwork bright and gleaming, he had never married himself.

'Wake up!' he said good-humouredly. 'You've still got an hour or two to do.'

'Oh—I'm sorry.' Quigley sat up straight, squared his shoulders. He glanced out at the misty street. Almost in the centre of town now, more cars about, people setting off for the evening's gaieties, lights shining out from hotels and cafés, a sudden flash of music. 'All right for some,' he said. 'Nothing better to do than enjoy themselves.'

'No thanks, I'm just off.' Owen Yorke raised a friendly hand, gesturing his politely firm refusal of another drink. He set down his empty tumbler and stood up, nodding farewell here and there. The lounge at the Independents' was pretty full this evening, many of the members in dinner-jackets, going on to some ritual feasting.

He looked about with satisfaction. A good club to belong

to, the finest in Milbourne, possibly in the whole county. And in no time at all he'd be standing in the ballroom, wearing his presidential sash, taking Zena by the hand, leading the first waltz at the inaugural ball.

He felt normal again, thank goodness, normal in the way he always used to feel until just lately, in the way he was pretty certain the great majority of the other members felt. Prosperous business and professional men, solid family men, ready long ago to settle for what might be reasonably expected from life, a sure and steady income, a sensible wife. Not men to chase a will-o'-the-wisp profit in tricky mining shares or be dazzled by a pair of smiling hazel eyes.

As he made his way between the tables he allowed himself to ponder for a moment on the home lives of these relaxed and jovial citizens. If any one of them had ever felt the pangs of passionate love, it was certainly not apparent now in the way they talked about their wives, in the whole of their attitudes, spoken or unspoken, about marriage. No one in his senses looked for pulsing happiness after the first year or two; a man who mentioned his wife often, with affection, was considered uxorious, soft, to be despised, even pitied.

His own marriage was not, after all, so exceptional. Quite run-of-the-mill, really. In the entrance hall he paused to read a notice on the green-baize board. A stray thought suddenly reared up in his mind. He looked back into the lounge at the urbanely smiling faces, wondering if any of his fellow clubmen, so like him in externals, were like him also in experiencing sometimes that painful, disturbing sense of having been cheated. Had any of them ever laid hold of a shining blade and longed, however briefly, to sink it into soft white flesh?

He gave a fragmentary laugh. Hardly likely, old boy, he said firmly to himself, taking the insane notion by the scruff of its neck and flinging it from him.

He exchanged a few friendly remarks with the hall-porter, slipping the fellow a handsome tip in expansive recognition of the season of goodwill. Down the steps, out into the car-park. A settled, highly-respectable citizen. He inserted a key into the car door. But . . . while he was actually out . . . and since he had definitely decided to close the shop . . . and as there was after all the matter of the surplus stock to be disposed of . . . he might perhaps just call in on Mrs Fleming.

Only five or ten minutes, certainly no more than a quarter of an hour. Purely and exclusively a matter of business.

He gave a little decisive nod of his head, opened the car door and settled himself with a brisk movement into the driving seat. He reversed the car and swung it smoothly out on to the forecourt, quite unaware that he was humming the waltz tune from *The Merry Widow*.

CHAPTER V

The bathroom was deliciously warm and steamy, the radio spun soft threads of music into the fragrant air. Oh . . . oh . . . I could lie here for hours, Linda thought, squeezing her sponge in the pale blue water.

For a moment she contemplated turning the hot tap on again, closing her eyes against the account books waiting for her in the desk downstairs. A loud rat-tat beat suddenly on the door panels.

'You still in there, Mrs Fleming?' Emily Bond's sharply accusing tones. 'I need some more scouring powder.'

Linda gave a long resigned sigh and pulled out the plug, seeing peace and leisure swirl away. She stood up and reached out for a towel.

'There's another canister in the cupboard under the sink. I'll be down in a moment,' she called placatingly.

'I can't stop above another twenty minutes or so,' Emily screeched with resolution.

Linda dabbed herself dry with speed. 'Yes, I know,' she called. 'I'm very grateful.' Oh, the weary necessity to keep the old duck in a good mood, on top of having to lash out high wages and handsome sweeteners. 'If you could just finish downstairs before you go, it would be such a help.' A mumbled grunt at the other side of the door as Emily took herself off again.

Linda wrapped a huge towel round herself and ran along the passage to her bedroom. She took a fluffy housecoat from behind the door, slipped her feet into feathery mules and attended rapidly to her face and hair. As she went downstairs towards the little room which she used as an office, she could hear Emily banging about in the kitchen. She wouldn't bother to make herself any supper just yet, for that would mean having to ply Emily with coffee and sandwiches, with a great waste of time all round.

She had just settled herself at the desk and begun to sort through the invoices when she heard a ring at the front entrance. Not the door leading into the shop but the one admitting visitors to the house. She threw down her pencil. Who on earth could it be calling on her? She went through the hall and opened the door.

'Why—Mr Yorke!' He was standing at the top of the short flight of steps, half turned towards the street, giving the impression that his call was made on the spur of the moment, that it was scarcely likely to be long.

'I happened to be passing.' His tone was friendly but impersonal. 'I thought I'd look in and see how you've been making out.' Crikey, he thought, a little taken aback by the sight of her in that pretty pink thing, her hair loosely taken up, her eyes still bright, her skin still faintly flushed from the bath—I'd certainly better not stay for more than five or ten minutes. 'But I expect you're busy.' He kept his voice light and easy.

'No, not at all. Do come in. As a matter of fact I was just starting to go through my books. There are one or two little matters I'd rather like to ask you about.' She opened the door more widely. At the mention of business he smiled and stepped inside. She closed the door and led the way along the passage.

'I use this room as an office. It's a bit cramped but at least it stops me scattering papers all over the sitting-room.' She would keep him in here out of earshot of Emily. No point in advertising to that old gossip the identity of her caller—or, she thought suddenly, in letting Owen Yorke know that his wife's charwoman was at that moment splashing about in the kitchen a few yards away.

She pulled up another chair. 'There's a question about discount that I don't altogether understand. Perhaps you know the firm?' She sorted the papers with a businesslike air. Time enough to relax with a glass of port in front of the sitting-room fire after Emily had been quietly despatched from the premises.

Owen ran his eyes over the invoices. 'Yes, I know this firm, very sound, been in the trade since the year dot. If you take the gross figure, here—'

Very bright, he thought with professional approval; she cottoned on at once to the somewhat involved explanation. And pretty too, really very pretty, sitting there in that pink negligée, smiling her gratitude. A pleasant, easy glow spread through him, he leaned forward and laid a hand lightly, casually over hers.

'I've decided to close down my High Street premises.' He liked the way she didn't break out into irritating Ohs and Whys but sat there with her head tilted, still with a smile on her lips, waiting for him to go on. 'There'll be a certain amount of stock left over at the end of the sale.' And he liked the way she didn't coyly withdraw her hand but let it lie peacefully beneath his own; not a woman who would argue every toss and turn with a man. 'If you were interested, I could let you have it very reasonably.' He gave her hand a fractional squeeze. The smile remained on her lips, her hand stayed where it was. 'At a purely nominal figure. You'd want to see the stuff of course, that could easily be arranged. I could take you over there one evening after the sale. Do you think you might be interested?'

She turned her head and looked him full in the eyes; her smile deepened. 'Oh yes. I might be very interested indeed.'

Ruth Underwood took the supper-plates from the trolley and began to stack them in the dish-washing machine. From upstairs came the bang of Jane's bedroom door, the sound of her feet running along the corridor, down into the hall. The sitting-room door thrust open, slammed shut again a moment later.

Ruth set the coffee-cups into a rack, ranged the saucers in position. Jane flung open the kitchen door.

'Father's gone! He might have waited for me, he knew I was going out!'

Ruth picked up a handful of used cutlery and inserted them into a container. 'Were you hoping for a lift? I don't think he could have understood, otherwise I'm sure he'd have waited. He's been gone ten minutes or more.' She stooped to take the tumblers from the lower shelf of the trolley. 'I imagined one of your friends would be calling for you. Can you get a bus?'

Jane frowned. 'Yes, I suppose so. But it's a rotten night to be waiting round for buses. You ought to have a car,' she said suddenly. 'I can't think why you don't. It would be very useful.' Her voice took on a friendly, animated note. 'And I could learn to drive, I could use it too.' She took a couple of steps into the room. 'Why don't you get one? Then we wouldn't always be so dependent on Father's car. If you had one now you could have run me to the party.'

'As a matter of fact I'm thinking about getting one quite soon.' Ruth crossed over to the table to pick up a couple of serving-dishes. What a pleasant manner Jane could switch on when she wanted to wheedle something out of her. And how cheerfully she was prepared to play her father and stepmother off against each other. She blinked away the thought. Only natural after all, in Jane's situation, any youngster would do the same. She smiled, 'I'll let you know when I make up my mind, you might come with me to choose it.'

'Oh, I'd love that. Do make it soon, won't you?' Jane glanced at the clock. 'I must go or I'll miss that bus.' She waved a careless hand and turned to the door.

What she needs is a nice steady boy-friend, Ruth thought with a wry smile as the echoes of departure died away. Someone to take her attention off her father and me.

She closed the machine and switched it on, then she sat down at the table and lit a cigarette. Monday, she thought, inhaling deeply, on Monday they'll announce the new appointments. Energy flooded through her; there was nothing she relished better than challenge, exciting change.

A senior executive had suffered a crippling heart attack early in December. There'd been temporary re-arrangements to tide them over the busy Christmas season; she'd been doing a job and a half herself for the last few weeks. She had no idea who the new man would be, he might be someone moved up from another branch or one of the Milbourne staff. She didn't much care who he was; it was the post of his assistant she had her eye on.

She stared down at the smoke rising from her cigarette, pondering again the coming reshuffle, the combinations and permutations it might give rise to. However she juggled the names and personalities in her mind, it always ended with the same result. No one in the department was better equipped for the assistant's job than herself.

She pushed back the chair and walked over to the whirring machine, she stood watching the jets of water rise and fall. They were certain to appoint her to the post, they must appoint her. It was surely totally out of the question that even for a single moment would they seriously consider promoting Anthea Gibbs.

'Never!' she said aloud on a derisory note. Anthea was turned forty, a watershed of an age in a firm that prided itself on the early singling out of talent; promotion must surely already have passed her by. Not that Anthea would see it. It would be another three or four years before she would finally swallow the unpalatable fact. Conscientious, hard-working, entirely competent at her own level. But a narrow, blinkered mind, not a spark of creative energy, no vision, no fire.

Ruth drew a little breath of satisfaction as if the matter had now been settled beyond dispute. She felt too stimulated, too restless to go into the sitting-room and stare at the television set. Coffee—she'd make herself some more. From a shelf she took down the percolator, discharging some of her thrusting energy in performing the routine actions with unnecessary force.

Promotion would mean quite a bit more money—though this thought sprang to her mind as very much a secondary consideration. She would definitely buy herself a car; it was ludicrous for a woman in her position to be dependent on buses and taxis. Or the convenience of her husband.

Her brow wrinkled into a frown. Odd the way Neil always nudged aside her suggestion of a second car. It could hardly be the money involved, he was if anything too generous in lavishing gifts on her. It was almost as if—she took out the notion and looked at it, not altogether liking its appearance at close quarters—as if he felt that a car would give her too much independence.

A tiny light glowed on the percolator, indicating that the coffee was ready; she poured out a cup and sat down again at the table, idly stirring the spoon in the steaming liquid. Another thought edged its way into her mind. Neil wasn't going to be all that pleased about a hefty increase in her salary, whatever she decided to spend it on. Nor was he likely to be wildly enthusiastic at her promotion.

With a shrug of her shoulders she abandoned that unprofitable line of thought; she'd have to deal with those consequences when they arose.

But the car—that was a more agreeable subject. She began to picture it in her mind. Nothing large or showy, a trim workmanlike runabout. It would be pleasant to have a car of her own again. She'd had a rather nice little foreign vehicle when she'd started out in the Liverpool branch but she'd had to get rid of it after her move to London. A car made life too complicated in London, what with the difficulties in parking, the nervous strain of all that traffic.

For a long moment she looked back at her time in London—and her reasons for leaving so abruptly. Anywhere, she'd decidedly suddenly and finally that sunny morning fourteen months ago, scanning the internal news-sheet lying on her desk with its list of vacancies in other branches—anywhere as long as it was far enough away from London. Anywhere had turned out to be Milbourne. And Neil. She'd met him a fortnight after she'd stepped down from the train; three months later she'd married him.

She closed her eyes against those London days, letting memory drain away in a long sigh, then she sat up briskly and raised the coffee cup to her lips.

'You surely can't mean you've run through the whole lot?' Zena linked her hands behind her head and leaned comfortably back against the pillows. There was no sharp concern in the look she gave her brother. He'd been reared as she was, with a healthy regard for money. The burst of folly—for so she chose to regard it—that had precipitated him into a hasty second marriage had certainly given rise to some wild spending but she couldn't for a moment believe he had made any really serious inroads into his capital.

Neil had been eighteen at the end of the war; in the years of his adolescence and young manhood there had been little encouragement or even opportunity for extravagance. Too young for active service, he had in due course been called up for a period of peacetime conscription. Afterwards he'd gone to London, begun his career in local government, married and settled down, returning to Milbourne when Jane was a child of ten.

Muriel had always seemed a careful, thrifty, undemanding wife; they had lived unshowily. Certainly he had never enjoyed a very handsome salary but Zena was sure they had always lived within it. Like many people with plenty of money and a strong taste for indulging their own extravagances while at the same time keeping a tight hand on the purse as far as other folk were concerned, Zena harboured the comfortable belief that less privileged citizens could and should manage very well on what they had.

'No, of course I don't mean anything of the sort.' Neil gave an easy little laugh. 'I'd scarcely be such a fool. It's just that I had rather a lot of expense over Christmas.' He contrived to make it sound as if the expense had been forced on him by some outside agency over which he had no control. 'You know what the stock market's like at this time of year.' A touch of flattery here towards herself as a shrewd judge of financial affairs. 'Not the best time for selling.' He smiled at her, the affectionate younger-brother smile that self-interest as well as habit had kept in practice. 'I thought perhaps you might be able to help me out.' Appealing to the old protective instinct of an elder sister. 'Just temporarily of course.' Establishing the correct attitude of retrenchment, the conscientious will to repay—without being inconveniently exact about the time or method of repayment.

'No.' Zena didn't bother to dress up her refusal. Neil had been little more than a boy when old Ralph died; he had had no interest in the gown-shop, he had been well satisfied to get his share of the inheritance in hard cash without any responsibility for running the business. He might very well envy the way in which her own capital had been put to work so that she now had a half-share in the whole Underwood enterprise, but his envy was no concern of hers.

She put up a hand to her mouth and gave a little yawn. 'You can borrow the money from Ruth. She must have a very good salary.' She saw the tiny instinctive shake of his head. 'And I dare say she'll have a better one very soon.' She knew about the illness and retirement of the senior executive at British Foods; it was no secret that there would be a reshuffle. 'I don't suppose she'll find her looks any hindrance to promotion.'

'Any promotion Ruth gets will be due to her ability and nothing else,' Neil said coldly. He wished fervently that he could be certain of that. 'And in any case I don't believe she's expecting promotion. She hasn't said anything about it.' But what if she was moved up? What if her salary was to take a leap beyond his? He didn't in the least care for the notion.

'You're besotted about her,' Zena said with contempt. 'That fur coat must have cost a pretty penny.' She had managed to get through the better part of the festive season without voicing an acid remark about the coat—or at least, not to Neil; she had said plenty about it to Owen. Now she no longer bothered to restrain her tongue. 'And then you come along here and expect me to hand over the money to pay for it.' She laughed aloud. 'It really is a bit much.'

Neil frowned. He drew a long breath in order to stop himself from blurting out a savage reply. It was as much as he could do not to spring to his feet and slam out of the room.

But he simply couldn't afford to quarrel with Zena. There had never been any outright discussion of the terms of her will but with casual hints and oblique references she had always led him to believe that a large share—or even perhaps the whole—of her interest in Underwood's would be left to him. She had no children and her husband looked all set to make a fortune on his own account. Neil believed she had a strong family feeling which would incline her to keep Underwood money where it belonged. And he had always taken care to see that Jane stayed on good terms with her aunt. He was only four years younger than Zena but she was in poor health and took no real care of herself; it certainly wouldn't pay him to create an open rift.

'I'm sorry you've taken it like this.' His voice held a note of mild surprise. He couldn't quite think what to say next so he said nothing.'

'What poor Muriel would have thought, I can't imagine.' Zena was by now enjoying herself. Whatever poor Muriel might have thought she wouldn't have been likely to disclose to her sister-in-law; there had never been much fondness between them, though it sometimes suited Zena now to talk as if they had been intimate friends. 'She couldn't rest in her grave if she could see the presents you've showered on that woman.'

Neil closed his mind to the sound of her voice running on. There had been moments in the last few months when he had himself fallen into the habit of remembering his first wife rather differently from the way she had actually been in life. 'Muriel would never have said that,' he would think after Ruth had uttered some casual remark that had wounded him. 'Muriel would have been kinder . . . or more careful . . . or more loving . . .' He had caught Jane in the same trick. 'Mother wouldn't have minded,' he'd heard her say more than once to her stepmother.

On Christmas Eve he'd driven to the cemetery as he'd done in all the five years since Muriel's death. He'd arranged the yellow and white chrysanthemums in the stone vase and stood looking down at the carved lettering of the inscription. It had struck him all at once with the force of revelation that if she could have walked in again through her own front door she would have found him changed from the man who had been her husband, her daughter grown into a tall stranger, even the furnishings and decorations of her home totally altered.

He had felt a terrible compassion for the loneliness and bewilderment of that imagined ghost. When he turned away from her grave it was as if at that moment she had at last ceased to exist. He had never since been tempted to compare her fancied behaviour with that of Ruth's.

Almost with a feeling of relief he switched his mind back from that bleak vision to the complicated present.

'. . . and without even a word to me,' Zena was saying in

a sharply hostile tone. 'My own shop, the foundation of the whole business.'

'Would you like me to make some coffee?' Neil asked abruptly. He had already had the pleasure of listening to the saga about the closing of the dress-shop. 'And something to eat, if you want? Sandwiches or biscuits?' There was no point now in hanging about any longer at The Sycamores; he clearly wasn't going to get any money. But he felt reluctant to drive back home just yet. In his own house there would be no escape from pressing thoughts of unpaid bills, from the whirlpool of emotions centring on the lovely figure of his second wife sitting opposite him in an easy chair.

'Oh yes, do! That would be nice.' Zena was pleased at the attention. 'As a matter of fact I am rather hungry. Turkey for the sandwiches, I think, there's plenty in the fridge. And some chocolate cake, in the blue tin.' Greed took her by the throat again. 'You could warm up a few mince pies. Switch the oven on high, they won't take long.'

Neil felt his stomach revolt at the mention of all that rich food. But he could do with a good strong draught of black coffee. He stood up.

'Ought you to eat all that kind of stuff?' he asked suddenly, belatedly remembering that she was supposed to diet. 'Surely Dr Gethin doesn't allow you—'

'What does Dr Gethin know?' She pulled a face. 'Silly old fool. He'd like me to starve to death, I suppose.'

'Why don't you change your doctor then, if you've got no confidence in him?' Impatience edged his voice. How on earth did Owen put up with her irritating ways?

'But I've always had Dr Gethin!' She was astonished at the suggestion.

You know perfectly well no other doctor would tolerate your nonsense for a single minute, Neil thought, looking down at her without pity. She likes things to stay as they are, as they have always been, he saw with clarity; even if they are muddled and senseless and disastrous, they are better in her eyes than the threatening face of change.

'But you do at least take your injections?' He would have liked to lean forward and take her by the shoulders, give her a good shake.

'Of course I do!' She grinned, a naughty little-girl grin. 'Well, most of the time. When I remember.' She threw some of her old teasing charm into her look. Good God, he thought with exasperated disbelief, it's all a kind of childish game to her. Here she is, in middle age, still expecting to be coaxed and wheedled, to be praised and laughingly reproved by everyone round her. Only now it isn't dolls and party dresses she's dealing with, it's serious, fundamental matters like good health, like life and death.

He went down the stairs and into the kitchen, switched on the oven, found the coffee and set about preparing a tray. How monstrously unjust his father had been in virtually excluding him from the family business. He might have been a very wealthy man at this moment if old Ralph had been fairer in his dispositions. Of course he had expressed himself as satisfied at the time. He had been a boy, little more than a child really; how could he have been expected to know where his best interests lay?

All the rancours and resentments of childhood, all the suppressed envies of the long years in which he had played second fiddle to his elder sister, gathered inside him into a single dark and driving force. As if, having in the last year discovered to his humiliation and astonishment that he was a man capable of violent jealousy, he saw now no reason to repress any longer the old hostilities and aggressions he had learned forty years ago to push down below the level of conscious thought.

He trimmed the sandwiches, taking a perverse pleasure in setting out the food elegantly. In addition to the chocolate gâteau oozing with cream he cut a large wedge from the ornate Christmas cake. If Zena wanted her fatal carbohydrates, then by heaven she should have them.

He opened the oven door and laid a testing finger on a

mince-pie. Not quite hot enough. He closed the door and stood waiting. His mind, stimulated, liberated, ranged without resentment over its fixed points of obsession. He conjured up a tormenting picture of the board of directors at British Food scanning names on a short list, pencils pausing at the name of Ruth Underwood, appreciative smiles exchanged, eyes mellowing into pleasure.

He clasped his hands, thrusting the palms fiercely against each other. How very swiftly Ruth had agreed to marry him, a mere three months or so after they had met. A beautiful young woman like that, the whole world to choose from, a good career before her—why him? He had never really understood it. At the time it had seemed like a miracle, a dream fantasy sprung to breathing life, he had closed his eyes to doubts and questions, grasping eagerly at what was so bewilderingly offered.

There had been another man, he had known that, had expected nothing else where such a lovely creature was concerned. He had believed he had accepted the fact like a tolerant man of the world, he had never probed, never again referred to the subject. Ruth hadn't been very forthcoming. She had merely sketched in a few details lightly, soon after their first meeting. A married man, no question of a divorce—no explanation offered why this was so—an affair that had drifted on into dissatisfaction on her part, terminating abruptly when she decided to cut her losses.

It was all over and done with, he had told himself. No reason ever to dwell on it. Ruth never showed signs of regret, no melancholy might-have-beens looked from her sea-green eyes. She never mentioned his name.

Neil jerked his head to one side. He had never known the man's name, she had never told him. Or wait now—she had, surely, used his first name, that evening when she had told him about the affair, sitting over dinner in the country club.

R—he was almost sure it began with R. Robert . . . Richard . . . He saw her there, opposite him, looking down at the tablecloth, he could hear her low tones . . . No, he had it now, it definitely began with M! He blinked his eyes open, clapped his hands in triumph. M! That was it!

With a curious compound of elation and misery he stored away the initial like a weapon he might need to produce at some crucial moment. The full name would come to him in a day or two, he was certain of that. It gave him a sense of power, almost of comfort, to know he would have it lying there ready for use.

He switched off the oven, snatched up a thick cloth and took out the dish of mince pies. The tray was so large and heavy that it took him all his time to carry it upstairs but he battled on without pausing for breath.

'Here we are!' he cried gaily as he kicked open the bedroom door. 'A regular dormitory feast!'

'Mm, it looks good!' Zena laughed back at him. 'A sandwich to start with, I think.' Fellow-conspirators, locked together for a brief delusive time in the sunny-surfaced world of their never-quite-forgotten childhood.

Neil handed the plate of sandwiches, set a cup of coffee richly laced with cream within easy reach of her, stooped and put a hand round her shoulders, dropped a kiss on her hair.

'Happy New Year, Zena!' He gave her plump shoulders an affectionate squeeze.

'Yes, I will be president of the Independents' in a week or two.' Linda Fleming heard the note of calm satisfaction in Owen's voice. 'Old Ralph was a member,' he added, 'but he was never president.' She gave him an enquiring look. 'Ralph Underwood,' he explained, 'my father-in-law.'

'Oh yes.' She nodded her understanding. They were still sitting in her little office but in the course of the last few minutes the conversation had drifted away from her business affairs and had turned into a monologue by Owen. He had enlarged on his own humble beginnings, had sketched in the expansion of the firm, taking some pains to indicate how matters stood—in relation to the property—between himself and his wife and brother-in-law.

She was aware of significance in all this, had done her best to follow, smiling and murmuring a suitable remark from time to time but more than half her mind was engaged in listening for sounds from the kitchen quarters. At some appropriate pause in Owen's flow she would slide out and dispose of Emily Bond. She forced her attention back on to what he was saying.

'Of course Zena's share would come to me in the event of . . . if anything happened . . .' He let the rest of the sentence tail away. 'She made a will, years ago, essential in matters of this kind.' He had never actually seen the will but was as certain of what it contained as if he had drawn it up himself.

'Quite so,' Linda murmured with a slightly abstracted look. He was aware that she believed he had married Zena solely because she was the daughter of his employer. He had in fact gone to some trouble in his narrative to give her that impression. It was totally untrue.

He had married for love and only love; it had simply been an additional blessing from the gods that Zena had money as well as beauty. Where once he would have fiercely resented the notion in other men's minds that he had gone courting with an eye to the main chance, he often caught himself these days, at the club or in business circles, deliberately fostering the idea. As if he would prefer to be judged a shrewdly unsentimental opportunist rather than be pitied as a man who had worshipped and married a beautiful girl who had turned into a caricature, a cartoon wife.

'There's to be a ball after the presidential election. Rather a grand affair.' He gave Linda an inviting smile. 'You'd enjoy it, do you good to get away from work for a while. I must see about a ticket for you.' His smile faded. Might be a bit tricky, that; he could scarcely include her in his own party, that would be the action of a lunatic.

He cast about in his mind for some satisfactory arrangement but could not for the moment hit on anyone he could ask to bring her along without giving rise to unwelcome hints and speculations. 'A big demand for tickets of course.' That was better, leaving the matter open; inspiration might strike him in the next few days. 'Can't absolutely promise, you understand, but I'll see what can be done.'

'That's very kind of you,' she said politely, half-registering the notion of some tedious and old-fashioned evening stiff with pompous formality. 'Would you excuse me for a moment?'

She slipped suddenly from the room. Owen stared round him at the walls. Better watch his step a bit, wouldn't do to get carried away like that, must take a harder look at the situation, think things out before opening his mouth again.

And then to his horror he heard from a few yards away the sound of a loud, argumentative voice. A voice he knew very well indeed. Emily Bond's unpleasing tones. He sprang to his feet. Recollection thrust at him, Zena saying something about the state of her bedroom, about Emily running off to Mrs Fleming's. Good God, if that old gossip knew he was here—his brain clicked into feverish action. Then he relaxed slightly. The stock of course, that was why he'd come, to see about the surplus stock. He tested the statement swiftly in his mind, it didn't have an altogether convincing air. Had the old devil seen him arrive? Could she have heard his voice? On the whole he thought not. But he'd clear off now, the moment Linda came back, he would infinitely prefer not to be put in the position of making any kind of explanation to his wife's narrowed eyes.

He was standing just inside the door when Linda came into the room. 'I thought we might have a drink.' She waved a hand in the direction of the sitting-room. She had paid off Emily, been forced to listen for a moment to her lively complaint about the lateness of the hour and the general unsatisfactoriness of the arrangement. She'd had to thrust another couple of coins into her hand in order to urge her on her way.

'Very sorry but I can't stop now,' Owen said in a rush. 'I've just remembered, there's a man waiting for me at the club. Simply must catch him, late already.' He gave her a mechanical smile, seized the door-knob and stuck his head out into the passage as if making sure all was clear. Could he have heard Emily? Linda wondered, taken aback by the swift change in his manner. Surely not. But if he went at this moment he would very probably bump into her.

He was already walking rapidly down the passage, he reached the front door. She went after him, she thought of saying, 'Wait a moment, your wife's charwoman is just leaving by the side door,' but at once rejected the words. They carried an implication of conspiracy; she knew instinctively they were better left unspoken. Before she could think of any other remark that would effectively detain him he had flung open the door.

'I'll be in touch.' He turned on the step and lifted a hand in abrupt farewell.

'There's that fellow again.' Constable Quigley looked idly out at the street. 'Pierson. The one we saw a while back.'

Cottrell turned his head, catching sight of the tall broad figure striding along. An air of disengagement, uninvolvement, he thought once again, as of an outsider permanently circling the perimeter of life. 'Often wanders about like that,' he said. 'Likes to be out in the open.' He understood that in a fashion. Been taken that way himself for a year or two after he got back from the war, he'd spring up suddenly from a fireside chair in the evenings and plunge out of doors, anywhere, just to feel himself actually, unbelievably free. But it had been twenty years or more since he'd been afflicted by those wild impulses. And Arnold Pierson still walked the night streets, driven by heaven knew what.

He pulled the car into the kerb, having spotted a shop

door that stood an inch or two ajar. 'Hang on a moment, I'd better take a look at that.'

Arnold hadn't noticed the police car. He had walked all round the shopping streets, pausing briefly sometimes to stare into a window, headed for nowhere. Now he glanced about him and saw that his feet had carried him to within a hundred yards or so of Linda Fleming's shop. He frowned, hesitated. What was he doing here? He had no intention of calling on her. Was he simply going to stand like a fool and gape at her premises? The cold began to strike at him; he moved on again, past a couple of parked cars, he reached the intersection where her shop stood on the corner opposite.

CHAPTER VI

Still foggy. And bitterly cold. Emily clutched her holdall in front of her, lowered her head against the icy breeze and set off at an awkward trot in the direction of buses and home.

She reached the crossroads and stepped straight off the pavement on to the treacherous road without a single glance to right or left.

A hiss of tyres, a shrill screech of brakes, the flash of lights, a voice crying out. An arm clamped suddenly across her chest, pulling her sideways and backwards. She fell on to a body, the hard muscular body of a man, her holdall slipped from her grasp and burst open on the roadway. A crunch of metal, doors slamming, running feet, calling voices. She let out a long astonished breath.

'Are you all right?' Faces looking down at her. She stared up at them, she began to laugh, she started to say, 'I will be when I get me wind back,' then it hit her—she'd almost been knocked down, run over, she felt a wild impulse to burst into tears, she began to tremble violently.

Behind her the man extricated himself with difficulty,

got to his knees and then to his feet, stooped and helped her up.

'Come on, better get off the road, don't want another car running into us.'

'Me holdall,' she mumbled, gesturing at the canvas bag, the assortment of food scattered around.

'That's all right. We'll pick it up. Don't worry.' She was back on the pavement, breathing more easily. 'No bones broken, at all events,' he said reassuringly. Why, I might have been smashed to pieces, she thought, still not quite able to take it in. Tears began to trickle down her face. She raised a hand, clumsy in its woollen glove, she tried to dab at her cheeks.

'Take it easy, Mrs Bond, you've had a lucky escape.' At her name she peered up at him; recognition filtered through the muddle in her brain.

'Why, it's Mr Pierson.' It came to her slowly that he had pulled her back from the path of the car, that he had very probably saved her life. An overwhelming tide of gratitude swept through her; she had a confused notion that she must say something, do something to show him how grateful she was, she was seized by a desire to shower him with the money she had just received from Mrs Fleming. 'If it hadn't been for you—' She looked distractedly about for the shabby old leather purse. 'Me bag—me holdall—'

He still had his arm round her shoulders, he gave her a soothing pat. 'Nothing to worry about, they've got your bag. It was a police car that nearly ran you down.'

'Here you are, mother, I've got your holdall. I've picked up some of the stuff that was in it but the rest of it—I'm afraid it isn't up to much now.' Constable Quigley held out the bag. She took it and scrabbled about inside, drawing out her purse, fishing for a handful of coins.

Sergeant Cottrell came up. Owen Yorke was walking at his side, he was talking in a protesting voice that held a strong note of repetition.

'I'm afraid I can't help you, I saw absolutely nothing, I

had my head turned the other way—' He broke off. 'Good God, it's Mrs Bond!' His brain jerked out a fresh stream of warning signals—she must have left Linda's at more or less the same moment as himself, by the other door—Cottrell had seen which house he'd come from, he'd run over and grabbed him at the foot of the steps as a possible witness—it was sure to be in the papers, Cottrell had run into the back of a parked car in his swerve to avoid Emily—but if he continued to deny that he'd seen anything—it would be all right—no need to panic.

He took a firm hold on himself. 'Are you sure you're all right?' he asked Emily solicitously. And of all people, Arnold Pierson standing there with his arm round her. He gave an inward groan.

'Yes, I'm all right, thank you.' She was beginning to feel a little more like herself. 'A lucky thing Mr Pierson was here, otherwise—' She tried to thrust the coins into his hand. 'Here you are, go on, take it.' Arnold gave a little surprised laugh and closed her fingers firmly over the money.

'There's no need for that, put it away.' He spoke soothingly, as if she were a child. 'But thank you all the same.' He looked at her anxiously. 'You really ought to sit down —is there anywhere—' He glanced about at the faces of buildings.

'I can run her home,' Owen said at once. 'The least I can do. I'll make her a cup of tea, I'll see she's all right.' The sooner he removed himself from the scene the better. 'I know where she lives, I've taken her home before.' He had a horrid fear that at any moment someone would suggest taking the old woman back into Linda Fleming's.

'Just hold on a bit.' Cottrell had his notebook out. 'Have to get one or two things down.' He despatched Quigley back to inspect the vehicle they'd run into; he made a formal request for names and addresses. 'I'm sorry about your car,' he said suddenly to Yorke, 'couldn't be avoided. We'll go over and take a look at it in a minute.'

'Oh—that wasn't my car you ran into,' Owen said with surprise. 'Mine is parked back there.' He waved a hand towards a side street some distance away. I thought he was taking it very well, Cottrell said in his mind, at the same time registering the fact that Yorke had for some reason left his vehicle quite a fair way off, tucked discreetly out of sight. Now why would that be? He looked across at the house Yorke had been leaving. Attached to that little draper's shop. Changed hands not very long ago. His brain searched automatically through the myriad fragments of accumulated data. A young woman, he rather thought, easy enough to check later.

Now what would Yorke be doing there? Business perhaps? Or not? He gave him a long considering look. He would have taken his oath Yorke had seen the accident. Persisted in saying he hadn't, a trifle eager to be on his way, by no means pleased to have his name entered.

Owen saw the look, he had also caught the sergeant's glance across the street. He assumed an easy, maty air—he knew Cottrell well enough, although they had never been anything as close as friends, their positions in the life of Milbourne were too far apart for that. But they had been at the same grammar school, although the few years between them had been sufficient to form a barrier. And their fathers had served together in the first war.

'I really ought to be getting along.' Owen glanced ostentatiously at his watch. 'There's someone waiting to see me at the Independents'.' Dropping the name of the club with just enough emphasis to remind Cottrell that he was dealing with a man of some consequence. 'I don't think you need me.' He smiled, frankly. 'Not a great deal of use, I'm afraid. I'll see Mrs Bond safely home.'

Cottrell put up a hand and massaged his chin. 'We'll have to take a statement from her of course, but that can wait till tomorrow. But she ought to see a doctor tonight. I know she says she's all right, but at her age—and one never knows with road accidents, doesn't always show at the time.' He shook his head slowly. 'There can be strains, something displaced. To say nothing of bruises. Or shock. Might be a question of a claim, loss of earnings, disability even.' His voice was politely resolute. 'I'm afraid I must insist. If you can't spare the time yourself it's of no consequence, we can run her to the hospital. Probably just as well that way.'

Yorke might have been expected to jump at that, Cottrell had said nothing about detaining him further. But he remained where he was. 'That's all right,' he said, still easy. 'I'll take her to the hospital myself.' His appointment had grown pretty elastic all of a sudden, the sergeant thought, seemed remarkably keen to deliver the old girl in person. Wanted to have a private word with her perhaps. But then he—or his wife—did after all employ the woman. Probably nothing more than a natural concern for her welfare.

'Very well. If you could see to that.' He glanced at Emily. 'Mr Yorke is going to drive you to the hospital, just for a check-up. Nothing to worry about. Either the constable or myself will call to see you in the morning.' His gaze slid to Pierson. 'We'll have to take a statement from you of course. Might as well come along to the station, warmer there than standing about in the street.'

It struck Owen suddenly that it was a bit of a coincidence, Arnold Pierson being there, poised on the edge of the pavement a few yards away from Linda's shop. Possible that the fellow was on his way to some unlikely gaiety of course. It wasn't conceivable—surely—that he had actually been about to call on Mrs Fleming? Had he seen her at the works? Been introduced to her perhaps? Were they already on friendly terms? Was Pierson by now a regular and welcome caller at the private entrance to the house? Owen stood with his head inclined to one side, waiting with some anxiety for Arnold's reply, for his mention of a pressing engagement, his offer to call at the police station tomorrow to make his statement.

But Arnold merely nodded 'Very well' to the sergeant.

Owen frowned, sliding him a keen look as an even more unpleasant notion bobbed up in his mind. Could Pierson by any horrid chance have posted himself on that precise corner in order to keep a watch on Linda's premises . . . or, more disturbingly still, on his own movements?

He was by no means unaware that some curious contact was maintained between Arnold and Zena, not altogether inexplicable in the light of a business relationship or even of their long acquaintance. Owen had never cared to probe this contact; there were many things about Zena—and if it came to that, about Pierson—that instinct had long ago warned him might be much better left unquestioned.

A swift succession of queries darted across his brain. Could Zena have somehow got wind of his interest in the young widow? Had she set Pierson on to watch him? But the notion was altogether too ridiculous . . . or was it? Had he let slip some unguarded word during his brief visit home? He bit his lip, striving to remember.

'No need to keep you here any longer,' Cottrell said suddenly, jerking Owen back to an awareness of Emily Bond looking at him with enquiry, waiting for him to lead her to his car. The sergeant had seen the glance Yorke had flicked at Pierson, the intent way he'd listened for Pierson's answer. His mind threw up an image of Pierson earlier in the evening, coming out of the lane that led to The Sycamores. One or two interesting speculations flashed across his consciousness. But there was no time to dwell on them now. Constable Quigley came back across the road with an urgent step.

'I think you'd better come and have a word.' He tilted his head in the direction of the damaged car and the owner, located and summoned to the scene. 'He isn't best pleased.' Which was in fact putting it very mildly; the man was hopping mad. A brand new car, the pride and joy of his heart, savagely run into by some lunatic policeman.

Cottrell sighed. 'I'm coming.' The little group broke up; Quigley led the way back to where the angry owner was running his hands over the battered coachwork. Going to be very late getting home, the constable thought with a stab of unease. His darling Sharon wasn't going to be at all pleased as another of her delicious little suppers slowly dried up in the oven.

'How long do you think we'll be?' he asked the sergeant in a low voice that held a note of stubborn hope. 'I'm thinking about Sharon—' A wild shred of possibility that Cottrell might drop him off on the way to the station, might offer to clear up the rest of the job himself, statements and all.

'I dare say you are,' Cottrell said without sympathy. 'I'd like to know when you ever think about anything else.' He saw Quigley's drooping look. 'Cheer up. She knows she's married to a copper, she doesn't expect office hours. Buy her a box of chocolates tomorrow. That'll sweeten her.'

Yes, I could, Quigley thought, briefly restored to optimism. An enormous box of chocolates. Or a piece of costume jewellery, she liked that sort of thing. That little fancy-goods shop over the road, might be something there. His shoulders sagged again as he remembered the leanness of his wallet after the holiday. He put up a despairing hand and pulled at his chin.

A couple of yards away the car owner wheeled about to face them. 'Come here and take a look at this! Cost a fortune to put this right!' Quigley thrust aside his visions of Sharon and his almost empty wallet and bent his attention to the inexorable call of duty.

At the other side of the road Owen piloted Emily towards the street where his car was parked. 'Bit of a nuisance for you, having to call in at the hospital.' His tone implied that she seemed perfectly all right now, was there really any need to bother with doctors and X-rays?

'Oh, I don't mind. Got to be done, the sergeant said. Quite looking forward to a bit more drama in fact. Not often she got the chance to be the centre of attention. And she hadn't missed Cottrell's reference to disabilities that might appear in the future. Might be an opportunity there for a nice little sum by way of compensation from someone or other.

They reached the car. Owen held the door open and she lowered herself into the passenger seat. As she settled the holdall on her knee she remembered with a wash of guilt the way the bits of food had burst out all over the ground. Had Mr Yorke spotted them? Could he possibly have recognized some of the contents of his own fridge?

'Bit late for feeding the birds tonight,' she said as he slid into the seat beside her. She hoped he wouldn't ask what birds were partial to legs of chicken and slices of cold plum pudding. He gave her a baffled look and switched on the ignition. 'First thing in the morning, though, I'll see they get their tit-bits,' she added virtuously. A trifle light-headed, Owen thought, pulling the car out, perhaps it's just as well she insists on going to the hospital.

It was beginning to look as if it might be quite a good party after all. Jane Underwood dropped into a chair against the wall and watched her partner shoulder his way to the buffet table at the other end of the room. Kevin Lang. She repeated the name in her mind, rather liking the sound of it. He hadn't been working very long in Milbourne, he was a trainee in the office of an estate agent; his home was in a village fifteen miles away, he was currently living in digs near the centre of the town.

Jane had felt at ease with him from the very first moment he had smiled and asked her name. It was partly the fact that he wasn't particularly good-looking, not utterly and frightfully ugly of course but rather plain in a wholesome, pleasant kind of way, the sort of face that made no very great demands on its owner but allowed him to be himself.

He was weaving his way back towards her now, both hands raised high above the jostling throng, carrying a large tray on which were perilously balanced two dishes of ice-cream and a couple of brimming glasses. He caught her eye and gave her a cheerful grin; he somehow managed to twirl the tray on his outspread fingers without spilling anything.

'How did you learn that trick?' she asked as he reached her.

He set his burden down on top of a low bookcase. 'I worked in a holiday camp for a couple of months last summer.' He laughed. 'Taught me how to carry food about at great speed. Probably stand me in good stead for the rest of my life.'

It won't last of course, she told herself, firmly rejecting hope as she selected a few sandwiches. But at least it's nice to have him just for this evening.

'Have you any brothers or sisters?' he asked as they began to eat. He'd already worked his way through the details of her school, her job at the library, her aspirations for the future.

She shook her head. 'What does your father do?' he went on, but not in a prying fashion, just with warm interest. 'Is he a librarian?'

'No, he's in the local housing department.'

He smiled. 'We ought to get on well then. Interests in common.' Only you won't be meeting him, she said in her mind, reaching out for a salmon sandwich, I'll take very good care you don't cross the threshold.

He opened his mouth and before the next words left it she knew what they would be; she raised her shoulders against them as he spoke.

'Does your mother do anything? Apart from being a housewife, that is?'

She gave him a long, level look. Here we go again, she thought. 'She has a good job with British Foods, she's an executive.' She raised her glass and took a sip. 'But she isn't my mother. She's my stepmother.'

By great good fortune the casualty ward was almost deserted, the festive rush of wounds and bruises not being due to start for another couple of hours. Owen paced restlessly about the corridors while Emily was being dealt with. At long last, when he was reaching the stage of emitting huge and unashamed yawns which threatened to dislocate his jaw, she materialized suddenly a couple of yards away from him.

'All finished!' she said brightly.

'And you're quite all right? Nothing to worry about?'

'Well, I wouldn't quite say that.' Her tone implied the possibility of grave but undisclosed disorders. She felt on the whole that it might be better not to reveal too precisely the doctor's opinion and advice. 'You've been very lucky,' he'd told her, only partly to her relief. 'Take it easy for a day or two, see your own doctor if you feel at all worried.' He'd given her some lotion to dab on her bruises and a couple of pills in case she couldn't sleep.

She whisked the bottle briefly in front of Mr Yorke without specifying its contents. 'Gave me this, the doctor did. Told me on no account to go to work tomorrow.' As Owen took her arm and drew her resolutely out towards the car she added on a sudden inspiration, 'That'll be a day's wages I'll be short.' She slid him a glance. 'You'll tell Mrs Yorke I won't be coming in the morning?' He nodded. 'And Mrs Fleming's expecting me in the afternoon.' She hadn't in fact intended to go near either lady. 'No way of letting her know.' She paused, tilted her head back and waited till he halted and looked at her.

'Will you be seeing her?' she asked in a voice bold with significance. 'Mrs Fleming, that is? Could you give her a message? Explain about the accident? Tell her I'm ever so sorry to let her down, but I don't rightly know when I'll be fit enough to go again.' Shan't bother going there at all, she added to herself, too much for me, let her find someone else.

Owen passed a hand across his forehead. Had the old crone seen him at Linda's after all? Or heard his voice? Could she be quite simply making a random and innocent suggestion? He couldn't tell.

'Don't worry about Mrs Fleming,' he said easily. 'I can make it my business to see she's given your message. Now, do come along.' He urged her to the car.

When they were settled into their seats he sat for a moment with one hand about to switch on the ignition, then he removed his hand and thrust it into his breast pocket. Emily stared ahead through the windscreen, listening intently to the little sounds he made, the rustle of notes, fingering them apart, counting them.

'Hard to manage, just on the pension,' she said, 'when there's no wage coming in,' and had the exquisite satisfaction of hearing an additional rustle, two rustles.

'Here you are.' He slipped the notes into her fingers. 'I wouldn't want you to go short.' He gave her fingers a little squeeze. 'No need to say anything about this to Mrs Yorke.'

'Why, how very kind!' she cried with surprise. 'I've always said you were a real gentleman.' She ferreted about in her holdall for her purse, contriving to get a squint at the money in the light from the lamps at the hospital entrance. Looked like five pounds, though she couldn't be certain, might be more. 'You can count on me,' she said with fervour, hinting at vast unshakable loyalties.

She stuffed the notes away; felt as if there were seven or eight. Mm . . . she thought as the car swung out into the road . . . a lot of money for Mr Yorke to part with so easy, he was never very free with his money, as far as she was concerned . . . a person might expect to buy a lot of silence for seven or eight pounds . . .

It didn't take them long to reach the little stone house. It had been a farm labourer's cottage, long ago, before Milbourne had moved into the industrial age. Now it stood on the edge of the town with only a field and a small belt of trees separating it from the onward march of expansion.

It suited Emily well enough, giving her a sense of country life. And she liked to keep herself to herself, no bother with tradesmen calling, she never had a newspaper de-iivered, made do with dried milk, bought her few odds and ends of groceries in town on her way home from work; once in a very long while the postman called with a letter.

Owen bounced the car over the rutted lane, up to the door, inwardly groaning in sympathy for his poor springs but feeling he could scarcely ask Emily to get out and walk the last hundred yards.

'I'll come in and make you a cup of tea,' he said without enthusiasm.

'I wouldn't hear of it.' Her tone was brisk, she'd had quite enough of his company for the time being. 'Not but what I'm much obliged,' she added hastily. 'I'll manage very nicely, thank you. You'll want to be getting off home.'

He watched her let herself into the cottage. No, he wouldn't go home just yet, he didn't in the least feel like encountering Zena at this moment, He frowned into the darkness. Might be as well to have a word or two with Arnold Pierson. A bit tricky, never quite certain what was going on behind that silent face. Could just drop in at the house, ask after old Walter's health, have a little chat with Sarah . . . not that he relished that notion either, recalling the business of closing the shop.

Pierson might still be down at the station, making his statement. If he drove back to the club for half an hour or so, that would be about right, wouldn't do to leave it too late and find the household retiring for the night.

'I'll give you a lift home,' Cottrell offered. 'I've got to drop young Quigley anyway, it isn't much farther on to your place.'

Arnold shook his head. 'No thanks, I'll walk.' He strode off at once, out of the station. Quigley looked after him with amusement.

'Rum fellow, that. Not exactly a brilliant conversation-alist.' The recurring thought of his bride and her ruined supper wiped the amusement from his tone. 'Come on,

Sarge, let's get going.'

As soon as the car turned the corner of the road that held his semi-detached love-nest he knew he was in for a soul-searing forty-eight hours. Every light was extinguished in that trim abode. He closed his eyes in despair. Sharon had taken herself off to bed then, had probably cried herself to sleep. In the morning she would be mute and red-eyed, levelling no spoken accusations but listening with the air of a downtrodden and brutally neglected wife to his pleading explanation. Now, suddenly, he knew he couldn't face another statutory two days of penance.

'You couldn't lend us two or three quid, could you?' Humiliation edged his tone. 'Let you have it back on pay-day.' This is abysmal folly, common sense warned him; she'll have to accept the fact that you can't always be punctual, she knew what job you had when you married her, she's not a child, she's a grown woman of twenty-two. Producing a present you can't afford every time she has a fit of the sulks isn't going to do anything except reinforce her petulant behaviour.

But it would take nerve and energy to sweat it out and he was always tired at the end of the day; he closed his ears to that acid voice.

Cottrell halted the car. He considered for an instant refusing the loan, handing out instead a few crisp words of advice, then he shrugged his shoulders and reached for his wallet. What did he know about it after all? An outsider, looking in through the windows at the face of matrimony. 'Four pounds do you?' he asked lightly.

'Thanks, Sarge, you've saved my life.' Quigley grinned at him cheerfully and thrust the notes into his pocket. 'See you in the morning.' He sprang jauntily from the car, letting the door slam with unprofessional loudness. Cottrell raised his eyes to the window of the front bedroom. But no sudden welcoming light switched on.

He shook his head slowly as he pulled away from the kerb. Women, baffling, unpredictable creatures . . . and pretty women the most infuriating of all. But what man in his senses wanted a plain wife?

His brain flung up before him the image of a face, beautiful, fine-boned, glimpsed a couple of days ago as he was driving through the Milbourne streets. She was coming out of a restaurant at lunch-time, she'd paused in the doorway and put up a hand to tuck away a strand of hair teased by the wind, she'd glanced out at the passing cars. Her eyes had met his for an instant, she'd given him a half-smiling look. Probably hadn't even seen him, had been thinking about something—or someone—else.

But he had been struck by the same wild blow that had laid him low on half a dozen other occasions in his life. That's the one, he'd thought, instantly, irrevocably, as he'd thought all those other times. Always the same face, the same figure. Tall and willowy, with the same necessary look, at once remote and potentially accessible.

Now he gave a little snort of amusement at his own recurring folly. He had thought himself cured by middle-age, more or less resigned to the prospect of solitary living, congratulating himself from time to time on the blessings of freedom and a mind free from emotional turmoil.

He reached the house where he rented a bedsitter and put the car away, pausing with one hand on the garage door. I am cured, he told himself with vigour, I am washed up on the shore, beyond the reach of the tossing waves.

But as he went up the short flight of steps and let himself into the house, calling out a greeting to his landlady who put her head round the kitchen door, it wasn't her broad and cheerful face he saw at the end of the passage but the face of his lovely dream-goddess with her faintly-smiling lips.

Owen Yorke sat in his car which he'd parked a few yards away from the Piersons' gate—in case he changed his mind about the wisdom of calling. Lights on both upstairs and down. He glanced about the street, half hoping that Arnold might suddenly come into view, allowing him a casual word or two out here, sparing him the awkwardness of going inside and possibly having to conduct his delicate business before the sharp eyes and ears of Sarah.

He felt profoundly irritated, not even being certain of the exact nature of his delicate business. He could hardly come out into the open and ask Pierson if he'd been spying on him. Nor could he imply that if the fellow wanted to keep his job it would be as well not to tittle-tattle to Zena. He couldn't get rid of Pierson without Zena having to know all about it. He gritted his teeth in frustration.

This is ridiculous, he told himself with force. I can't sit out here dithering all night. I'll just go in and have a pleasant little chat with Arnold, easy enough to tell from his manner if he intends to make trouble. All my imagination most likely, I'll be laughing at myself ten minutes from now.

He seized the door handle and then withdrew his fingers. He'd never been able to read Pierson's mind before, why should he find himself suddenly gifted now? In all probability he'd be no wiser at the end of his visit than he was at this moment. A memory of Emily Bond and her swift grasp at the pound notes sent his hand uncertainly towards his breast pocket.

Money . . . had it any voice that spoke with meaning to Pierson? He was well aware that a self-made businessman could be tempted to overestimate its absolute importance to everyone . . . and yet, there were few men he knew who wouldn't cup a palm to a generous hand.

Twice he took out the wallet and twice he thrust it fiercely back again. The third time he opened it and counted the remaining notes. Seven pounds might bring a delighted gleam to Emily's eye but it wasn't likely to have much influence on Arnold.

Fifty-four pounds in all; he'd fallen into the habit of carrying a certain amount of money in the days of unconventional dealings after the war. Tens and fivers mostly;

he restored the singles to the wallet and folded the remaining fifty, putting them for easy access into the pocket of his overcoat. The sum struck him as just about right—if the central idea had any validity. Anything less smacked of insult and anything more might invite downright blackmail.

The word gave him pause for a moment. Was he about to commit an act of outrageous folly? No way of being absolutely sure—there never was in tricky negotiations.

He stepped out of the car and walked briskly towards the Piersons' gate. Sarah answered his ring at the door; he asked at once for Arnold, with an air of urgency assumed in order to avoid being led into a casual exchange with Sarah, when he could scarcely prevent the subject of the shop coming up.

She stood aside. 'Won't you come in?'

Arnold was standing by the hall table. He looked up in surprise.

'I happened to be passing,' Owen said as soon as Sarah had discreetly disappeared. 'I thought I'd look in and see how your father is.' He assumed the easy air of a man addressing an employee. 'And I also wanted to thank you for rescuing my charwoman from a sudden death.' He gave a pleasant, friendly smile; his tone held the faintest overlay of patronage.

He slid his hand into his pocket, maintaining his frank and kindly expression. 'Totally inadequate of course . . . but I'd like to show my appreciation . . . I'm sure Emily would wish me to express her gratitude . . . the merest token . . .' His brain, working now in high gear, registered the beginnings of puzzlement in Arnold's eyes. Owen drew his hand smoothly from his pocket and laid the roll of notes on the table without a downward glance, at the same time keeping up his disarming flow of reassuring utterances . . . 'your father's illness . . . many extra expenses just now . . . some little delicacy . . .'

Well done! his brain cried—the money had manifested itself in the dim light of the hall without being openly given or received; its purpose had been skilfully clouded over and yet its association with Emily's accident clearly stated. All the fellow had to do was smile and murmur something.

But Arnold turned his head and looked at the roll, even leaning forward a trifle to make sure what it was. Just as he was about to speak, Owen turned and swung the door open, saying as he did so, 'Really must go . . . someone waiting at the club.' He closed the door behind him and was off down the path with a feeling of elation like a man leaving the dentist's. As he reached the car he gave a little laugh, realizing suddenly that from start to last Pierson hadn't spoken a single word.

CHAPTER VII

'Just a cup of tea for me, I'm not hungry.' Owen had spent Saturday morning and the best part of the afternoon in his almost empty factory, glad to be able to attend in peace to the papers that mounted relentlessly on his desk, pleased also to be out of Zena's way. She had risen grumbling from her bed at breakfast-time, feeling somewhat better, although not openly advertising the fact. Irritated—but not surprised—that Emily Bond hadn't seen fit to turn up for work, she had spent the day dealing in a slapdash fashion with inescapable household chores.

She helped herself now to a thick slice of Christmas cake. 'I'm not sure that it's as good this year,' she said after a couple of mouthfuls. 'Not as moist as it should be.' Owen gave a grunt that might mean anything; he was listening for the sound of the news-boy at the front door. Ah—surely that was the crunch of feet on gravel. He stood up.

'I'll take my tea into the study. One or two things to see to.' He escaped from the room, just in time to see the evening paper drop on to the mat. He snatched it up and went down the passage into the study. Five minutes later he sat back in his chair with a profound feeling of relief. Twice he'd been through the entire paper and not a solitary word about the accident; he could scarcely credit his luck. All he had to do now was hang about on Monday morning till Emily showed up and indicate to her with some force that there was no longer the slightest necessity for her to mention the incident to Zena at all.

Might it be as well to flash a little more money about? He shook his head slowly. Not the wisest of actions. Some pressure he might apply? His brain flung up all at once a picture of the food scattered on the road; he remembered with a sudden nod of comprehension the uneasy way Emily had kept on about feeding the birds. He smiled, lifted his cup and drained the stone-cold tea. A word or two about her pilfering would ensure she kept her mouth shut; she wouldn't be in the least anxious for that little matter to reach Zena's ears.

He settled his shoulders comfortably against the upholstery, leaned back and closed his eyes. Might slip down to the club later for an hour or two. But just for the present—he opened his mouth in a luxurious yawn—what better than a little nap?

Ruth Underwood sat at her desk in the office she shared with Anthea Gibbs. In the half-hour they had been at work they had exchanged scarcely a word after the customary greetings. Monday morning was never a relaxed and chatty time but the atmosphere today was charged with tension. Each carefully avoided meeting the other's eyes, not wishing to read there hope, expectation, hostility peering through the surface calm. Anthea looked diligently through a file; a thin, pale woman, with a dried-up look and a nervous habit of twitching her lips.

Footsteps, voices in the corridor outside. A light rap on the door, the handle turned at once without any waiting for a reply. In her seat near the window Ruth drew a deep breath; a couple of yards away Anthea Gibbs sat rigid, both hands outspread on her desk.

The marketing director came into the room without haste, a tall thin man with a look of impersonal amiability.

'I'd like you to meet your new head of department.' He glanced at both women in turn but his eyes came back to rest on Ruth. There was a brief scraping of chairs as they stood up. The director moved a few feet farther into the room, turning his head back to the door, raising one hand in a courteous gesture of invitation. He looked again at Ruth. 'I'm happy to inform you that you've been appointed to the post of assistant.' He gave her a pleasant smile.

'Thank you,' she managed to say, aware of the fierce pounding of her heart. She shifted her gaze and saw the face of the new man, standing behind him, a little to one side. Maurice! A wave of faintness swept over her, she thrust out her hands and steadied herself against the desk. Maurice Turner! Looking exactly the same as when she'd last seen him, fourteen months ago in London.

'Mr Turner,' the director said in a voice that seemed to have developed a curious echo. With a strong effort she forced herself to draw a long deep breath. To her unutterable relief her pulse began to slacken, strength returned to her limbs, the director spoke again in his normal voice. 'I'm sure you'll find Mrs Underwood a very able and loyal helper.'

'I'm sure I will.' Turner stepped forward, came right up to her desk and leaned across with his hand outstretched. He smiled at her with a teasing edge to his look. She murmured something, hardly knowing what she said; she felt his fingers clasp hers with a strong warm pressure. 'We might have lunch together,' he said easily. 'There'll be a good deal to discuss. I'll be busy the rest of the morning but I should be free by one o'clock.' He released her hand. 'I'll look in here then.'

She thought of saying she couldn't make it, she had another engagement. But from two o'clock onwards they would begin to work together; there was no way of avoiding that. It would be just as well to have a talk with him first, get matters straight. She felt a thrust of confidence. It would be all right, she could cope. She nodded. 'Yes, I'll be here.' Not returning his smile but flicking him a cool level look.

Nothing so very terrible had happened after all—and she had been promoted. Until this moment she had scarcely taken in the fact. Pleasure rose in her mind, and a brief thought of the car she would buy. Something else succeeded pleasure, a trace of excitement and an exhilarating sense of challenge, stimulus, almost of danger.

Turner walked across to where the director was exchanging a casual word with Anthea Gibbs, unaware of the savage blow he had just dealt to that lady's last hopes of promotion. Turner threw in a polite remark or two and then they were gone.

Ruth dropped into her chair as soon as the door began to close behind them. She felt deeply elated, powerfully alive. Maurice Turner in that incredible moment suddenly here, in her own office, her new boss—calling for her in less than four hours' time!

'Congratulations,' Anthea said in a voice chipped from ice. 'You must be very pleased with yourself.'

An unpleasant thought struck Ruth suddenly like a physical blow. Was it conceivable that she hadn't after all been promoted on merit—that she owed her good fortune to the skilful manipulations of Maurice Turner?

'It's ten minutes to one. Surely you can knock off now.' Kevin Lang leaned across the curved counter of the library and seized Jane's hand. 'Come on, there won't be anything fit to eat if we don't get to the café by one o'clock.'

'Sh!' Jane pulled her hand away, frowning at him. 'Keep your voice down!' she added in a fierce whisper. 'I've another ten minutes to do.' They had spent a good part of Saturday and Sunday together, walking down by the river, eating sandwiches in the Milbourne snack bars, dancing in cellar discothèques, and talking, talking, talking. Already she felt as if she had known him for years.

She gestured him aside as a man came up to the counter with an armful of books. 'Quite a collection you've got there, Mr Pierson.' She smiled in a friendly fashion as she wielded the date-stamp. Travel books, the memoirs of a field-marshal, a couple of light romances, some popular detective novels. 'Something for all the family.' She remembered his father, old and ill. 'Better news at home, I hope?'

Arnold gathered up the books. 'Not too good, I'm afraid. Thank you for asking.' As he moved away Kevin came back to the counter.

'It's one o'clock now. Get your coat and come along.' She rather liked the way he seemed to think he had some right to order her about; it gave her a soothing sense of security.

'All right, I won't be a moment.' She went swiftly off to the staff cloakroom.

Five minutes later they were standing squashed together in the gangway of a bus carrying them towards the café. The bus halted suddenly, throwing her off balance. 'Steady on!' Kevin slipped an arm round her shoulders. She looked through the misted windows at the crowded pavements, the shoppers hurrying home.

'I know that man—he came into the office on Saturday morning.' Kevin glanced out through the open door of the bus, over the heads of descending passengers. 'He wants to buy a house, he's taken a furnished flat for a few weeks while he's looking.' Jane turned her head without any very compelling interest. 'Rather a gorgeous creature he's with,' Kevin added lightly. 'I wonder who she is.'

Jane followed his gaze with keener attention and saw with an abrupt dampening of her spirits the blonde head and graceful shoulders of her stepmother. Ruth was talking animatedly to a tall heavily-built man, the pair of them just about to enter the doors of a restaurant.

'He's taken up some new position in the town,' Kevin said as the bus jerked off again. 'I showed him over the flat. Quite a pleasant fellow. He just wants a small house, he's a widower, no children.'

'Did you really think she was very beautiful?' The day began to look grey and cheerless to Jane.

'Who?' Kevin drew his brows together.

'The woman he was with.'

'Oh—her. Yes, I suppose so. Not my type of course. Too old. And anyway I never go for blondes.' He grinned at her. 'I prefer them young and brown-haired.'

A shaft of sunlight shone through the bus window. Quite a bright day after all. 'She's my stepmother,' Jane said gaily, recklessly. 'The woman you saw. You must come along and meet her sometime. And you must meet my father too. I think you'll like them both.'

At five o'clock one of the engineering staff put his head round the door of Maurice Turner's office. 'You might like to take a look at this.' He waved a newspaper. 'The local evening rag. It's got a piece in about the new appointments.' He came up to the desk and dropped the paper in front of Turner. 'That photograph you gave them must go back a year or two.' He smiled with a trace of malice. 'Makes you look a good deal younger.'

'You know how it is,' Maurice said with easy charm. 'Detest having my picture taken.' He ran his eye over the column.

Sarah was already at home when Arnold walked up the garden path. They had shared the purchase of a small car a few years back but as often as not it was Sarah who used it to drive to and from work. Arnold preferred to walk, even in the worst weather.

'Do come up here,' she called out when she heard the sound of the front door. 'Have you seen the evening paper?'

'No.' He didn't raise his voice by very much, disliking her habit of opening a conversation from several yards away. 'I'll be up in a moment.' He hung up his coat and went slowly up the stairs to his father's room, glancing past Sarah towards the bed. Walter lay propped against the pillows; he looked alert and pleased.

'How are you, Father? Feeling a little better?'

Walter gave an impatient nod. 'We've just been reading about you in the paper.' Arnold frowned. 'About the accident,' Walter said. 'A nice little piece. They put in a bit about me as well.' Delighted to know folk hadn't forgotten the time he'd gone out under fire with Yorke, after Cottrell.

Sarah looked critically at the column. 'A pity they've used that old photograph. I suppose they unearthed it from their files.' She held the newspaper out to him. 'Don't you want to see it? It seems you're quite a hero.' She flicked him a sardonic glance but there was a tinge of pride and pleasure in her voice.

Arnold took the paper, bending his head and making a show of reading it. But the word *hero* had roused in him such a strong wave of revulsion that it was all he could do to remain in the room. As soon as it was decently possible he laid the paper down on the chest of drawers.

'Has the doctor been again?' he asked with concern. 'What did he have to say?'

'Never mind the doctor.' Walter waved the question aside. 'I'll have that paper again if you've finished with it, I want to take another look, read it properly.'

'I'll go and have a wash then.' With a deep sense of relief Arnold made his way past Sarah, out of the room.

It was nearly ten when Owen Yorke let himself into The Sycamores. He was feeling relaxed and cheerful. A companionable evening at the club—he hadn't bothered to go home after work, he'd had a civilized meal in the members' dining-room, getting his secretary to phone Zena and deliver a message about an important appointment. And there had been a meeting afterwards, very satisfactory, they'd settled the final arrangements for the Presidential Ball. He'd even managed to fix up a ticket for Linda Fleming, had contrived to get her included in another party. Very skilfully done, he was pleased with the way he'd handled that, casual, the air of a man suddenly remembering a request from a customer, a hint of universal benevolence for those engaged, however humbly, in the same trade, a notion of goodwill towards newcomers to the town, a suggestion of fatherly—and nothing more than fatherly—interest in the welfare of a struggling young widow.

He would ring Linda in the morning, as soon as he got to the factory, tell her the good news. The possibility of a discreet little run out somewhere quiet tomorrow evening crossed his mind; one or two snug hostelries he knew, well out of sight of Milbourne eyes. He was smiling as he opened the sitting-room door.

Zena had fallen asleep in front of the television set. For a couple of minutes he stood looking down at her with compassion and a kind of tolerant friendliness that rose sometimes from the ashes of old and passionate love. He touched her gently on the shoulder.

'Wake up, Zena.' She stirred and opened her eyes.

'What time is it?' She yawned and glanced at the clock.

'Would you like some coffee? And a few sandwiches?' He spread his hands in a gesture of generous goodwill. 'Just say what you fancy.'

When he had gone off to the kitchen she glanced round for her cigarettes; they were lying on the carpet beside her chair—and beside them, the evening paper, still precisely folded. As she exhaled a long spiral of smoke she turned the pages idly, her fingers suddenly arrested by the sight of a face from long ago.

'Turner!' she said aloud on a note of pleased surprise. 'Maurice Turner!' One of the old crowd, the gay lads of her dancing days. She read the paragraphs with avidity. Back in the county after all these years! Actually working in Milbourne now! Well, well, well . . . Her brain began to take in the other details, the brief mention of a less important appointment, Mrs Ruth Underwood to the post of Mr Turner's assistant . . . Twice she read the column; speculation, deduction chased across her mind.

She stood up, crossed to the corner cupboard and poured herself a tot of brandy, then she settled herself comfortably into her chair and let her mind range over a host of notions.

How would Neil take Ruth's promotion and the fact that in all probability she would now be earning a good deal more than himself? London . . . Turner had been working in the London branch, according to the paper, that would surely be the headquarters of British Foods . . . why would he want to come to Milbourne? Drawn back to the haunts of his youth, perhaps? She sat up suddenly. Ruth had worked in London . . . and now Ruth was to be his assistant . . .

Memory flicked up all at once another item from its complicated files, Arnold Pierson in that odd, unstable time after the war, kneeling by her chair, gripping her fingers so tightly that she almost cried out, talking, talking . . . smashing down the dam and releasing the torrents . . . it had been Turner! Of course! Turner had been his captain!

A fierce current compounded of pleasure and excitement flowed through her. She sprang up and almost ran over to the phone, snatched up the receiver and dialled Arnold's number; it was engaged. She sighed with disappointment; the current began to ebb. She waited for a minute and then dialled again, no longer quite certain of what it was she had wanted to say. She heard again the engaged signal and in the same moment the sound of the trolley being wheeled from the kitchen. She replaced the receiver, feeling suddenly rather tired and flat.

Owen thrust the door open, came smiling in with the laden trolley. 'Here you are! Quite a delicious little spread. Hope I haven't been too long!'

'I did know there'd been some kind of accident,' Linda said into the receiver. 'One of my customers told me her husband's car had been run into. But I'd no idea either you or Mrs Bond had been mixed up in it. I've just been reading about it in the paper.' She paused briefly, then added, a little shyly, 'I was very interested at what it said about your getting a medal in the war.'

The image of Arnold had recurred to her several times since she'd firmly despatched him on his way on Friday evening. More than once she'd found herself regretting not having accepted his invitation to the theatre. And then—the piece in the paper—the realization that when the accident happened he'd been only a few yards away from her door, about to call, perhaps, or even, more intriguingly, simply drawn back to the neighbourhood that housed her. But above and beyond all, Linda dearly loved a hero. She hadn't been able to prevent herself from seizing the phone as soon as she'd digested the news.

'I liked the photograph,' she said lightly. 'I suppose it was taken during the war.' A very good-looking young man—and Arnold still had a fine, solid, prepossessing appearance. A man to be relied on, an arm that would snatch one out of the path of danger. She began to feel relaxed; a pleasant glow spread through her.

'All that happened a very long time ago.' His voice, level, unemotional, reached her ears. 'It was all rather exaggerated.' The warm glow began to fade; a sensation rose in her as of having reached joyfully out for something precious that had dissolved into mist before her fingers.

'Mrs Bond's accident wasn't a long time ago.' Mildly surprised at her own persistence. Accustomed to the pressing attentions of the male; something of a novelty, being driven to take the initiative. She half smiled at herself as she spoke. 'I don't think they exaggerated about that.' She laughed. 'Even if they're not going to give you a medal for it.'

She wished fervently that Arnold would say something but he merely made an indeterminate sound that might have meant anything. She hesitated. If she wound up the conversation—as he seemed to wish she would—it would very probably be the end of any intimate contact between them; the idea struck her as oddly chilling. Without giving herself any further time to ponder she plunged on.

'I find now I have a little more free time than I'd expected. I managed to deal with all my paperwork over the week-end.' She gave a tiny shudder of distaste for the inescapable unsubtlety of her words. 'I could have accepted your invitation after all.' And he said not a single, solitary word! 'It was so kind of you to think of asking me.' A slow blush crept up over her cheeks; her forehead throbbed with fire. She could say nothing more, she thought wildly of simply dropping the receiver back on its stand.

'I believe it's quite a good play,' Arnold said suddenly. In actual fact he hadn't the faintest idea of its quality. His mind was a battleground of conflicting emotions. He'd been resigned to her refusal, accepting it as permanent and total. Startled to hear her voice when he'd answered the phone. Momentarily pierced with happiness at the warmth of her tone. Horrified to realize she saw him as some kind of noble figure.

He saw clearly that she was providing him with an opportunity to renew his invitation. Could he? Dare he? He clutched at delay. 'I'd like to suggest another evening—now that you find yourself a little freer—but I'm afraid my father's very ill at the moment. I really don't feel—'

'Oh, I quite understand,' she cried on a long trembling breath. 'I didn't know. You mustn't think of leaving him in the evenings, I see that.'

'Later on, perhaps, when he's better, I could call and have a word with you, we could fix something up.'

'Yes, do.' She smiled into the phone. 'I'll give you a cup of coffee.' And this time, she thought, washed over by amusement, I'll actually let you taste your drink. 'I do hope your father makes a good recovery. I read what they said about him in the paper. He sounds a fine old man.'

When she replaced the receiver a couple of minutes later

she sat down and stared into the fire, feeling at once calm and pleased, as if something had been settled, something had begun. She remembered Owen Yorke holding forth about a ball, vaguely suggesting that she might like a ticket. She wondered if Arnold ever went to a dance; it seemed a trifle unlikely. But perhaps he might be gently coaxed, Owen's tentative offer might transform itself into a pair of tickets. Owen Yorke, she thought suddenly, seeing his speaking glance. She put up a hand and touched her lips. There was after all, Owen Yorke . . .

CHAPTER VIII

'Something very interesting in the evening paper. I'll show it to you.' Zena set down her cup and fished up the paper from the floor. She began to search for the bit about Turner.

'What's that?' Owen jerked his attention away from the television set.

'It mentions Ruth. She got the job.' Zena flashed him a look of knowing malice. 'Not that we need enquire exactly how she set about it.' She returned to the pages, running her eyes over the columns. 'Where is it—I thought it was on this page. You'll never guess who her new boss is. Maurice Turner!'

'Turner?' Owen frowned. 'Who's Maurice Turner?'

She turned a page impatiently. 'You remember Maurice Turner. He used to come into Milbourne a lot. Before the war. He had that little sports car.'

'Good heavens, yes.' Owen laughed. 'I remember him. And he's—what did you say? Ruth's new boss?'

'Yes, it seems he works for British Foods, been with them a long time—' She broke off. 'What's this?' she asked in a totally different tone, her voice sharp, rising. A cold finger of apprehension laid itself on Owen's brain. He rose instantly to his feet, putting himself instinctively into the fight-or-flight position, knowing from long and painfully-acquired experience that when Zena spoke like that a wise man didn't remain seated.

'Emily Bond,' Zena said on an even higher note. 'Arnold Pierson.' Her brows gathered in a fierce frown. 'Friday evening.' She flung him a glance full of concentrated thought. 'Here, in my own house, working here the best part of today and she never said a word about it.' Her eyes pinioned Owen to the spot; he could almost see the rapid working of her brain. Now if ever was the time to make use of his feet.

'If you've finished with your plate.' He dredged up a mirthless smile, contrived to set his legs in motion. 'I might as well begin to clear away.' He got as far as picking up his own cup and saucer before her voice struck out again.

'Leave those things, I haven't finished yet.' Friday—she flashed on the screen of her mind an embracing vision of the evening. Emily Bond running off to Mrs Fleming's. The interview with Arnold. Owen telling her he was going to the club. Coming back pretty late. She set about a rapid piecing together of the jigsaw. What was Arnold doing over there by Mrs Fleming's shop? Was he carrying out her instructions about following Owen? Or engaged in some ploy of his own?

'Where were you on Friday evening?' she barked like an examining magistrate.

'I was at the club, of course. I told you.' Owen measured the space between himself and the door, set himself resolutely in motion, allowing one sentence for each yard to freedom, picking up speed as he saw the door-knob miraculously within touching distance.

'I'll just take this into the kitchen. Got an abominable headache.' With his free hand he struck himself on the forehead, blessing, not for the first time, the invention of headaches with their absolute lack of susceptibility to proof. 'I'll take a couple of pills and get off to sleep.' His fingers on the knob. 'Got a long day ahead of me tomorrow.' The door open, through it, pulled to behind him.

From the other side he heard Zena's angry cry—'Where do you think you're off to?' He banged down the cup and saucer on the first available surface and mounted the stairs two at a time, never slackening his pace until he was safely in his bedroom with the door snicked against intrusion, knowing Zena immobilized, for the moment at least, by weight and a strong disinclination for speedy movement.

Within three minutes he had ripped off his clothes, snatched on his pyjamas, sprung into bed and extinguished the light. He opened his mouth suddenly and exploded into a long and powerful laugh. Men had been decorated for less.

Downstairs Zena frowned yet again over the newspaper. Owen needn't think his precious headache had put paid to the cross-examination. There had been no need to pursue him up the stairs, there was always tomorrow, and the day after that. But she felt a restless need for some kind of action; she tilted back her head, bit her lip, considering. What about ringing Arnold? Demanding his account of Friday evening? Yes, that ought to settle a few points. She glanced at the clock and saw with reluctance that it was getting a little late to phone a house where there was after all a sick old man. First thing in the morning, though, catch him before he left for work.

Ah—of course! She could ring Neil! They could have an absorbing conversation about Ruth's promotion and the reappearance of Turner. She levered herself up and went to the phone. Of course Neil couldn't be expected to remember Turner; Maurice was four or five years older than Neil, who had really been little more than a child in the days when Maurice Turner swooped into Milbourne in his sports car.

She lit a cigarette and made herself comfortable in

the chair by the phone, then she lifted the receiver, confident that Neil would be eager to listen to everything she had to say.

As soon as Owen opened his eyes next morning he knew what he was going to do. Remove himself from the whole schemozzle for the entire week. He often went away on business trips, buying, selling, creating or maintaining goodwill. Reasonably convenient to depart just now. He pulled at the light cord, glanced at the clock. Seven-thirty.

Zena wouldn't be about for some time yet. Pack a suitcase silently, no need to bother about breakfast, get off to the office and deal with one or two pressing matters and then into the car and his foot down on the accelerator.

He was about to throw back the bedclothes when he remembered Emily Bond. He clicked his tongue in irritation. He definitely had to catch the old girl before Zena had a chance to talk to her. What time did she normally show up at The Sycamores? Assuming of course that she intended to show up at all today. The accident had probably done little to improve her reliability.

He jumped out of bed as an inspiration struck him. Of course! All he had to do was drive over to her cottage, he would either meet her on her way to the bus or, if she had decided not to go to work, call at the house and speak to her.

In a little under half an hour he had washed and shaved, dressed and packed his bag; he tiptoed down the stairs and let himself silently out into the dark chill of the morning. He had left no note informing Zena of his business trip; his secretary could phone her later in the morning, when he was well away, making mention of urgent matters suddenly arisen. It struck him all at once that Zena would soon realize he had formed the intention of departing long before he reached the office—how else explain the fact that he had no need to return home to pick up some clothes?

He lifted his shoulders in a careless shrug. He'd be away

the whole week; by that time she'd have forgotten the trifling detail. He began to hum a tune as he sent the car swiftly along the road in the direction of Emily's little cottage.

Arnold Pierson was coming downstairs a few paces behind Sarah when the phone rang in the hall. He halted with one hand on the banister rail as she went forward to pick up the receiver.

'Oh—it's you, Mrs Yorke.' Sarah turned and flashed a glance at Arnold. 'I was just about to phone you myself.'

'I want to speak to your brother,' Zena said briskly. 'Is he there?'

'I'm afraid I'll be a little late getting in to work this morning.' Sarah firmly continued to say what she had to say. 'My stepfather died in the night.' Her voice wavered. 'Yes, it was rather sudden in the end. But it was quite peaceful.' She put her free hand up to her eyes. 'Was it something urgent you wished to speak to Arnold about?' she asked when Zena had finished her conventional murmurs. 'There is, as you can imagine, a great deal to be seen to.' She raised her eyebrows at Arnold in a look of enquiry. He shook his head and spread both hands in a gesture of refusal.

'Well, I would like to speak to him.' Zena couldn't at once accept the fact that she could scarcely in all decency fire a succession of questions at Arnold just now.

'Actually I don't think he's available at this moment,' Sarah said. 'I dare say it can wait until . . . all this . . . is over.' Really, she thought, that woman! Absolutely no sense of what is fitting. 'I'll go into the shop about ten, Arnold is taking time off to deal with things.' No point in both of them being away from work. She'd be glad to be compelled to occupy her mind. 'I'm sure you'll understand if I leave early or come in late during the next few days.'

I'm free of you now, Arnold thought; the notion came to him flatly, without emotion. He need never again as long as he lived pay Zena any attention whatever. He had a brief flash of Linda's face, her hazel eyes. He stroked his jaw. I suppose I ought to phone her, let her know about Father, I wouldn't like her to hear it casually from a customer. And telling her would create a sense of family between them, a hint of intimacy. His fingers pressed his lips; he was conscious again of a dull feeling of vacuum, of deep and permanent loss.

'Yes, of course, that will be perfectly all right.' A notion of obligation, fitting behaviour, nudged at Zena. 'Would you like me to go down to the shop?' A marked absence of enthusiasm in her tone.

'That's very kind of you but there's really no need.' Sarah managed with difficulty to restrain an abrupt refusal. 'It's only a question of an hour or so from time to time. And the head saleswoman is very capable. I'm sure you must have a great many calls on your time.' Be a pity to have to cut down on the naps and siestas, she thought sourly, laying down the receiver a few moments later.

And now—she squared her shoulders and looked up at Arnold. 'We've a lot to do,' she said. 'We'd better begin.'

'I think that's more or less everything,' Owen said aloud. He ran his eye over the page in his desk diary, making a final check. No need to ring Linda yet about the ticket for the ball; that would keep till he got back. Something a little too formal and businesslike about a phone call so early in the day.

As if in response to his thought the phone shrilled beside his hand. He picked it up, half expecting to hear her voice. But it was Arnold Pierson, ringing to say he'd have to take a few days off work, his father had died.

'I'm very sorry to hear that,' Owen said with genuine sympathy, though without any very great sense of surprise. So old Walter had gone at last . . . one never heard without emotion of the passing of someone known all one's life, there was always this feeling of the links that bound one to the past, to the carefree days of childhood, being relentlessly severed, one by one. My father will be upset to learn of it, he thought, deeply startled a fraction of a moment later to remember that his father had been dead for over thirty years.

'The funeral will probably be on Thursday,' Arnold said. 'We very much hope of course that you and Mrs Yorke will be able to come.'

'I'm afraid I shall be away, I'm going off on a business trip, I won't be back at all this week.' He must phone the florist as soon as Arnold had rung off, order a handsome wreath. 'But I'm sure Zena will wish to be there. I'll let her know right away.' Awkward, that; he had no wish to speak to her personally but it didn't seem decent to leave it to his secretary.

'She already knows, Sarah spoke to her. I shall be able to come into work on Friday as usual.'

'No need for that.' Owen sent his mind rapidly over dates. Nothing very urgent at the moment and the audit wasn't due till the first of March. 'Take Friday off as well, make a whole week of it, I'm sure you'll need it.'

Zena sat on the stool in front of her dressing-table, tugging a comb crossly through her disordered locks. She didn't yet know that Owen had taken himself off for the week.

From downstairs she heard the sudden drone of the vacuum cleaner. Ah—Emily had seen fit to show up, then. She pushed back her stool and stood up, her face pleased and animated. Now she could get to the bottom of that business about the accident.

In the sitting-room Emily held the snaking hose in one hand and with the other guided a sectioned metal tube with a nozzle at the end of it over the floral carpet. Her brain was in a state of conflict.

Mr Yorke had banged on the door of her cottage while she was still buckling herself into massively-reinforced stays which would have done much to put at rest the mind of a knight of old departing on a Crusade. He had made it extremely and repetitively clear to her that as far as Mrs

Yorke was concerned he had never been anywhere near the accident; he had made highly ungentlemanly references to valuable items of food missing from the fridge at The Sycamores.

Just before banging his way out again he had however slapped down a couple of pound notes on the table, causing Emily now to look back on his visit as more in the nature of a belated call from Father Christmas than anything else. Indeed it was beginning to occur to her that the accident was by far the most fortunate thing—in the way of money —that had happened to her in a long while.

As she directed the carpet nozzle under an easy chair she caught sight of a folded newspaper on the lowest shelf of an open bookcase. That would be it—last night's paper.

She switched off the cleaner and bent down. Sure enough the paper was folded so that the bit about the accident was staring right up at her. She sat down and began to read with avid attention.

The door burst open. Zena stood on the threshold, glaring at her.

'Get up!' she cried. 'Put that paper down!' Emily did as she was told. 'And now, there are one or two questions I want to ask you.' Emily stood with her hands folded and her head lowered. Here it comes, she thought, stiffening her old limbs to meet the challenge.

'In the first place, why did you say nothing to me yesterday about what happened on Friday evening?'

'Well, you never asked.'

'Of course I never asked! How could I? I didn't know anything about it! The point is, why didn't you tell me about it?'

'I thought you knew. And when you didn't ask I thought—' a rather good little martyred sniff—'you weren't interested. Never was one to bore other folk with me troubles,' she added with brilliant inspiration.

'How could I know? It wasn't in Saturday's paper.'

'I fancied Mr—' Emily broke off in horror at what she

had so nearly come out with. Only went to show how careful you had to be, get a little confident and you got carried away.

'Mr Who?' asked Zena with triumphant emphasis.

Emily smiled; her brain made a wonderful recovery. 'Mr Pierson. I fancied Mr Pierson would have told you. Knowing how friendly you are with him.' Oh, that was good, that was.

Zena jabbed a finger in the air. 'You were going to say Mr Yorke. I know, don't try to lie to me.'

'Why ever should I say Mr Yorke? It was Mr Pierson who saved me.' She jerked her head at the newspaper. 'It's all in there. How he grabbed hold of me.' It was beginning to look after all as if she was going to be able to get in a few words about that thrilling moment. 'Flung his arm round me neck. From behind. Like this.' She threw herself about in violent attitudes.

'Do stop jumping up and down,' Zena said crossly. 'And talking of Mr Pierson, does he call on Mrs Fleming? Have you ever seen him in her house? Or in her shop?'

'That I couldn't say, mum.' Emily reverted suddenly to pure Victorian kitchen-maid, pursing her lips primly.

'And why couldn't you say?'

'Not in a position to, that's why.'

Zena remained angrily baffled for a moment. 'Got a couple of bruises on me body,' Emily said almost with gaiety. 'When he took me home I got me things off—'

'When who took you home? How did you get home?'

'In a car. Not fit to walk. One on me leg and one on me arm, turning black and blue, I'll show you—'

'Whose car? Who took you in a car?'

'A gentleman.'

'What gentleman?'

'A gentleman who was passing.'

'One of the police?'

Emily put up a hand and fingered her ear. Getting a bit tricky now. 'Well no, not exactly police, he wasn't.'

Zena gave a sarcastic little laugh. 'Only partly police, was he? In what way did he resemble the police? Did he for instance have big feet?'

'Big feet?' Emily could make nothing of this. 'Not as I've ever noticed. I never pay no attention.' She let out a long breath. 'And now if you don't mind. I'd like to get on with me carpets.'

'Was it or was it not,' Zena said very loudly and clearly, 'Mr Yorke who drove you home?'

Emily glanced at her with an air of great surprise. 'Why, whatever makes you say that, mum? He never went and told you that, surely?' There's two pounds stuffed under me mattress back at the cottage says he didn't, she added in her mind, almost smiling at the memory.

'Yes, he did!' Zena cried triumphantly, believing she had at last bowled a winning ball.

'Oh, Mrs Yorke, mum!' Emily fielded it neatly, levelling at her a look of reproachful accusation. There was a brief pause. 'Me mother always told me to speak the truth,' she added pointedly. 'Speak the truth, Emily, she used to say, and God will look after you.'

'Then speak the truth now!' Zena shouted. 'Who drove you home?'

Emily raised her eyes to the ceiling, 'A gentleman who was there with his car.'

'What was his name?'

'I never thought to ask.' She flung a level look at Zena. 'And that's the one hundred per cent truth.' She drew a finger across her stringy throat. 'And hope to die. And now, I'll get on with them carpets.' She switched on the machine and began to wield the tube with determination.

CHAPTER IX

The day of Walter Pierson's funeral was brilliantly clear and cold. As David Cottrell drove through the streets he glanced out at the pavements, hoping he might catch sight again of the woman he now habitually thought of as the blonde goddess. But there was no sign of her. Was it conceivable she might be at the service, might be acquainted with the Piersons? He blinked away the thought, a little ashamed of such speculations at a time like this.

Several hundred yards ahead of Cottrell's car Arnold and Sarah were driving to the church. Arnold turned his head and looked out at the tail-end of the lunchtime crowds. An ordinary day for them, returning from the shops, going back to work, setting off for the cinema. He saw suddenly a man walking along, facing the car, pausing to look in a shop window, a tall, middle-aged man inclined to heaviness. The face—he couldn't place it but it teased at his mind as if he ought to have been able to recognize it. It was the walk though, the swing of the shoulders, the movement of the arms, that really pricked at recollection. Already the car had moved past, the man was lost to view. Someone from the factory perhaps? A buyer—a salesman? A local shopkeeper, unfamiliar out in the streets?

But they were drawing near the church. Other cars appeared from side roads, turning towards the gates. He had many details to attend to now, the face and figure dropped away from his mind.

Emily Bond walked into the church with an air of assurance as of one who had every right to be there. She took her place in a pew at the back, watching with lively curiosity everyone who came in, noting their clothes, the depth of grief expressed on each countenance. All her life she had been an ardent devotee of christenings, weddings and funerals, the primitive landmarks of existence. And the greatest of these was funerals.

She had laid out a good part of Owen Yorke's two pounds on a wreath. Not that she had known the dead man, not even to nod to in the street. But he had been the father of her rescuer and it was a feeling of intense loyalty to Arnold that had made her part with the money, brought her to the church and would despatch her to the graveside to stand in the bitter weather with the rest of the mourners. The least she could do by way of gratitude was to see Mr Pierson's father respectfully on his way.

'What on earth made you bring that old woman back to the house?' The last of the funeral guests had departed; Sarah was worn out at the end of the afternoon, inclined to asperity. She knew Mrs Bond of course from her own business visits to The Sycamores; she had never cared much for the creature, slovenly, unmannerly, argumentative. What Arnold could have been thinking of—naturally Mrs Bond had leapt at the chance of a free spread, she'd jumped into the back of the car with surprising agility.

But what had above all irritated Sarah was the way the old crone took it upon herself to help to do the honours, handing food around, gathering up empty plates, refilling cups and glasses. And insisting afterwards on staying behind to help with the washing-up, talking non-stop although Sarah had indicated more than once that she had a headache.

There had been nothing for it in the end but to suggest to Arnold that he drive her home; otherwise Sarah feared she might actually bed herself down for the night on some pretext or other.

'I thought she looked as if she needed a good hot drink,' Arnold said mildly, rather surprised at Sarah's sharpness; he'd thought Mrs Bond had been very helpful, waiting on the guests, clearing away, waving aside his offer of payment.

'Always glad to oblige *you*,' she'd said, looking up at him with meaning. 'Call on me any time. I'll come from the ends of the earth,' she'd added, briefly startling him.

'Why don't you sit down now and have a rest?' he said. Sarah did look tired. The whole thing must have been a tremendous strain for her; there had been the responsibility for nursing his father even without the sorrow and upheaval of the funeral.

'Oh, I'm all right, really.' She gave him a half-apologetic look. 'But I will sit down and close my eyes for half an hour.' She lowered herself into a chair, sitting upright as usual.

'I've one or two things to see to,' Arnold said vaguely. He felt restless but didn't feel he could follow his usual practice of going out and roaming the streets; he couldn't very well leave Sarah alone at this moment.

The notion thrust at his mind as he walked up the stairs and into his father's bedroom. He stood looking down at the bare mattress, glanced round at the table and shelves already stripped of Walter's belongings. For all the evidence that remained, his father might never have passed an hour between these four walls. When we are gone, how truly and finally we are gone, he thought with sorrow. His gaze searched about, striving to conjure up some sense of the man who had loomed so large in his life but the room offered him nothing but emptiness.

He turned his mind back to Sarah. I am free, he thought again; he felt all at once that it was true. Inhibition had slipped away from him, lying now under a weight of icy earth. Free to pay court to Linda Fleming. Was it conceivable that she would ever agree to marry him? If he could ever get as far as asking her. He strove to imagine himself opening an evening door, seeing her come towards him along a passage. It seemed just faintly possible.

But what of Sarah? Could she be left alone? Would there be any justice in that after she had devoted the greater part of her life to looking after himself and his father? He closed his eyes against the notion of her sharing an establishment with himself and Linda. Totally out of the question.

He walked to the window and looked out at the darkening evening. Arrangements could no doubt be made about Sarah, arrangements might have to be made . . .

Downstairs Sarah sat unrelaxed in her chair, her eyes closed against fatigue. Her lips moved in the merest suggestion of speech; she was addressing her thoughts to the image of her mother, a habit she had increasingly fallen into with the passing of the isolating years. Over a quarter of a century since she had stood in this very room and handed round the plates of cakes and sandwiches after her mother's funeral and yet it seemed to her still that her mother was the only person to whom she could fully and frankly open her mind.

I looked after him, she said to that beloved shadow, I looked after them both, I kept my word. She had been a woman of thirty-two when she stood beside her mother's grave—in the same plot where Walter had now joined her. On that day she had said goodbye to her last frail hopes of marriage, children, a place of her own. Never a beautiful girl, scarcely even a pretty one, she had grown up in a time when there were women to spare, when men could pick and choose.

But if her mother had never married a second time, if there had never been any deathbed promise, things might have been very different. Sarah had been a mere eighteen when she had moved with her mother to Walter's house and the footsteps of an eighteen-year-old girl might have gone down paths that were closed at thirty-two.

Her own father had worked for Ralph Underwood; there had been a great deal of argument after his death about pension rights. Such matters hadn't been so precisely formulated then, there had been some technical flaw. Old

Ralph had never been a man to part with a penny more than the law compelled him to disburse; humanity and moral justice were considerations outside the realms of hard cash. And so in the end her mother had got nothing except the return of her husband's contributions, which had just about served to pay the expenses of the funeral and the bills that had piled up since he drew his last breath.

Sarah clasped her hands on her lap, pressing the fingers tightly together. If there had been a pension, if old Ralph hadn't been such a skinflint, her mother would never have remarried—or at least would never have married Walter—and Sarah would have been as free as air. Her lips moved in a faint smile. At least I'm to get a pension, she thought, time has brought about some improvements.

Not that it would be exactly princely. Her salary—on which the pension would be based—had never been exceptionally generous; there had been talk a few years ago of an annual bonus as a percentage of sales but it had come to nothing. The question had been raised by Owen Yorke in a moment of expansiveness, but there had been a credit squeeze, the shop's figures had begun to dwindle after the appearance of more fashionable boutiques. And Zena had put her foot down. Not that credit restrictions seemed to affect the Yorkes' standard of living very much, Sarah thought, they did well enough.

She passed a hand across her eyes. If Arnold had married, his wife would have been expected to take over the responsibility for Walter and Sarah might yet have spread her wings. And he might have married, she thought, if it hadn't been for the curious and complicated ties that kept him bound to Zena. It seemed highly unlikely that he would marry now, too set in his ways, too locked inside himself.

But her promise to her mother had surely not been meant to extend as far as looking after a man of Arnold's age, a man who had deliberately chosen not to marry and who could if it came to the point, pay a housekeeper. If she and

Arnold continued to inhabit the same house it would be from mutual convenience, habit, a lack of attractive alternatives, and not from obligation.

So she opened her eyes at last on the thought: I am free, I have done my duty. But no exhilarating sense of liberation followed, only a deep weariness, staleness, the feeling of a vast section of life being over and done with and little to show for it but greying hair and a habit—all that was left of youthful courage and hope—of greeting each day with a kind of optimistic pessimism.

She tilted back her head and glanced up at the ceiling, hearing Arnold walking restlessly about upstairs. She wondered for a moment if he was experiencing any sense of release. She remembered all at once something that had been driven from her mind by the pressures of the last few days. There had been a phone call for Arnold—when was it? Yes, Monday evening, she had answered the call herself. A woman's voice, light, attractive; she had given her name . . . it came back to her now . . . Linda Fleming. Fleming . . . surely that was the name of the young woman who had taken over that little draper's shop. Could it be? Why should she be ringing Arnold? He had said nothing about it to her afterwards. It occurred to her suddenly that there might be a great many things she didn't know about Arnold . . .

He came downstairs and into the sitting-room. 'How's the headache? Any better?'

'About the same, thank you, it isn't a very bad one.' She wouldn't even consider taking an aspirin. 'Mrs Yorke never troubled to come to the funeral,' she said suddenly. Zena hadn't bothered to attend the funeral of Sarah's mother either.

'They sent a very handsome wreath,' Arnold pointed out.

Sarah made a contemptuous sound. 'Lift a telephone and pay the bill, that's all a wreath involves. And even that was probably done by Mr Yorke. I know he couldn't come to the funeral, he's away on business, I'm certain he would have come if he'd been in Milbourne.' She got to her feet, feeling the need for movement. 'I'm going to make some coffee—would you like a cup?' She gave a grim little laugh. 'If I can find where anything is after Emily Bond's kind assistance.'

CHAPTER X

Linda Fleming yawned delicately and glanced at the clock. Half past two. She felt bored and restless, all the busy activity of the week dwindled into this somnolent stretch of time before Sunday tea.

Not a word from Owen Yorke in over a week; he had very probably forgotten all about his impulsive offer of a ticket for the ball. She sighed. She couldn't in any case now think of coaxing Arnold to go with her; there would be no question of his going anywhere very festive for some considerable time.

And then the phone rang sharply. She sprang to her feet with a smile of lively anticipation.

'I hope I'm not disturbing you.' Arnold's voice, hesitant but tinged with resolution. 'I wondered if I might perhaps call to see you.'

'I should be very pleased,' Linda said. 'I'll give you some tea.' As soon as she had replaced the receiver she bustled about the room, restoring order. As she straightened the magazines on a side table she saw the week-old copy of the evening newspaper folded open at the report of Emily's accident. She sat down and read it through again with pleasure before going off to change her dress and do her face.

Quite a useful week's work on the whole; Owen had drummed up some good business, and it had been a relief to be away from home. But I don't think I'll bother hanging on here for tea, Owen thought, glancing round the hotel lounge with its scatter of winter residents, sleepy after Sunday lunch; I think I'll push off now. It would only take an hour or two to get back to Milbourne, not much traffic at this time of year.

But the prospect of an endless evening at The Sycamores with Zena likely to be in a highly combative mood, seemed little more alluring than tea and inane chat among the potted palms.

I'll call and see Linda, he decided. A pleasant drive out into the country, maybe a civilized dinner somewhere . . . perhaps it might be as well to phone first. He pushed back his chair and got to his feet, rousing a couple of elderly ladies into accusing wakefulness; he strode cheerfully over to the reception desk and brought his hand briskly down on the bell.

Things so far had gone rather well. Arnold still sat a little stiffly in the easy chair but he was beginning to experience an unusual and very agreeable feeling of relaxation. The room was a good deal brighter and gayer than the sitting-room at home. A bowl of daffodils bursting into bloom stood on a low table, a vase of tulips, delicate mauves and pinks, graced the top of an elegant little bureau.

And Linda looked so pretty in a white dress that emphasized the dark softness of her hair, the porcelain quality of her fine skin. She hadn't unnerved him by any brittle gaiety of manner that would demand an equal liveliness in response. Everything about her, her voice, her movements, her look, seemed gentle and fluid.

He had the comforting notion that she would be an easy person to live with, not given to importunate demands, understanding, soothing, softly-spoken. Impossible to imagine her in a rage or even sourly irritable.

They had chatted in a companionable way; the question of an evening out had been lightly touched on but nothing definitely settled yet.

'I'll go and put the kettle on,' Linda said, getting to her feet. 'I won't be long.' She waved a hand at the side table. 'The Sunday papers are there if you'd like to look at them.'

When the door had closed behind her Arnold went over and looked at the pile of newspapers, seeing with a slight thrust of surprise that the topmost one was a copy of last Monday's evening paper with his own long-ago face staring solemnly up at him.

He carried it back to his chair and began to read the paragraphs with keen interest. When Sarah had given him the paper a few days ago he had merely made a show of running his eyes over the column. Now he was pleased to find he was able to study it without revulsion, almost with detachment, striving to see it as it would have appeared to Linda.

When he had sufficiently taken it in he looked up with a faint smile beginning to touch his mouth. Perhaps after all the present might be allowed to close over the past, life could be permitted to move forward again, unclouded by ancient shadows.

In the distance he heard the soothing domestic sounds of a woman moving about a kitchen, preparing tea. A feeling of peace washed over his mind; he turned the pages idly, skimming the reports of meetings, football matches, golden weddings, half-registering the faces, known and unknown, conventionally gay or averted in shyness.

He stopped abruptly at one face looking straight out at him with an expression of direct enquiry. His mouth opened in a swift intake of breath; at the back of his neck he felt the hairs bristle with shock. He closed his eyes for a moment against that uncompromising glance; in the pit of his stomach the muscles twisted in apprehension. The years dropped away in a single flash, around him the air seemed humid with tropic heat, alive with the calls of exotic birds. He let out a long shuddering breath.

Turner! Captain Turner! He opened his eyes and forced his attention back to the page. Here in Milbourne, an appointment in British Foods, transferred on promotion from the London headquarters. All at once his mind threw up an image of a tall, heavily-built man pausing to glance at a shop window on the afternoon of the funeral, the face altered and matured, but the gait, the movement of the shoulders, familiar to him, touching some old, deep knowledge. So it had been Turner, sprung out of the war days, materialized here on a winter pavement, walking the Milbourne streets, likely to be encountered in the turn of a road, a halt at a crossing.

He got to his feet, the newspaper slid to the floor. He must go, must get out of this suffocating room into cold bright air under a soaring sky. He took a couple of steps towards the door and felt vitality begin to return to him. He seized the door-knob and heard from the kitchen the sound of the tea-trolley being wheeled into the passage.

Linda glanced up in surprise as he suddenly appeared on the threshold.

'I can't stay,' he said abruptly. 'I have to go.' He became conscious of her puzzled eyes. 'I'm afraid—' he raised a hand in a vague gesture. No explanation presented itself to his searching brain. 'The time—I'd no idea—' He wheeled about, strode swiftly down the passage, reached the front door and was gone.

For a couple of moments Linda remained where she was, motionless with astonishment. 'Well!' she said at last on a note of blank incomprehension. She resumed her journey, pushing the trolley into the sitting-room. She sank down on to the sofa, still trying to work it out, to arrive at some answer.

The newspaper obtruded itself on her baffled gaze; she stooped automatically and picked it up, folded the sheets, frowning down at them as if they might offer a solution.

Last Monday's evening paper, he had been looking at it then. The account of Emily's accident perhaps? A face looked briefly up at her as her eyes slid over the columns, an unknown face with a level, almost accusing glance. But it meant nothing to her, her gaze flicked past it, she continued to skim the pages.

Then she raised her shoulders and abandoned the matter. If Arnold chose to behave in that unceremonious fashion—she turned to the trolley and selected a little sponge cake decorated with pale pink icing; might as well have something to eat. She lifted the teapot and then paused, throwing back her head and laughing aloud. It seemed as if Arnold Pierson was destined to be forever offered cups of tea in her house and forever fated never to drink them.

When Owen Yorke phoned an hour or two later she was hard at work in the shuttered shop, checking old stock in the crowded storeroom, doing her best to hold at bay the long tedium of the evening.

'Dinner?' she echoed with pleasure at his invitation, 'I'd be delighted! What time will you be calling for me?'

Sarah came down the stairs on her way to the kitchen. She threw a brief glance at Arnold who was standing by the hall table, talking into the phone; his face wore a closed and weary look. Zena's at her games again, Sarah thought irritably, I suppose she fancies enough time has elapsed since the funeral to allow her to resume her puppet-play.

'So many things I would like the opportunity to talk over with you,' Zena said lightly into the receiver.

'I wasn't proposing to give myself the pleasure of talking anything over with you.' Arnold's free hand clenched itself into a fist. 'Ever again.'

'Your bravery at the time of poor Emily's accident,' Zena said as if he hadn't spoken. 'I should like to congratulate you on that. Not that one would expect anything but gallantry from a man with your war record.' Her voice took on a gay and intimate note. 'And there's the matter of an old acquaintance of ours. Come to live in Milbourne after all these years.' She rather thought he knew nothing of Turner's re-appearance, she waited for him to frame a question. When he said nothing she added, 'Your old captain,

Maurice Turner.' She listened intently for an exclamation of dismay, for an intake of breath, but there was only silence. 'I'm so looking forward to seeing him again,' she said in a lively tone. 'So much to chat about. I'm sure he'd be pleased to have news of you.'

Without a word Arnold replaced the receiver on its rest. A single insistent thought began to beat against the edges of his mind . . . as long as Zena lives there will never be an end to inhibiting fear . . . there will never be freedom or the possibility of joy as long as she remains alive . . .

CHAPTER XI

In the spacious and ornately-gilded room at the Milbourne Assembly Hall, brilliant with light from crystal chandeliers, pulsing with music from the finest dance-band in the county, the Presidential Ball of the Independents' was in full swing.

Owen Yorke was standing near the buffet, half-listening to the slightly heated exchange taking place between the two men beside him, Dr Gethin and Detective-Inspector Venn, both long-established members of the Independents' who knew each other so well and had had so many professional dealings over the years that a little set-to here and there could have no effect on their mutual regard. Some minor trouble now over a parking-ticket that had been slapped on Gethin's car by an over-zealous warden new to the job.

Owen let their conversation slip past his ears; his gaze travelled over the dancing couples, the leaders of Milbourne society and their decked-out ladies, and came to rest on his own reflection held out to him by a glittering mirror opposite. A fine figure in full evening dress, resplendent in the royal blue presidential sash; he could scarcely prevent himself from flashing a look of delighted recognition, exuberant congratulation at the successful citizen confronting him.

He turned his head a fraction and saw the back view of his wife as she leaned over the buffet table to indicate a particular delicacy to her brother who was obediently spearing appetizing morsels on to a large plate at her command. Owen felt the fierce glow of his mood begin to waver and slacken at the sight of those ample curves only partly restrained by a shimmering gown of amethyst-coloured wild silk that had been specially made for her in his own workrooms. A little sigh escaped from his lips; he pivoted himself round a little and returned his attention to the men at his side.

'Don't give it another thought,' Venn was saying with his customary air of wary affability. A tricky path to tread, official watch-dog, fellow-clubman, professional colleague; and all directed by a temperament naturally inclined to easy-going goodwill and an instinct to avoid rather than seek for trouble. Many a time in his earlier years Venn would wake in the cheerless night and ask himself if he had chosen the right career; now he had abandoned that pointless question, comforting himself instead with the prospect of approaching retirement. One good thing about growing older was that he had been able to stop worrying about further promotion; he had reached a position in the force where he was just about competent enough to hold his own without fear of disgrace. He had wedged himself into this final niche with thankfulness, determined to remain there until the releasing day brought him his pension and a suitably-engraved silver tray.

'I'll have a word with the fellow myself,' he said to Gethin. 'You can forget about the parking ticket. And I'll see you're not bothered in future.' He had a little notebook at home in which he now actually worked out from time to time the detailed count of years, months and days until the moment of liberation. Deep down in his mind he was aware that retirement would present him with another and perhaps more intractable set of problems but he always dropped a shutter over that notion, preferring to leave it in deliberate obscurity until the day when it would inexorably spring out to confront him in stark reality.

Owen saw now with a touch of irritation that Zena was coming towards them with Neil a pace or two in the rear. She called out a gay greeting to Gethin, smiled at Venn, threw a casual glance at Owen.

'You're not going to stuff yourself with all that?' Gethin demanded, nodding his head at her plate and then fixing Zena with an accusing eye; Zena gave him a defiant look, just sufficiently tinged with gaiety to rob it of open offence. 'And you'll forget your injection as well, no doubt.' Gethin saw at once from the way her eyes jerked open that the matter had indeed totally slipped from her mind. 'I knew it!' he said with a kind of angry triumph. He swung round to face Owen. 'You'll be ringing me up in the morning, crying for help. I'll be expected to go running here and there, picking up the pieces. Can't you drum any sense into that wife of yours?'

Neil gave the doctor a cold glance of reproof, then he put a hand under Zena's elbow and steered her between the knots of revellers who closed instantly over their passage, mercifully obliterating them from view.

Owen stood at a temporary loss, submerged in a feeling of guilt at the notion that he was somehow responsible for Zena's self-indulgence, but at the same time resentment began to thrust its way up into his mind. He couldn't trust himself to say something civil to Gethin so he said nothing, but Inspector Venn, who had averted his head from the little scene in uneasy embarrassment, now stepped forward and tried to press Gethin to take some food.

'I don't want anything,' Gethin said with an unceremonious wave of his hand. 'I'll go to the bar and get a drink.' He pushed his way through the throng without a backward look.

Venn put a comradely hand on Owen's arm. 'Come on, he said in a friendly tone, 'have something to eat. You don't want to pay any attention to old Gethin. He's getting past it, that's his trouble, he ought to have retired years ago. His nerves aren't up to it any more, he's inclined to fly off the handle these days.'

Owen felt a wave of gratitude begin to wash away his resentment. He took a plate and helped himself from one or two of the dishes, then he followed Venn to an empty table and sat down. After a few mouthfuls of food calm returned to him and he was able to make casual conversation with the inspector and two or three other men who paused beside them for a brief chat; by the time his plate was empty he was quite cheerful again. He let his eyes rove round the room and saw with a sudden smile of pleasure the pretty figure of Linda Fleming walking gracefully towards the buffet beside her partner, a member of the party Owen had arranged for her to join.

Venn's sharp eyes observed the alteration in Yorke's mood; he turned his head and followed Owen's gaze. He saw a good-looking, dark-haired young woman flash a smile at Yorke, raise her hand in a greeting that seemed to hold a note of intimacy, of secrecy, then her companion took her arm and they disappeared from sight.

'Who was that?' Venn asked in an idle tone, 'I don't think I know her.'

Owen gave him a frank, bright glance. 'Who?' He looked briskly round at the crowded room as if he had no idea what Venn was talking about.

'It doesn't matter,' the inspector said, lifting his fork and stabbing at a morsel on his plate.

Several yards away, at the other side of the room, Zena sat at a table with her brother and his wife. She was sipping at a tall glass, her eyes never ceasing to wander round the room while at the same time she kept up an animated conversation with Ruth about the merits of the new car her sister-in-law had driven proudly home on the previous day.

'I can't say I ever cared for small cars myself. Not enough leg-room. But I dare say it will do well enough for getting you to work and for running Jane here and there.' She sent a little needling glance at her brother. 'I take it you've solved your difficulty with money then?' She smiled gaily. 'You'll have to be careful, being in the housing department, people might say you're taking bribes—or cooking the books.' She raised her glass and took a long drink.

'I don't think that's very funny.' Neil gave Zena an angry look.

'I don't know that it was meant to be all that funny,' she said serenely. 'A man in your position, you must be aware how people talk in a place the size of Milbourne.'

'Difficulty about money?' Ruth tilted her head back and looked at Neil with a slight frown. 'Surely it wasn't anything serious?' But apparently it had been serious enough for him to go running round to discuss it with Zena. 'I thought you said—'

'Whatever I said, this is hardly the time or place to discuss it.' He drew a deep breath, relaxed his shoulders, forced himself to smile. 'Anyway, there is no difficulty, I thought I'd made that clear.'

'I'm delighted to hear it.' Zena took another drink from her glass. 'I imagine Ruth's promotion has done a lot to help. Must be a load off a man's mind to be able to count on a good income from his wife.'

'Look here.' Neil's eyebrows came together; his voice rose. 'You know perfectly well I'm not the kind of man—'

'Oh, there's Maurice Turner!' Zena waved a hand. 'He must come and join us. Oh good, he's seen me, he's coming over.' She turned to Ruth. 'How do you get on with your new boss? I suppose Neil's told you he's an old friend of mine?'

'No, he didn't mention it,' Ruth said in an easy tone. She leaned forward and picked up her beaded bag; she opened it and began to search about inside it.

'You must have known him in London of course,' Zena said lightly. 'Was he your boss there? Did you know him well?' Neil moved his head and gave Ruth an intent look. A silence fell over the table; it seemed a tiny island in the eddying currents of talk and laughter. 'Did you know Maurice well?' Zena persisted.

'Oh, there it is,' Ruth said with triumph, fishing up a lipstick from her bag. 'I thought I must have left it at home.' She removed the gilt top, took out a powder compact, flipped it open to look into the mirror while she delicately touched up her lips. When she had finished she snapped the compact shut. 'I'm sorry, Zena—you were saying?'

But before Zena had time to frame her question again Turner was beside them, smiling genially down at the trio. Zena looked up at him with a lively expression.

'Are you enjoying yourself? I suppose you're meeting a lot of old friends and acquaintances.'

'One or two,' Turner said easily. 'Can't always recognize old faces after a number of years. People change a good deal.' And none of them as much as Zena Yorke, he added in his mind. He had met her in the receiving line at the beginning of the evening, she had proclaimed her identity with instant friendliness. It had been as much as he could do not to betray his deep sense of shock when this total stranger revealed herself as the ravishing Zena Underwood of his bachelor days. He looked at her now with fascinated scrutiny, striving to see in that bulging figure, the fleshy contours of that over-made-up face, the lovely girl who had sat beside him in his sports car.

'You know my sister-in-law of course,' Zena said. 'And this is her husband, my brother Neil. I don't suppose you remember him.'

Turner gave Ruth a formal little nod, leaned over and held out his hand to Neil. 'I do vaguely remember that Zena had a young brother,' he said with a smile. 'But I don't believe we ever met.'

'No, I don't think we did, I was still at school in those days.' Neil's fingers touched Turner's in the briefest grasp, his eyes looked intently up into Turner's face. Maurice, he thought, casting fiercely into the depths of memory, was that the name Ruth had spoken over the dinner-table a year ago? M . . .M . . . ? Or had it been an R? He stood up suddenly and pushed back his chair. 'If you'll excuse us now—' he laid a hand on Ruth's arm—'come and dance.' He felt a sharp sense of humiliation at his own absurd need to establish a proprietary claim; he threw Turner a cool look. 'I'm sure you'll have a lot to talk about with Zena.'

Ruth got to her feet, half glad to escape and half resentful of the peremptory way Neil had touched her arm. As she moved out on to the dance floor she saw with irritation that Anthea Gibbs was sitting a yard or two away, focusing her undisguised attention on the four of them. Anthea's face was pale and her eyes had a watery look; as their glances met she turned away and took a handkerchief from her bag, her shoulders shook in a violent sneeze.

Behind her Ruth could hear Zena's friendly tones. 'Do sit down, Maurice,' she was saying. 'I believe you worked with Ruth in London. Were you in the same department?'

Ruth took Neil's hand and drew him out into the dancing throng. Over Neil's shoulder she caught sight of Owen circling gaily to the music with a very pretty young woman with a fine pale skin and soft hazel eyes. 'Owen seems to be enjoying himself,' she said lightly. 'Who's that he's dancing with?'

Neil turned his head without much interest. 'I don't know, I've never seen her before.' Surely there was something rather strained and brittle about Ruth's manner, she had an air of catching at any random topic as if to distract his attention from some other unwelcome subject.

'She's very good-looking,' Ruth said with animation. And the same thought presented itself forcefully to Zena a few yards away. She broke off in the middle of saying something to Turner, she sat silently for a few moments, watching her husband, her fingers tapping the table. Turner followed her gaze.

'That's a pretty girl Owen's partnering. I was introduced to her earlier on, I had a couple of dances with her.'

'I can't quite place her.' Zena's fingers continued to beat time on the table. 'Do you remember her name?'

'Fleming,' Turner said. 'Mrs Fleming, I didn't get her first name. She's a good dancer, moves very lightly.'

How airily she floats in my arms, Owen thought with pleasure, pressing his hand into the back of Linda's waist. 'You're looking very beautiful this evening,' he murmured, putting his cheek against hers. 'You're by far the prettiest woman in the room.'

Linda laughed. 'You mustn't exaggerate. Actually, I'm beginning to feel a little jaded, I always find this time of year rather wearing, the cold, the fog, everyone coughing and sneezing. Now that the sale's over I'm going to take a couple of days off shortly.'

'What about the shop? Can you leave it to your assistant? She's very young, isn't she?'

'Oh I couldn't leave her on her own for long, I'll just take a week-end, I can close the shop at lunch-time on Saturday and come back early on the Monday morning. I'm not planning to go very far away—Seahaven, I expect you know it.'

'Yes, of course I do.' Thirty miles away, on the coast, a pleasant enough place in the summer though probably a little bleak in the middle of winter; he had often been there on business. 'Is it this coming week-end you're taking off?' he asked casually. He felt a tingle of excitement begin to prickle along his nerves. He could quite easily slip down to Seahaven himself; always some business to be drummed up in that area. He normally went and returned in the course of one day but there would be nothing to prevent him staying overnight, even a couple of nights. The break would do him good; a man couldn't be too careful with all this flu about.

'No, not this week-end,' she said, 'the next one.'

'And have you found yourself a good hotel?' he asked in a light impersonal tone. 'If not, I can recommend one or two.'

'I've already found one,' she said with equal casualness. 'One of my customers told me about it. Cliff View, apparently it's not too expensive out of season.'

'Yes, I know it, I've called in there for lunch once or twice, the food's very good, I think you'll be comfortable there.' If I went down on the Friday morning, he thought, or even the Friday afternoon, that would give me plenty of time to fit in a little business. His imagination conjured up an intriguing picture of Linda coming down the hotel stairs after her unpacking and himself rising to greet her from a seat in the lounge, seeing the expression on her face as she recognized him. His attention wandered briefly from the dance and he missed the beat, stumbling awkwardly and catching his foot against the leg of a chair set a little too close to the circling couples.

'Oh—I'm sorry, do forgive me—' He steadied himself, glanced down with an apologetic smile and saw Dr Gethin's eyes looking back at him. 'Clumsy of me,' he said. 'I hope I didn't—'

'That's all right,' Gethin said. He stood up and moved his chair back a few paces. 'Serves me right for sitting so far forward.' He seemed anxious to offer amends for his discourteous behaviour earlier on. 'The evening's going very well.' He gave Owen a little smile. 'You must be feeling very satisfied with yourself.'

'Indeed I am.' Owen's voice was warmly emphatic. 'You must have a drink with me later.' He was pleased to see Gethin nod and he swung Linda back into the dance.

As he negotiated a tricky turn he caught sight of Zena still seated at her table, chatting to Turner, who was staring out at the dancers with a look that even at this distance seemed to Owen to be eloquent of boredom. A surge of pity rose inside him; only ten or fifteen years ago any man who sat beside Zena at a ball would have given her his full and undivided attention. His arm closed round Linda a little more tightly; he felt as if he could turn and circle with her for ever to the dip and lift of the music, under the glittering brilliance of the chandeliers.

At the small table Maurice Turner shifted in his seat and did his best to suppress a sigh.

'I don't believe you're listening!' Zena leaned over and tapped him coquettishly on the arm.

'I'm sorry.' He managed a look of friendly apology. 'What was it you were saying?'

'I was asking if you remembered Arnold Pierson. He was in your regiment during the war.'

'Pierson?' Yes, he remembered him; and he'd read a little piece about him in the paper the other day, some accident in the street. 'We were taken prisoner together,' he said, looking back at those incredible days.

'He works for Owen now, has done ever since the war.'

'Yes, I gathered that, I saw his photograph in the local paper, there were a couple of paragraphs about him, he'd saved some old woman's life.'

'Oh yes,' Zena said with significant emphasis. 'Quite the hero, dear Arnold.'

Turner frowned. 'He was decorated in the war, you know,' he said shortly. 'And he deserved it.'

'Did he indeed? I wonder.' Her voice held an odd note of pleasure.

'Just what are you getting at?' Turner asked, all his instincts springing up in defence of one of his own men against the sneer of this useless civilian for whom the war had probably been little more than an annoying interruption to her butterfly days.

'I believe I know considerably more than you do about Arnold Pierson's war record.' All the subtle shades of tone had left Zena's voice, she spoke now with ruthless directness. 'And what happened to one of your precious companies as a result of his—' She was interrupted by someone halting by her chair, trying to edge a way past her; she uttered a sound of irritation, glanced up and saw a woman looking down at her with apology.

'If you could just move your chair a little,' the woman said with quiet persistence. Turner sprang to his feet, glad of the interruption; in another moment he might have said something to Zena that he would later regret.

'Why, it's Miss Gibbs!' A member of his department at British Foods, a little unfamiliar now in an elaborate gown of dull gold silk that did little for her sallow complexion. 'I hope you're enjoying the ball?' He addressed her with considerably more interest than he would normally have employed and her expression brightened with remarkable swiftness.

'Oh yes, thank you,' she said effusively. 'It's a very good band, isn't it?' The music ceased and the dancers began to make their way back to the tables. It struck Turner with dismal certainty that he was going to have to ask Miss Gibbs for the next dance; a sense of mounting exasperation rose inside him, he seemed to be surrounded by astonishingly unattractive females.

'I don't know if you've met Mrs Yorke,' he said desperately.

'No, we've never met,' Anthea said, fishing about in her bag and giving vent to a shattering sneeze before she managed to snatch up a handkerchief. 'Oh, do excuse me! I believe I've caught a cold.' She exploded into another sneeze, this time mercifully into a square of lace-edged lawn. 'Of course I know you by sight,' she said to Zena with determined friendliness as soon as she had finished dabbing at her nose. 'I suppose everyone in Milbourne does.'

Zena gave a little grunt, her eyes slid over Anthea's face, her bony shoulders, pausing with a faint increase of interest at the sweeping folds of her dress which struck her as very probably coming from her own shop, there being no other establishment in the town supplying quite such expensive gowns cut in so intricate a style.

'I work with your sister-in-law, Ruth Underwood,' Anthea said, trying to ignore the coolness of Zena's manner.

'Is that so?' Zena tilted back her chair, put up a hand to her mouth and yawned. A flush rose in Anthea's cheeks, her eyes began to shine brightly. And then Neil came up with Ruth and the moment dissolved into a general exchange of remarks. The music struck up again and Turner's face assumed a look of cheerfulness.

'Ah, a waltz!' he said gaily. He took a step forward, smiling, one hand stretched out; Anthea's mouth lifted in pleasure, she moved to join him but something impeded her, she gave an impatient tug at her skirt and saw in the same moment that Turner was looking past her at Ruth. There was a ripping sound as the threads of the gold silk parted; she glanced down to where the hem of her dress was pinned under the foot of Zena's chair.

'Now look what you've done!' Anthea said in a low trembling voice. A yard or two away Turner was already moving expertly to the music, his arm round Ruth's waist. Neil stooped and took hold of the torn skirt. 'Move your chair,' he said to his sister who got grudgingly to her feet.

'It's nothing to do with me,' Zena said. 'You should look where you're going.'

Neil released the strip of material. 'I'm afraid it's well and truly torn,' he said, looking up at Anthea. Her cheeks were a fiery red, she looked as if at any moment she might burst into tears. 'If you went to the cloakroom,' he said with an attempt at kindliness, sorry for the wretched woman, 'someone might be able to sew it up.'

Anthea jerked the folds to her side, clutched her bag to her thin bosom and plunged off without a word towards the haven of the ladies' room. Neil got to his feet and stood looking after her.

'Don't you think perhaps you ought to go with her and see what you can do?' he said to Zena.

'Why on earth should I?' she said loudly. 'It was no fault of mine. Clumsy creature!'

'Poor Anthea!' Ruth murmured, glancing over Maurice's shoulder at her colleague's departing back. 'It's probably ruined her whole evening.' She had glimpsed the little episode as she turned to the beat of the waltz.

'I shouldn't worry about Miss Gibbs,' Maurice said lightly. 'Shall we go and have something to eat? I'm beginning to feel hungry.'

'Yes, I would like an ice, it's so warm in here.'

He kept his arm round her waist as he piloted her in the direction of the buffet. At the other side of the room Neil watched them with a frown. He turned to Zena. 'Do you want something more to eat?' he demanded abruptly. 'Would you like to come along to the buffet?'

She shook her head. 'No, I don't feel like anything.'

'Shall we dance then?' He could steer her down to that end of the room, keep an eye on Ruth and Turner.

Again Zena shook her head. 'No, I'll stay here.' So he was compelled to stay beside her; he remained standing, doing his best to look between the heads of the crowd but unable to catch a glimpse of his wife. Zena made no attempt at conversation; she was beginning to feel a little unwell, she had eaten and drunk too much, the room was very warm, and the exchange with Anthea Gibbs had brought an unpleasant sensation of fullness to her temples.

The waltz ended but Ruth and Turner didn't reappear; after a brief interval the music began again and Neil's eyes searched among the swirling throng without finding them. At last the dancing came to another stop but still there was no sign of them. He felt unable to remain rooted to Zena's side for another moment.

'Do come and have a drink,' he said urgently. She made no reply and he bent his head to look at her. She was leaning back in her chair with her eyes closed. 'Are you all right?' he asked with a trace of anxiety, irritated that she should choose this moment to play the invalid.

She opened her eyes and gave him a weary glance, she passed a hand across her forehead. 'I feel a little faint.'

She drew a long breath. 'A touch of giddiness. It's so hot in here.'

'I'll find Ruth,' he said at once, 'I'll get her to take you to the rest room, I won't be a minute.' He made his way briskly between the chairs and tables, down to the end of the room, scanning the clusters of people at the buffet. Neither Ruth nor Turner were anywhere to be seen. He forced a passage to the bar and stared round at the laughing and chatting groups but nowhere could he catch sight of Ruth's blonde head.

He left the bar and began a resolute circuit of the dance-floor, until his feet brought him at last before a little alcove and there they were, smiling at each other, talking with careless enjoyment, never a thought of himself.

'So this is where you've got to!' he said in a low fierce tone. Ruth glanced up in surprise, taken aback by his intent, accusing gaze. She had finished eating and was just about to raise a glass to her lips. 'I've been looking everywhere for you,' Neil said on the same note of outrage. 'I'd no idea you'd hidden yourselves away in here.' Turner's face took on a veiled, withdrawn look; he closed his eyes in a moment's resignation. Milbourne society seemed to offer a variety of emotional encounters, each a little more wearing than the last.

'Did you want me for any particular reason?' Ruth asked with detached courtesy.

'I certainly did!' Neil said. 'Zena isn't feeling very well, I want you to come and look after her, take her off somewhere quiet for a while.' His manner implied some huge and unnamed fault in Ruth for not being constantly at hand to watch over Zena's welfare.

'I don't suppose it's anything very much,' Ruth said in an unconcerned fashion. 'You know what Zena is, she's always fancying she feels ill.' She gave Maurice a smiling look. 'I'm sorry, I'd better go and take a look at her, do excuse me.'

'Of course, I quite understand.' Maurice stood up as Ruth

rose to her feet; he watched the two of them go, Neil with his hand firmly on Ruth's arm. He picked up his glass and drained it, then he set off towards the bar for another, stronger drink; he felt very definitely that he needed it.

Zena was still sitting with closed eyes when Neil returned with his captive wife. She really looks far from well, Ruth thought with a blend of exasperation and pity; she took her sister-in-law gently by the arm. 'Come along,' she said quietly. 'You'll feel a lot better as soon as you get out of this stuffy atmosphere.' Zena allowed herself to be urged to her feet, she followed Ruth obediently round the edge of the dance-floor, past the musicians' dais out into a passage where at once the air was cooler and fresher, into a pleasant rest-room with a row of wash-basins along one side, comfortable chairs dotted about and an archway leading to a smaller room.

'Oh dear!' Ruth said under her breath as she caught sight of Anthea Gibbs standing with her back to them, facing a long mirror set in the wall by the archway. An elderly woman was sitting on a stool at Anthea's side, diligently stitching the long rip in the hem of her dress. She glanced up with a look of enquiry as Ruth settled Zena into a chair. 'It's all right,' Ruth said quietly, 'we just want to sit here for a while,' and the woman returned to her task. Ruth was pleased to see that Zena paid no attention to Anthea but sank back against the cushions, exhaling a long breath of relief. 'That's better!' she said, 'I shall be all right in a few minutes.'

At the sound of their voices Anthea moved her head and studied their reflections in the mirror. She stood up a little straighter and flexed her shoulder muscles as if nerving herself for a fresh encounter; she drew in a steadying lungful of air.

'I shall take this dress back to Underwood's next week,' she said to the attendant in a loud defiant voice. 'I shall demand every penny of my money back.'

Zena jerked herself upright in her chair, flashed a glance

at Anthea's back and then addressed herself to Ruth. 'People can't expect a refund,' she said clearly, 'for goods they have damaged by their own stupid clumsiness.' Oh dear, Ruth thought in dismay, casting about for some way to put an end to the exchange but finding no immediate solution.

In the mirror Anthea saw her own face, glowing cheeks and shining eyes; exhilaration rose inside her. It was astonishing how much better and bolder you felt once you snatched at courage and stood up for your rights. 'Damaged articles ought not to be sold at full price,' she said, still shafting her words at the attendant who plied her needle with exaggerated care, removing herself spiritually if not physically from the scene. 'I'm positive it's against the law,' Anthea added, growing braver every moment. 'False pretences or misrepresentation.'

Zena gave Ruth a brilliant smile; she looked well and energetic again. 'No imperfect garments are ever sold at full price in my shop.' She enunciated every syllable distinctly and precisely. 'They are put twice a year into sales and disposed of at a fraction of their cost. If people wish to pay five pounds for a ball gown—'

'I gave thirty-five pounds for this dress,' Anthea broke in; her voice took on a ringing quality as if she were standing on the platform at a meeting of the Ladies' Guild. 'This is only the second time I've worn it. And for thirty-five pounds I do not tolerate flawed material.'

Perhaps there could have been a flaw in the cloth, Ruth thought; Zena had paid very little attention to the running of her business for some considerable time. It was quite possible for a substandard garment to be overlooked. She laid a hand on Zena's arm. 'Don't you think perhaps—' But Zena shook away her touch with a brusque movement.

'Women who indulge in slanderous statements,' she said, with enjoyment edging her tone, 'must expect the full rigour of the law.' A middle-aged woman in evening dress came out of the archway and walked towards the wash-basins; she glanced with curiosity from Anthea to Zena. Neither of them gave her so much as a look.

'I'm sure if Anthea calls into the shop next week,' Ruth said desperately, feeling things had gone far enough, 'the matter can easily be settled. Perhaps another dress, part exchange—Miss Pierson could see to it.'

Anthea whirled round from the mirror, dragging her skirt out of the attendant's grasp; there was a crisp sound as the tear lengthened. 'Oh dear!' the attendant said. 'You've gone and made it worse.'

Zena threw back her head and laughed out loud. 'One can hardly credit such natural clumsiness,' she said in between spasms of mirth. At the wash-basin the middle-aged woman ran the taps and soaped her hands with care.

'If you take the dress into the shop,' Ruth persisted, 'I feel quite certain—'

'You keep out of this!' Anthea cried, levelling at her a look bright with anger. All the accumulated resentment she felt at her years of unrewarded service at British Foods, her failure to secure promotion, her position now actually as a subordinate to Ruth Underwood, bubbled up inside her. 'What business is it of yours?'

'How dare you speak to my sister-in-law in that fashion!' At once Zena closed ranks against the outsider.

A laugh escaped from Anthea's lips. 'Sister-in-law!' she said. 'A fine sister-in-law!' A warning light flashed in her brain but she blinked it away. She'd done a little ferreting in the last couple of weeks, had made one or two phone calls to an old friend in the London branch, had got a long and highly interesting letter from her only the day before, full of absorbing items of gossip about the goings-on between Ruth and Mr Turner when they had worked together at headquarters, when Mr Turner was still a married man. 'Ask your precious sister-in-law how she wangled her present job!' she said to Zena with deep pleasure. 'Ask her what she gets up to behind her husband's back!'

Ruth stood up; her face looked pale under the clear white light. The door from the passage opened and three women came in, chatting gaily. 'If you're feeling better,' Ruth said to Zena in a low voice, 'we could go back and join the others. Or would you rather go home?'

'Indeed I will not go home!' Zena said fiercely. 'But I've had more than enough of Miss Gibbs's company.' She got to her feet and walked to the door with Ruth thankfully at her elbow. The three newcomers had already vanished through the archway; the woman at the wash-basin had completed her toilette and now dropped some coins into a saucer on a table.

'Thank you, Mrs Venn,' the attendant said, still seated on her stool. 'Now that that's all over,' she said to Miss Gibbs, 'perhaps I can get on with stitching up your hem.'

Anthea felt all her vitality drain away; she began to shiver, her shoulders shook in a sneeze. 'Actually I don't feel very well,' she said in between dabs at her nose with a moist handkerchief. 'I think I'll go home.' It had been a disastrous evening; there had been scarcely ten minutes that had given her any pleasure at all. She lived in a village ten miles away, had been given a lift to the hall by a member of the Independents' who lived in the same village. But he would be sure to stay till the very end and she couldn't possibly endure another two or three hours of this wretched festivity. 'I'd better go and see if I can find a taxi.' She took some money from her purse and gave it to the attendant; she had a sudden horrid feeling that she was about to burst into loud, undignified tears.

'What a ridiculous creature!' Zena said as she walked back into the hall with Ruth. She felt for the moment almost kindly disposed towards her sister-in-law, being left with the impression of having fought side by side with her against the foe. 'Demand her money back indeed! I'll speak to Sarah, I'll make very sure she doesn't get a penny.' As they edged their way towards their table she caught sight of Maurice Turner dancing with that dark-haired young woman. He raised his hand and waved at her; she gave him a little nod in return.

'By the way,' she said to Ruth, suddenly recollecting Anthea's final shafts, 'what was that about Turner? That Gibbs creature, what was she saying about you—'

'Oh, I shouldn't pay any attention to her,' Ruth said easily. 'She talked a great deal of nonsense, I think she'd had a little too much to drink. Poor thing, she probably isn't used to it, she'll be very sorry about it all tomorrow. And I shouldn't think you'll hear any more about the dress, she'll calm down, she's that type, she'll let it drop. Are you sure you feel all right now?'

'Yes, I feel fine.' Nothing better than a good argument to stimulate Zena back to a sense of well-being.

I'm glad I managed to escape from her clutches, Maurice thought, glimpsing Zena's rear view again as he revolved with Linda Fleming. He smiled down at his partner. 'We'll slip along to the bar as soon as the music finishes, we'll have a little drink.' He pressed her close to him. A remarkably pretty woman, an agreeable and soothing companion; it occurred to him with pleasure that it would be a very good idea at the end of the evening to offer to drive her home.

CHAPTER XII

'And suppose I'm taken ill again while you're gallivanting by the sea,' Zena cried above the sound of music from the radio on her bedside table. 'I could die for all you'd care!'

Owen put his head round the dressing-room door. 'I'll leave a note on the table with the name of my hotel and the phone number. You can always ring me.' He hadn't bothered to mention the name of Seahaven, he'd allowed Zena to believe he intended making a trip to several places along the coast. 'Anyway, you'll be perfectly all right.' She was certainly very much recovered from the attack that had laid her low immediately after the ball; there'd been a day or two when old Gethin had looked gravely concerned, had shaken his head in the passage outside her room. But thank goodness that was all over now. 'You can always get Emily Bond to stay the night if you want to, she won't mind.' Owen returned to his packing.

'Emily Bond!' Zena spat out the words with distaste. 'I'm not having the pleasure of her company for the night!' Returning strength was beginning to unleash in her a host of old animosities and resentments.

In the dressing-room Owen took shirts and pyjamas from a drawer, folded them neatly into his suitcase. A stream of words from Zena washed against the edge of his mind but his thoughts were very pleasantly occupied with a vision of tomorrow evening, Linda Fleming coming gracefully down the stairs of the Cliff View Hotel, the way her face would break into a delighted smile when she caught sight of him.

As he tucked his hairbrushes in among the clothes he became aware of a certain note of repetition in Zena's shrill utterances. He stood still and allowed the unlovely sounds to formulate themselves into intelligible sentences.

'For the third time!' Zena roared. 'Have you or have you not dealt with the matter of the surplus stock? What's wrong with you? Have you gone stone deaf?'

Scarcely surprising if I have, Owen thought, hastening to the door and flashing his wife a conciliatory look. 'So sorry, my dear, I didn't catch what you were saying.'

'Didn't catch what I was saying!' She was astounded. As well she might be, he thought; folk a quarter of a mile away had doubtless been able to make out her drift. 'I was asking you if you've made any arrangements about the rest of the stock from the shop.' Tomorrow evening the shutters would go up for the last time; she still hadn't forgiven Owen for high-handedly taking the decision to close down the shop without consulting her, although she had realized after due reflection that it was a sensible move.

'That's all taken care of,' Owen said smoothly. 'Don't fret yourself about business, you just want to concentrate on getting your strength back.' Though she seemed particularly well supplied with strength this morning. He vanished back into his sanctuary and finished packing. Zena's questions continued to bombard him but he didn't bother to register them; in another minute or two he'd be safely downstairs and out through the front door. He glanced round the room, making sure he'd forgotten nothing, snapped the suitcase shut and went in to say goodbye. Zena's cheeks were bright pink with rage.

'It may have escaped your notice,' she said as he put down his case and approached the bed, 'that I am still joint owner of the whole business and that I am quite capable of telephoning my solicitor and getting him to draw up a new will.' She saw the weary way his eyelids drooped for an instant, implying a bored disregard of her threat; it jerked her into fresh fury. 'I will do it!' she cried. 'I'll ring him as soon as he gets to the office, I'll have a new will signed and sealed before the day's out.' It seemed to her now that she would actually translate her idle words into forceful action; Owen would see that she wasn't to be trifled with.

He stooped and kissed her cheek. 'Goodbye,' he said in an abstracted fashion. 'Take care of yourself.' She called something after him as he went downstairs but he had already switched his attention off; he didn't even turn his head in the direction of her voice.

A few minutes later he was snugly seated in his car, driving gaily into the pale grey morning and the music which came lilting and singing from his radio, the very same music which upstairs in Zena's bedroom had struck him as tasteless and irritating, now fell upon his ear like the carollings of angels and the rhythm of glittering blue seas beating on enchanted shores.

'Come in here at once!' Zena cried fifteen minutes later when she heard Emily Bond's step down the hall. Like that, is it? Emily said to herself stoutly, her trained ear at once interpreting with keen accuracy the particular note and quality of that displeasing call. Had a row with the old man, she diagnosed with soundly-based confidence; looking for someone to take it out on. She sent back no answering screech but allowed her heavy unhurrying footfall to signal her approach.

'You've certainly taken your time!' Mrs Yorke said as soon as she'd got one toe across the threshold.

'Can't go hurrying at my age,' Emily said calmly. 'Not wise.'

'No,' Zena said with emphasis, 'and can't go pilfering either at your age, not in the least wise.'

'Pilfering?' Emily asked on a totally different note. 'What do you mean? Pilfering?'

'I'll tell you precisely what I mean.' Zena embarked on a catalogue of missing objects, all more or less trivial, the kind of item Emily had come to look on as one of the perks of the job—and heaven knew there weren't many others. The irritations and frustrations of the last day or two of her convalescence, plenty of time to brood over grievances real or fancied, had prompted Zena to dredge up from the depths of her memory various peccadilloes on Emily's part that she'd let pass at the time but which struck her now in her angry and dissatisfied mood as important and monstrously reprehensible.

'No one is going to call me a thief!' Emily said, fiercely virtuous. Within another five minutes the situation had slipped from Zena's control; there were accusations and counter-accusations, words like prosecution and slander began to pepper the air. And in yet a further five minutes Emily was being despatched down the stairs with her insurance cards and a week's wages in her handbag; and Zena found herself abruptly without a daily woman.

A quarter to ten. Arnold Pierson glanced at his watch and decided it was a convenient time to go along to Owen Yorke's office to settle a few points that had arisen in connection with the annual audit, due in another four or five weeks.

'I'm sorry,' Owen's secretary said when he looked into her room, 'Mr Yorke isn't in today, he's gone down to Seahaven on business, he won't be in till Monday. Is it anything urgent? I've got the phone number of the hotel.' She glanced down at her notebook. 'The Cliff View Hotel. I could contact him there if it's really necessary.'

'No, it's not urgent.' Arnold turned to go. 'It can quite easily wait over till Monday, no hurry at all.'

At lunch-time Neil rang his sister from the office to ask how she was.

'You may well ask,' Zena said in a dramatic tone. 'In the first place Owen has suddenly seen fit to take himself off for the week-end—' She enlarged on her husband's neglect, callousness and all-round deficiencies in character and feeling. Neil opened his mouth in a huge silent yawn. 'And then, if you please,' Zena went on, 'Emily Bond has the cheek—' Another two minutes crawled by while she devoted herself to the old woman's sins of omission and commission. My, my, Neil thought, we have been having a right royal time, haven't we? He began to sketch an intricate pattern on a memo pad. He realized suddenly that Zena had switched from the subject of Emily to another topic, she was saying something about her solicitor. He sat up in his chair.

'What was that?' he asked. 'I couldn't quite catch—'

'I said I've already seen my solicitor,' Zena said distinctly. 'He came over at eleven o'clock, he's calling in with the draft some time this afternoon, and if it's in order, it will be signed tomorrow morning.'

'Draft?' Neil asked on a rising inflection.

'The draft of my new will, of course,' she said impatiently. 'What's the matter, aren't you listening? You ought to, it concerns you.'

Neil's pencil remained rigid in his fingers. 'In what way?' he asked gently.

'Never you mind.' A teasing edge to her tone. 'Are you coming in to see me this evening? I'll be all on my own.'

'I'm afraid I can't this evening, Ruth and I are invited out to dinner. But Jane could come over and keep you company, she could stay the night if you like.'

'She needn't bother staying the night, but you could ask her to look in for a bit if she's got nothing to do.'

'I'll tell her,' Neil said. He would make quite certain Jane had nothing better to do if there was a question of new wills being made.

'Let me see,' Zena said, 'isn't she going off abroad somewhere soon?'

'Yes, she's going on a coach-tour for a week with her godmother.' A sister of Neil's first wife—a retired schoolmistress, fond of travel, glad of the company of a lively young girl.

'When is she going?'

'Not for another five or six days. What time would you like her to come over?'

'Not too early,' Zena said. 'Say about half past seven or a quarter to eight.'

At eleven o'clock on Saturday morning Anthea Gibbs stood on the damp pavement outside Underwood's dress shop and rallied her forces for the attack. She had spent the greater part of the past two weeks in bed with a severe bout of influenza; it was only the knowledge that this was the final day of the shop's trading that had prompted her to leave the house at all this morning. She still felt a little weak and wobbly but there was no help for it; if she wanted her money back she would have to march through the door today, Monday would be too late. And she was absolutely determined to get her money back.

She looked up at the red and white stickers proclaiming the closing-down sale; under one arm she clutched a large cardboard box wrapped in brown paper. She glanced about at the harassed shoppers, then she squared her shoulders and walked resolutely forward. Might as well go in, she was never going to feel any bolder than she did now.

She let the door swing to behind her and strode up to the counter. 'Good morning,' she said to a young assistant in a voice that struck her own ears as being extravagantly loud, possessed of a curious ringing tone. 'I wish to speak to Mrs Yorke.'

The assistant's eyes blinked open in a look of wariness. 'I'm afraid that's not possible,' she said. 'Mrs Yorke isn't here, in fact she hardly ever comes into the shop nowadays. And in any case she's ill.'

'Then I will speak to whoever is in authority,' Anthea said with unflagging spirit. 'The manageress. Or head saleswoman.'

'If you could just indicate what it's about,' the girl persisted courteously.

'It's about criminal misrepresentation.' Anthea slammed the cardboard box down on to the gleaming mahogany surface. 'False pretences,' she said. 'Among other things.'

'I'll get the manageress,' the girl said hurriedly, moving swiftly towards a distant curtain. She re-appeared a few moments later with Miss Pierson at her side. Sarah halted and levelled a long look at Anthea.

'All right,' she said to the assistant. 'I'll deal with her. I know the type, trouble-maker. You can finish clearing up in the stock-room.' She made an unhurried progress to where Anthea stood with both hands resting on the cardboard box. As she approached, Anthea turned her head and caught sight of the straight-backed figure, the uncompromising glance. Oh dear, she thought, remembering now that this was the woman who'd served her when she bought the dress last summer; how had she forgotten that unflinching eye? Not exactly a person before whom one might utter the words 'false pretences'. Anthea turned her head and threw a longing look at the door.

'Good morning,' Sarah said with icy calm. 'I believe you

feel I might be able to help you?'

Anthea drew a long breath and withdrew her gaze from the door. She was beginning to feel she had bitten off rather more than she could comfortably chew.

Shortly after half past twelve Zena phoned Sarah to discuss one or two final details about the closing of the shop.

'Are you sure you're well enough to be worrying about these matters?' Solicitude showed through the formality of Sarah's tone. 'They're very minor points.'

'Oh, I'm feeling a great deal better.' Zena was pleased all the same at a little fussing about her health. 'I particularly wanted to ask you about the surplus stock.'

'There's no need for you to bother about it. It's all being jobbed off in a single lot. Didn't Mr Yorke tell you?'

'He probably mentioned something,' Zena said carelessly, 'but I haven't been in much condition lately for troubling myself about business. And he isn't here at the moment for me to ask him.'

'It's all to go to Mrs Fleming.' At the other end of the line Zena made no reply; only the faint sound of a radio, playing light and joyful music, reached Sarah's ears. 'I expect you know who she is,' Sarah added after a brief pause. 'She took over that little shop—'

'Yes, I know who she is,' Zena interrupted. 'When was all this arranged?'

'I couldn't tell you exactly. Mr Yorke mentioned it to me a couple of weeks ago. I did ring her earlier today, to ask if she could call in this evening and get things settled, but it appears she's going away for the week-end.'

Again there was a short pause; then Zena asked idly, 'Where's she off to? Somewhere gay?'

'I don't really know.' Sarah did her best to remember. 'I think she said something about the sea.'

'Well now.' Zena spoke with a brisk change of tone. 'We must settle a time for you to come over with the rest of the accounts, we can go over them together—' She broke off suddenly. 'Oh, I was nearly forgetting—has a Miss Gibbs been into the shop recently? Anthea Gibbs, the name is. I meant to warn you about her but of course I was taken ill and it went out of my head.'

'As a matter of fact,' Sarah said, 'she called in this morning, she said she'd had flu or she'd have come in before.'

'You didn't refund her any money?' Zena cried. 'You didn't go and pay her the thirty pounds or thirty-five or whatever it was she said she paid for the dress?'

'No,' Sarah said soothingly, 'I did nothing of the kind.'

'Oh, good! For one awful moment, I thought she'd got away with it.'

'Now, Mrs Yorke,' Sarah said, 'you've known me a very long time. Would I be likely to do such a thing without consulting you?'

'No, I suppose not. What did you do then?' Hardly likely that Miss Gibbs had tamely accepted a polite refusal to countenance her demands.

'I told her that I would discuss it with you when you were fit again and that in due course we would let her know what had been decided.'

'Oh yes,' Zena said with pleasure, 'that was exactly right. As a matter of fact I'll see her about it myself when the time comes.' She would enjoy the encounter. 'You must be certain to look out the sales slip for the dress. I don't know what tale she told you but she had the nerve to imply that the material—' She plunged into an animated account of Miss Gibbs's behaviour at the ball.

But when she rang off a few minutes later it was not Anthea Gibbs's sinewy figure that rose up in her mind but the graceful curves of Mrs Fleming. She seized the telephone directory to look up the number of the shop—it would still be listed under the name of the previous owner, of course; her fingers trembled in agitation as she turned the pages, it was several moments before she could with certainty recall the name. At last she heard the double ring of the phone; another minute crawled by before the receiver was picked up.

It wasn't Mrs Fleming who answered but the high, impatient, young-girl voice of her assistant.

'Actually we're closed,' Iris said, glancing down at her watch, mindful of her bus. 'It's gone one o'clock. And Mrs Fleming isn't here.' The blinds were already down at the windows, Linda had gone off a few minutes before to the self-drive car she had hired for her trip.

'Then I'll ring again after lunch,' Zena said.

'There won't be anyone here,' Iris replied without undue courtesy. 'We're closed until Monday morning. Mrs Fleming's going away for the week-end.'

'Somewhere nice, I hope?' Zena said, striving for a note of casual interest.

'Depends on what you call nice,' Iris said with a laugh. 'Seahaven, not my idea of a gay week-end, not at this time of the year. Still, everyone to her taste, I always say. Oh, just a moment—' She caught the sound of a distant door opening and closing, footsteps in the rear of the premises. 'I think Mrs Fleming has come back in again, she's probably forgotten something. If you'd like to hold on a minute, I'll go and see if she can speak to you.'

Zena waited at the other end of the line, sitting rigid in her chair. She had a sudden clear vision of Owen at the ball, dancing with Mrs Fleming, holding her in a close embrace. Some other questing section of her mind threw up a memory of Emily's accident—it had taken place at the intersection by Mrs Fleming's shop; she remembered the way Emily had fenced with her about whether or not Owen had been on the spot. She was certain now that he had been there, that he had been calling on the young widow. A profound sense of astonishment mounted in her brain; it was one thing to suspect and another thing altogether to have suspicion confirmed.

'You might run upstairs and see if I've left my brown

gloves on the dressing-table,' Linda said as she caught sight of Iris.

'There's someone on the phone for you.' Iris turned towards the stairs. 'I didn't ask the name.'

'All right, I'll take it.' I hope it isn't going to be long, Linda thought with irritation as she picked up the receiver. 'This is Linda Fleming,' she said. 'Who is that, please?'

No coherent line of conversation presented itself to Zena's mind; she heard herself saying, 'This is Zena Yorke. I was going to suggest that you come over to discuss the question of the stock but your assistant tells me you're going away for the week-end.'

'Yes.' Just that one syllable, nothing more.

'Somewhere pleasant, I hope?' Zena said.

'Nowhere very exciting.'

'My husband is also away for the week-end.' A distinctly sharp edge now to Mrs Yorke's voice.

'I'm afraid you'll have to excuse me,' Linda said. 'I really must go.'

'Quite a coincidence, don't you think, my husband choosing this particular week-end to go away?'

Linda looked at her watch. 'If it isn't anything special, I must—'

'Stealing my husband's special,' Zena said with force.

'I really can't engage in this kind of conversation. You must excuse me.' Linda laid the receiver on its rest with an abrupt movement. She stood for a moment frowning down with concentrated thought. There was a sound of hurrying footsteps as Iris came back holding out the gloves.

'Here you are, they were on the bed.'

'Oh—thank you. You will be sure to lock up carefully, won't you?' Linda took the gloves and went rapidly out to the car.

I knew it! Zena thought, they're spending the week-end together! She still could not quite credit it. She clasped her hands together and tried to steady the turmoil in her brain. The hotel—Owen had said something yesterday morning—yes, he'd said he'd left the name and phone number of the hotel on the table. She looked down for a memo pad or a piece of paper but there was nothing there. She went into Owen's bedroom and then back to her own room, searching rapidly, pulling open drawers, running her eye over the carpet in case a scrap of paper had slipped to the floor. But there was no note.

She sat down again by the phone, consumed by the sense that she must take some kind of action. Arnold, she thought suddenly, I'll ring Arnold. She almost smiled with relief.

'Owen's gone off for the week-end,' she said as soon as she heard his voice.

'Yes, I know,' he said guardedly. 'His secretary told me.'

'Did she tell you exactly where? He said he'd leave a note of his number but it isn't here. All he told me was that he was going down to the coast.'

'No, I don't know where he's gone.' Instinct warned Arnold to keep his mouth shut. Seahaven, his mind recorded, the Cliff View Hotel.

'I'm absolutely certain he's meeting Mrs Fleming,' Zena said. 'She's going to Seahaven for the week-end, I'm sure that's where Owen is too. I want you to go down there, you can easily find him.' Only three or four hotels in Seahaven that might tempt Owen by their size and comfort.

'Look here,' Arnold said with protest. 'You don't expect me to go—'

'It wouldn't take you long in the car,' she broke in. 'You could call in to the big hotels, ask if he's there, you'll soon find him.'

'I'll do nothing of the kind.' Is it possible? he was thinking with a disturbing sense of shock. Linda and Owen together. He put up a hand to his face.

'You will go,' Zena said with a mixture of command and pleading. 'You must. You wouldn't need to spend the night there. Just get hold of Owen and make him phone me.

Tell him I'm ill.' She was certain that if only she could get in touch with him, let him know she was aware of what was going on, it would be all right, she could still snatch him back.

'It's no use, I won't go,' Arnold said with deep distaste. 'I'm not going to get mixed up in this kind of situation. And in any case,' he added with inspiration, 'I have work to do this week-end. I've had to bring papers home from the office—'

'Oh yes,' Zena said with a significant inflection, 'it's coming up to the audit, isn't it?' There was a brief pause. 'I think you'll find you'll be able to spare the time after all,' she said with authority. 'You'll be back in plenty of time to work on your accounts.'

When she rang off a few minutes later she remained for some time seated in her chair by the phone. Her brain felt clear and active, she was full of a sense that events were in her grasp again. She levelled a cool, assessing glance at the rest of the day, at tomorrow. Neil had said he wouldn't be able to look in at all today, he was attending a one-day course for local government officers; it was being held in a neighbouring town and there was to be a supper afterwards at some hotel, he wouldn't be home till about ten. But he'd asked Ruth to call in on her during the afternoon, to see that she was all right. I'll tell Ruth that Neil must come over for a few minutes, however late he gets back, Zena decided; she was beginning to experience a surge of elation at the plan forming in her mind.

She stood up and walked briskly into the bathroom, took from the cabinet the box of ampoules Owen had brought her on Thursday evening, unopened, still in its chemist's neat white wrapping. Three ampoules had remained in the old box which now lay empty and discarded in the waste-bin beside the wash-basin. She had used the three for her evening injection on Thursday and the morning and evening injections on Friday. She should already have taken an ampoule from the new box for this morning's injection but with so much to occupy her thoughts she had forgotten all about it, in spite of old Gethin's angry lecture last week.

She stared down at the box, weighing the degree of risk she was running. If she omitted the injection this evening as well . . . She conjured up a dramatic picture of Neil letting himself into The Sycamores at half past ten or eleven, calling out as he came up the stairs, getting no reply . . . She smiled and put the trim white parcel back into the cabinet.

With any luck Arnold would get hold of Owen some time during the afternoon or early evening. If Owen phoned her, if she was able to prevail on him to return, would there be any point then in 'forgetting' the evening injection, in letting the little drama run its full course? On the whole she was inclined to think there would; Owen might put down the phone with the best intentions, ready to pack his bag, and on the staircase he might run into Mrs Fleming dressed and coiffured for the evening, he might very well change his mind, might decide to postpone his return till the morning . . . And even if he didn't, if he got into his car and drove home, it wouldn't do him any harm at all to find his wife in a state of semi-collapse . . .

She made her way slowly back towards the bed. Time enough to make a final decision about the injection after Owen—or Arnold—telephoned; in any case she must be sure to write down the name and number of Owen's hotel as soon as she knew them, leave the sheet of paper prominently displayed by the receiver. Then, if Owen failed to appear, if she was alone and possibly comatose when Neil bounded up the stairs, he would be able to put through an urgent call to Seahaven, disturbing Owen at what might be a very interesting moment . . .

'But it could be quite late by the time Neil gets back.' Ruth set down a cup of tea on the bedside table, close to Zena's hand. 'Don't you think it would be better if either

Jane or I stayed the night with you?'

'No, that isn't in the least necessary.' Zena picked up the knife and fork from the tray Ruth had prepared for her. 'I don't care if it is late. I won't be asleep. He needn't stay long, he can just see I'm all right for the night, have a little chat and then go back home. He won't object to that.'

'Very well, if that's what you want,' Ruth said reluctantly. 'He's going to give me a ring at seven, to let me know what time he'll be back, I'll tell him what you said, I suppose it will be all right.' And really Zena did appear well on the road to recovery now. Her face wore a reasonably healthy colour and she was certainly tucking into the food with a good appetite.

Zena buttered a piece of toast. 'You must make it quite clear to him that he's to call in, however late it is.' She gave Ruth a commanding glance. 'Then I'll be able to settle down quite happily to sleep, I won't mind being on my own.'

'Yes, I'll make sure he understands.'

Zena gave a satisfied nod. 'Tell him I'll leave the front door on the latch.'

'Is there anything I can get you in Milbourne on Monday?' Ruth asked in a friendly fashion. 'I don't suppose Owen will have much time for shopping.'

'Well now, there are one or two things. Let me see.' Zena wrinkled her brows in thought. 'I'll need some more cigarettes. And some bath essence—'

'Just a moment, I'll jot it down.' Ruth opened her bag and took out a notebook. 'Cigarettes—what brand do you want?'

'By the way,' Zena said when the list was completed, 'your Miss Gibbs marched into the shop this morning and demanded her money back for that dress.' She recounted with energy the confrontation between Anthea and Sarah Pierson.

'I must say I'm a little surprised,' Ruth said. 'I was

sure she'd have thought better of it when she got home. And she's been away from work with flu, I imagined that wouldn't have done much for her nerve.'

'She'll need all her nerve before the matter's settled,' Zena said with enjoyment. 'I'm going to deal with her myself.' But the memory of her encounter with Anthea at the ball brought with it more disagreeable recollections. She did her best to blink away the picture of Owen holding Mrs Fleming in the close embrace of a waltz but it remained obstinately etched into the forefront of her mind.

'Would you mind taking the tray and putting it over there?' she said at random, and then, to her dismay she heard herself add as Ruth stood up and bent over the bed, 'Owen's gone off for the week-end with that wretched Fleming woman, what do you think about that?'

There was a brief pause. Ruth stood arrested with her hands just about to clutch the tray, then she flashed Zena a little disbelieving smile, straightened up and carried her burden across the room, setting it down on top of the chest of drawers.

'I'm sure you're wrong,' she said easily. 'Whatever put such a foolish notion into your head?' But in that moment before she picked up the tray a look had flashed over her face; Zena had seen it clearly. And the look had said as plainly as words, 'So! I'm not in the least surprised! And I can't say I blame him!'

'You knew all about it!' Zena cried accusingly. 'You knew he was running after her! You probably encouraged him!'

Ruth halted by the chest of drawers, she turned to face Zena. 'Oh, come now!' she said calmly. 'You know that isn't true. Why should I wish—'

'Your own morals aren't very much to boast about.' All the resentments of the day gathered themselves up inside Zena, she felt a fierce compulsion to strike at someone. 'Maurice Turner hasn't been a widower all that long.' A jumble of facts, conjectures and deductions swam up before her. 'You thought nothing of carrying on with a married man. It means nothing to you if a marriage is going to break up, you probably think it very amusing.'

With an effort Ruth steadied her voice. 'I don't think we'd better continue this conversation,' she said quietly. 'You're not well, you don't know what you're saying.'

'I know what I'm saying all right,' Zena said with venom. 'Do you think everyone doesn't realize how you got your precious job? Everyone except Neil, that is. And the sooner he knows, the better.'

Ruth couldn't restrain herself any longer. 'How dare you talk such stupid nonsense!' she said, approaching the bed. 'You deliberately go and make yourself ill, to draw attention to yourself or for some other devious reason of your own, then you lie there in bed inventing mischief about everyone concerned with you, you won't be satisfied till you've set everyone at each other's throats.' She broke off abruptly. Oh dear, she thought with a thrust of remorse, that was a mistake, I should never have let fly like that.

She opened her mouth to say she was sorry but it was more than she could do actually to frame an apology, so she merely said, 'I'd better go.' She took a couple of steps towards the door and then paused, a little surprised that Zena had made no reply to her outburst.

She turned her head and threw a look at the bed. Zena was lying back against the pillows, staring at her with a shocked, incredulous expression; she seemed about to burst into tears. For an instant Ruth considered going back and taking her hand, saying, 'Let's forget it, let's be friends.' But it would be a useless gesture, there could never be any real understanding between them. She caught sight of her handbag lying forgotten on a chair, she stooped to pick it up and walked without another word out of the room and down the stairs.

When she reached home she put away her car and let herself into the house. She switched on the light in the hall and saw a note speared on one of the hooks of the coat-stand. She unfolded it; a couple of sentences from Jane to say she'd gone out with Kevin, wouldn't be back till late, not to wait up for her. Ruth stood for a moment with her head tilted back in thought, then she went to the phone and dialled Maurice's number.

Quite a long time later Zena awoke from an uneasy doze. The radio was still on; a disc-jockey was laughing loudly at his own jokes.

Downstairs the front door opened and closed. She cocked her head, listening. The sound of unhurried footsteps reached her ears.

'Who's that?' she called out. 'Is that you, Ruth?' She threw back the covers and pulled on her dressing-gown. 'Neil, is that you?' The footsteps advanced without haste towards the bedroom door. She stood up and thrust her feet into her slippers. 'Who's there?' she cried. 'Owen! Is it you?'

'Hope I didn't alarm you,' said a familiar voice from the head of the stairs. 'It's only me.'

It was well after eleven when Neil got home. The house was in darkness; there was no sound either upstairs or down. It had been an agreeable evening, a very good supper, excellent wine, cheerful company. A picture of Ruth began to float into his mind; she would be lying peacefully upstairs, wrapped in sweet dreams, her blonde hair spread out over the pillows. He smiled as he went silently towards the staircase.

He didn't switch on the bedroom lamp but made do with the shaft of light coming in from the landing. But Ruth stirred and yawned in the half-darkness. 'Neil?' she said sleepily. 'What time is it? You never phoned.'

'I'm sorry,' he said lightly. 'I intended to but with one thing and another I forgot. Did it matter? You weren't worried, were you?'

She burrowed down again under the covers. 'No, I wasn't worried,' she said drowsily. 'I hope you had a good time.'

He eased himself into bed and slipped an arm round her shoulders. 'I thought about you,' he said. 'I kept wishing you were there.'

A long time later, just as she was drifting off again into sleep, Ruth was suddenly roused by the feeling that there was something she ought to have remembered. 'Oh—what was it?' she murmured, screwing up her eyes in the darkness. Then it came back to her. 'Zena most particularly wanted you to call in and see her this evening. I meant to tell you if you rang.'

'I can't go now,' Neil mumbled, already almost asleep. 'It must be well after midnight, I'll go round first thing in the morning. She must be all right or she'd have phoned you.' His voice tailed off, he drifted away on a feather-soft cloud into bright and peaceful regions where birds sang sweetly, the sun shone in a brilliant sky and no one ever posted or received such things as bills.

CHAPTER XIII

Jane surfaced next morning from a deep trough of sleep to hear the insistent sound of the telephone ringing downstairs. She threw back the covers, pulled on her dressing-gown and went downstairs; she yawned as she picked up the receiver.

'Why, Uncle Owen!' she said a moment later, recognizing his voice. 'I thought you were away for the week-end.'

'I am,' he said. 'I'm ringing from the hotel. Is your father there? Or Ruth? I'm worried about Zena. I've been trying to phone her but I can't get through, I get the engaged signal every time.'

'That just means she's talking to someone,' Jane said easily.

'But it was ten to nine the first time I tried to get through. That's nearly an hour ago. She wouldn't be talking all that length of time. Go and get your father, Jane, he must go round there and see if anything's wrong.'

'Yes, all right, hang on while I get him.' She ran upstairs and banged on the bedroom door, flung it open and switched on the light. 'Father, wake up!' She crossed over to the bed and seized him by the shoulder. He shook himself free from her grasp and sat up, blinking at the light. 'It's Uncle Owen, on the phone.' She gave him the message rapidly. At his side Ruth stirred and came awake.

'What's the matter?' she asked. 'Is something wrong?'

Neil jumped out of bed and seized a garment from the back of a chair. 'I'll get over there right away,' he said to Jane. 'You go down and tell Owen. Get him to ring off and then you try to phone Zena.' He struggled into his shirt as Jane ran off again downstairs.

'What is it?' Ruth asked in an urgent tone.

'It's Zena, Owen's been trying to get through to her but all he gets is the engaged signal, he thinks something's wrong. I should have gone round there last night.' He snatched at his trousers. 'You get up and put something on, anything, run down and start the car.'

She sprang up, seized her dressing-gown, thrust her feet into a pair of leather brogues and vanished through the doorway.

'I can't get any reply,' Jane called out to Neil as he came running down the stairs a few minutes later. 'Just the engaged signal. Shall I come with you?'

'No, you stay here. Owen might ring again. Tell him I've gone. I'll phone you from The Sycamores.' He ran out to where Ruth already had the car ticking over.

'All right,' he said. 'You'd better get back inside and get dressed.'

'No, I'll come with you.' She moved over into the passenger seat, glanced down at her dressing-gown. 'It doesn't matter, I'll come as I am.' She drew the cord more tightly round her waist, put up a hand and smoothed her hair.

Neil swung the car out into the road. 'I'll never forgive

myself if anything's happened to her,' he said in a low intense voice. Ruth threw him a glance, opened her mouth as if she would speak, then she sighed, raised her shoulders and let them drop again, turned her head and looked out in silence at the almost-deserted Sunday-morning road.

Neither of them spoke during the remainder of the drive; in the light scattering of traffic Neil was able to send the car along at a good deal more than the permitted speed. As the wheels crunched at last over the gravel beneath the great trees, Ruth leaned forward in her seat and scrutinized the front of the house. The curtains were still drawn across the windows of Zena's bedroom.

Neil brought the car to a halt and ran with silent haste towards the front door. He turned the handle but the door wouldn't yield; he pressed the bell and heard it ringing some little distance away. They stood together on the top step, heads at an angle, listening. He pressed the bell again, more loudly. Nothing stirred.

'Run round to the back door,' he said to Ruth. Again he put his finger on the bell. She pulled her dressing-gown round her as she ran, hindered by the sweeping skirt. Outside the back door two bottles of milk stood on the step. She turned the handle without success, tried to raise the lower half of an adjacent window, but the catch was snicked inside. She hurried back to the front of the house; Neil was stooping to pick up a handful of gravel.

'Zena!' he called in a clear level tone as the gravel rattled against the pane. 'It's me, Neil. Are you there, Zena?' He picked up another handful and repeated his action, calling out more loudly and urgently.

'It's no good, we'll have to break in,' he said after another few seconds. His face looked pale and drawn. He glanced at the front door, solid, unyielding. 'I think a window would be better.' He snatched up a large stone from the edge of a flower-bed.

Ruth followed him round to the window of Owen's study, watched as he smashed the glass, put in his hand

and released the catch. He swung himself into the room, turned and helped her in over the sill.

'Zena!' he called out again as they went up the stairs. 'Zena! It's me, Neil!' The faint sound of music came to their ears. He threw open the bedroom door, stood for an instant on the threshold, then ran towards the bed. The radio played a sweetly mournful tune; a girl's voice sang of the pains of love. Zena lay back against the pillows in a relaxed attitude of deep and peaceful sleep; one arm was stretched out on the coverlet, her lips were curved in a faint smile.

Neil bent down and touched her forehead; with his other hand he felt for the pulse in her wrist. 'She's dead,' he said over his shoulder in a flat matter-of-fact voice. He pulled back the bedclothes and laid a hand over her heart. 'She's been dead a long time, she's cold.' He stood up and gave a deep sigh. On the radio the music ceased and a man's voice began to speak, cheerful and intimate. Neil glanced at the radio with a frown and switched it off. 'I'd better phone Gethin,' he said. 'Not that there's anything he can do.'

Ruth drew back the curtains and turned off the light as he went through into the dressing-room. 'No wonder we couldn't get through,' he called. 'The receiver wasn't put back properly on the rest.' She heard him dialling the number, talking to Gethin. She looked at the bed, at Zena with that gentle smile; she dropped into a chair and put her face in her hands. She was suddenly seized by an uncontrollable fit of shaking.

'Gethin's coming over as soon as he's dressed.' Neil came back into the bedroom. 'He's not well, he thinks he's sickening for flu. I told him he could send his partner but he insists on coming himself.' In the dressing-room the phone rang suddenly and he went back to answer it; it was Owen, able at last to make contact.

Ruth stood up and went over to the window; in the other room she could hear the sound of Neil's voice. She had stopped shuddering, she was beginning to feel steadier now. She looked up at the sky which was showing a small patch of blue; a pale winter sunlight straggled through the thin grey clouds. She heard Neil ring off, his footsteps coming towards her.

'Owen's leaving at once,' he said. 'It won't take him long.'

'How did he take it?' she asked without turning round.

There was a tiny pause. 'He seemed to think it was our fault,' Neil said in a level tone. 'That we should have come over last night. I didn't enter into any arguments, people say things at a time like this—'

'If there's any question of allotting blame,' Ruth said, still watching the slow dispersal of the clouds, 'he might start by asking himself why he wasn't here himself to look after his wife.'

'No, no sherry, thank you, I'd better not,' Dr Gethin said. 'I've dosed myself with something pretty potent, I'm afraid I'm in for an attack of flu.' If there was one thing he wanted at this moment above all others, it was to be lying down in a well-warmed bed with his eyes closed and his housekeeper standing guard between himself and the battering demands of the world outside. 'But I would be glad of some coffee. Very hot and strong, please, no milk or sugar.' He settled himself back into his chair in the comfortable sitting-room of Neil's house, he stole a glance at his watch. Almost one o'clock. Another five or ten minutes and he could set off for home.

'I'll get Jane to make some coffee, it won't take long.' Gethin looks ready to drop, Ruth thought as she went off to the kitchen. It struck her suddenly that he wouldn't be at Zena's funeral, he would very probably be tucked up in bed, battling against fever. All those years he had attended Zena, watching over the measles and chicken-pox of childhood, the more serious illnesses of her adult life, and now, when it came to the last attention of all, he wouldn't be there; the notion seemed inexpressibly sad as if Zena would somehow be aware in that final moment of the absence of a long-familiar face.

'If only I'd gone round last night,' Neil said yet again.

'You mustn't start blaming yourself,' Gethin said. 'Doesn't do any good.' But he saw the look Owen flicked at Neil. He felt a great weariness well up inside him. If Owen was going to harbour resentment against Neil and Ruth—he'd observed the same reaction in relatives after many another death. And it was often those who felt themselves to be guilty of neglect who cherished the strongest grudge against others close at hand as if striving to deflect the voice of conscience towards more acceptable targets.

Gethin had a pretty shrewd suspicion that Owen wasn't at all anxious for it to come out exactly where and how he had passed the previous forty-eight hours; in spite of the feverish muzziness in his brain he could recall quite distinctly a moment at the presidential ball when Owen and that pretty young woman had stumbled against his table, he remembered clearly what they had been saying to each other, and the way Owen had been looking at his partner.

But that was something that could be left to Owen to mull over in the restless hours of coming dawns. I can't honestly blame him, Gethin thought, looking back dispassionately at the long muddle of Zena's life, many another man would have done the same.

He had no intention of making things worse for an old friend, a fellow clubman, the son of his youthful comrade-in-arms, a highly-respected citizen of Milbourne. Zena might very well have guessed at something, might have staged her dramatic scene once too often. He hadn't missed the significance of the unopened box of ampoules in the bathroom cabinet at The Sycamores; he'd already gone over with Owen the matter of how many ampoules had been left in the old box. He could see no need whatever for these questions to be aired in public. Zena had expected Neil to walk in and summon help and she had relied on him in vain; it was no one's fault but her own. There was no need for an inquest; she had been seriously ill and he had been in attendance on her within the last few days. And now she was dead and nothing in the world could bring her back to life.

Ruth came back into the room. 'Jane will bring the coffee in a minute.' She glanced round at the silent group. 'Have you—' She hesitated. 'The funeral—is it—?'

Neil shifted in his chair. 'No, we haven't settled it.' He looked at Gethin, then at Owen. 'Today's Sunday. I suppose Tuesday or Wednesday—' He looked back at Gethin. 'I take it there's no need for an inquest?'

It seemed to Owen that the air in the room came suddenly and cracklingly alive. He couldn't see how the others could be unaware of it, it was like a fierce current of electricity flashing from every surface.

The powerful, pulsing headache of influenza began to throb inside Gethin's skull, he felt an ache in every limb. 'An inquest,' he said with distaste, remembering the pursed lips and self-righteous air of the local coroner. Fifty per cent of all human activity is either totally unnecessary or actively dangerous, he thought with savage sourness. 'I see no reason for an inquest.' He gave Owen a level glance. 'If you could call at my house later on today, you can pick up the certificate from the housekeeper, I'll sign it as soon as I get back, I'll leave it with her.' He let out a deep sigh. 'You won't see me, I'll be in bed.' He closed his eyes briefly. What was the death certificate after all but the last stamp on a lifetime of meaningless folly, the passport to final oblivion? It came to him abruptly and with total certainty that he would never practise again, that when he rose up from his bout of influenza he would at last see sense and retire.

I hope to God I haven't left it too late, he thought with a deep uneasiness twisting the muscles of his stomach; he had a moment's appalling vision of another doctor in another room picking up a pen to record a date and reason for death, entering with careful neatness the name Gethin.

'Thank you,' Owen said. He moved his shoulders under the smooth cloth of his jacket. 'I'll look in before tea.' The air in the room had dropped into its customary state of peaceful warmth; he felt a kind of languor seep through his bones. The door opened and Jane came in with a tray of coffee. 'I think perhaps Wednesday would be best.' Owen looked enquiringly at Neil and Ruth.

Not that he intended it to be a large and showy funeral; he was going to limit it to members of the family, otherwise, with a man in his position, there was no reason why the occasion shouldn't spread out to include half the town. He expected some opposition from Neil, who would very probably be all for a vast turn-out, but he certainly wasn't going to enter into an argument about it now, in front of Gethin; time enough to tell Neil of his plans in the morning.

Jane poured out the coffee. 'Black for you, I think, Dr Gethin?' She smiled at him. 'And no sugar.'

'Thank you, my dear.' He took the cup and began to drink the coffee at once, scaldingly hot as it was. In four or five minutes at the most he could be out through the front door and sliding into the seat of his car.

'And black coffee for you, Uncle Owen.' Jane carried the cup across, touched his hand gently as she set the saucer down beside him. He looked up at her with a grateful glance. A sympathetic, understanding child.

As he raised the cup to his lips it suddenly occurred to him that Zena would have disapproved loudly and protestingly at the arrangements for her own funeral.

CHAPTER XIV

The atmosphere at the breakfast-table on Thursday morning was so silent that each of the three people might have been alone in the room, absorbed in compelling thought. From time to time Ruth got to her feet to remove plates or bring more milk but her actions had an abstracted quality as if she were moving about in her sleep. Neil held a newspaper in front of him but he didn't appear to be turning the pages; he refused everything except a piece of toast and drank several cups of strong coffee.

Jane was glad of the quiet which allowed her to run over in her mind the intricate details of exactly which garments she was going to pack for her trip with her aunt. She assumed that the other two were still sunk into natural despondency after the funeral yesterday, although her own spirits had reverted to their usual buoyancy almost as soon as she had stepped into the car outside the cemetery gates.

Should she or should she not pack a raincoat? And then there was the question of money. Aunt Dorothy was paying all the main expenses of the holiday but there would be presents to buy, postcards, sweets, occasional refreshments. She had saved up what she could from her not very large salary, she had some travellers' cheques upstairs in her bag and a little money in sterling. Would it be enough? She bit her lip, considering. Her father had offered to supply any deficiency a few weeks back but she had cheerfully refused, feeling grown-up and independent, confident of being able to manage, not realizing the deep inroads Christmas would make on her savings.

'I was just wondering,' she said at last, peering round the newspaper at Neil, 'if I'm going to be a bit short of cash. On the holiday,' she added, seeing his puzzled look. 'I thought perhaps it might be better if I borrowed a little from you—' Borrowed was a good word, with its sturdy implication of repayment. 'I wouldn't want to have to ask Aunt Dorothy, she's being very kind about taking me—'

'No need to ask Dorothy.' Neil smiled expansively. 'And I don't think we need discuss borrowing. I did offer to give you something before. How much do you need? Ten pounds? Twenty?' The phone rang sharply and he stood up. 'Think about it, let me know, I can call into the bank this morning.' He went briskly out of the room.

'Neil?' said Owen's voice at the other end of the line. 'I've just remembered—Ruth very kindly said she'd go round to The Sycamores today.' To restore order, clear things up, tidy away distressing reminders. Owen had installed himself at a Milbourne hotel after lunch on Sunday; it seemed to him utterly impossible that he could ever again walk through the front door of The Sycamores, let alone live there. 'I forgot to give her the keys. Would you ask her if she'd mind calling in here on her way to the office?'

'Yes, I'm sure that will be all right,' Neil said. Something very cool and formal in Owen's tone, not at all his normal friendly voice. 'Is there anything I can do?' Neil asked. 'Just say the word.'

'No, thank you, not at present anyway. By the way,' he added as if at a casual after-thought, 'Zena left you a thousand pounds in her will. I thought you'd like to know.'

Neil put up a hand to his chin. 'A thousand pounds,' he said. 'That was very kind of her.' After a tiny pause he asked in a careless tone, 'When was the will made? Just out of interest.'

'Several years ago. I'd have to look at it to give you the exact date.' Neil gripped the receiver tightly and frowned down at the carpet. 'I spoke to the solicitor over the phone on Monday,' Owen went on. 'Apparently there was some talk of Zena changing her will, she got as far as having a draft made and then she changed her mind, rang him up and told him to tear up the draft.' His voice indicated the irrational whims of a sick woman. 'It wasn't the first time that had happened of course. It will be quite some time before the bequests are paid out. But I don't suppose you're in desperate need of a thousand pounds.'

'No, of course not.' Neil got a light inflection into his voice. 'Anyway, I'll give Ruth your message.'

'I've been working it out,' Jane said when he came back into the room. 'Fifteen pounds ought to give me plenty of margin.'

Neil threw her an unsmiling look. 'I'll give you five,' he said brusquely. 'I'm not a millionaire.' She looked at him in surprise but the expression on his face didn't invite further discussion.

'Oh—well—thank you,' she said. 'Five pounds will be a great help.'

'Any more coffee?' Neil pushed his cup across to Ruth. 'That was Owen on the phone. He wants you to call into the hotel to pick up the keys to the house.'

Ruth poured out the last of the coffee. 'Actually, I wish now I'd said I'd go in a little later on. Things are a bit hectic at work just at the moment.' And she'd had time off yesterday for the funeral. 'Do you suppose I could leave it till Monday or Tuesday? I can't really see there's any urgency about clearing up.'

'You did offer,' Neil said abruptly. 'And I told Owen you'd go round for the keys.' He felt in no mood to countenance the shifts and whims of the female temperament.

'I'll go,' Jane said brightly. 'I'll have plenty of time, it won't take me long to do my packing.' She wasn't going in to the library at all today.

'I don't know,' Ruth said dubiously.

'Oh, let her go,' Neil said irritably. 'All perfectly straightforward, no need to make a song and dance about it.' Simply a matter of putting things into order, nothing unpleasant or upsetting likely to be encountered. 'Get your coat on,' he said to Jane. 'You can come with me now in the car and pick up the keys.' He glanced at his watch. 'Then I'll run you over to The Sycamores. You can find your own way home afterwards by bus.'

She jumped up. 'Yes, all right. I'll just run upstairs for my coat.'

'No need to be over-fussy,' he said as he dropped her ten minutes later in the drive of The Sycamores. 'Just leave the place looking presentable.' He turned the car round, raised a hand in farewell and drove off towards the main road.

Jane inserted the key in the lock and opened the front door. She gave a little jump of astonishment as she felt something brush against her legs. She looked down and saw a very thin black cat contorting itself into an attitude of supplication.

'Hello.' She knelt down and stroked the dull-looking fur. 'Are you hungry?' The cat uttered a plaintive mew. 'Come along then, I'll find you something to eat.' She carried it inside and closed the door. As she turned to go along the passage to the kitchen the cat suddenly sprang from her arms and ran with great speed and an air of concentrated cunning up the stairs.

'Come back!' she cried, half-laughing. She ran up after it and saw it disappear through the open door of the front bedroom. 'Come here!' she called. 'Good pussy, come on!' Without a backward glance at its pursuer the cat insinuated itself under the floor-length folds of the bedspread. 'Come along then, I'm not going to play hide-and-seek, if you want something to eat you've got to come down to the kitchen, I'm not feeding you up here.' As she spoke she kept lifting the edge of the bedspread, now at the foot, now at the side, thrusting in a sudden hand, trying to take the animal by surprise. But it managed to elude her every time.

Then she heard a little clink, something falling over beneath the drapes. She lay down almost flat, raised the heavy cloth and peered underneath. The carpet reached only half-way under the length of the bed; an expanse of floor-boards stretched between the end of the carpet and the wall. She could just see a glass, a tall tumbler, lying on its side on the polished wood, with a pool of milk beside it. The cat was crouching over the milk, lapping it up swiftly and with whole-hearted attention.

Jane let the bedspread fall back into place and scrambled to her feet. 'Oh, all right,' she said, 'have it your own way. Come down to the kitchen when you want something more substantial.' She went out into the passage, leaving the bedroom door open for when the cat chose to accept her invitation. I suppose there's still food in the fridge, she thought, bound to be. She could chop up some cold meat, the cat would enjoy that.

The milk must have been very far from fresh, it suddenly struck her, it must have been there since—since Saturday evening at least. The notion presented itself to her with distinct unpleasantness, she wrinkled her nose in distaste, shook her shoulders with a little eerie feeling.

She came down into the hall, opened the doors, glanced into the rooms. How still and silent the house was. She had a curious feeling as of having stumbled on some terrestrial version of the *Marie Celeste*; it seemed as if the inhabitants of The Sycamores had been abruptly snatched away, as if no one would ever live there again. An open magazine on a table, a little pile of novels, a packet of cigarettes on a mantelpiece, a saucepan on the draining-board in the kitchen. She had a sudden horrid sensation that she was about to burst into sobs.

Come now, she told herself sternly, this won't do, mustn't let the place get on your nerves. Bustle about, find some cleaning tools, switch a radio on and fill the empty spaces with gay music. She squared her shoulders and set about her work.

There seemed to be a very great deal of time and not all that much to do with it. On the fourth day of her retirement Sarah had not yet grown accustomed to the vast desert of leisure. Barely ten o'clock and the breakfast things already washed up, the beds made, the rooms spick and span. Arnold was taking a day off work; she had asked him if he would like to go with her into town.

Now she looked round for something to occupy her until it was time to leave for the bus. Ah yes, there was that cupboard under the stairs; for years she had been saying to herself that one of these days, when she had time, she'd look through it. Well, now she had the time, so she might as well make a start.

One of the first things she came across was an ancient gramophone encased in a heavy wooden box, and beside it a pile of old records. Her mouth curved in amusement as she looked down at the labels. My goodness, she thought, how many years it is since we played those! She was seized by a sudden desire to hear some of them again.

She didn't summon Arnold but managed to carry the gramophone into the sitting-room where she gave it a good dusting before fitting a needle and setting one of the records in motion. The tune, tinkly, nostalgic, with its dated, regular rhythm, a man's voice, tinny, scratchy, like a communication from an older, simpler world, brought back so sharply and powerfully the far-off time of her youth that it seemed for a moment that she was seventeen again and none of it had ever happened, her mother was still alive, not yet remarried, the second war was only a shadow of fear in the eyes of knowledgeable men and she herself still charged with optimism, the certainty of joy.

She raised a hand and beat time to the music. Her gaze fell on a pottery dish propped up on the mantelpiece, the dish Arnold had given her three days ago on her birthday. Her fifty-eighth birthday. She ceased to beat time, the smile left her face. She was no longer a young strong girl, she was an ageing spinster facing the last stretch of existence.

She took a step forward and picked up the dish, turned it over, examining it. What a curious present for Arnold to have given her, but then in the whole of her fifty-eight years no one had ever given her any present she had really wanted. When she was a little girl she had gone every summer to the church fête, she had saved her money to spend it on the tombola; every year she had stood and looked at the prizes, knowing for certain that this time she would win one of the mysteriously-shaped parcels. But every year she had drawn a blank.

And there had been a ruby pendant in the corner of a shop window in a little side street on her way to school; for months she had yearned for it, had dropped her careful pennies into the back of a china pig on her dressing-table. A ruby, she had thought with expectant pleasure, rattling the pig week by week, a real glowing ruby to wear round my neck. And when at long last she had brought it home and unwrapped it in the kitchen, she had held it out on her palm, showing it to her father with a depth of pride that made her voice tremble.

'Look, a real ruby! It's mine!'

He had given it a smiling glance, had lifted the chain on a careless finger and said with good-natured contempt, 'It's just a bit of red glass. I hope you didn't go wasting good money on that.'

Behind her she heard Arnold come into the room. She turned and caught his puzzled look at the massive gramophone, the enquiring smile he gave as of someone witnessing the amusing antics of a child. She walked over and removed the record.

'I was just trying it out to see if it still worked,' she said. 'The Scouts might like it for their jumble sale, there's always someone interested in old things.' She closed the lid of the gramophone. 'Still plenty of time. We needn't leave till eleven. I'm clearing out the cupboard under the stairs.' And she went unhurriedly past him, back to her dusty chore.

Jane left the best bedroom to the last, having developed a mild aversion for the room, in spite of her efforts to divert her thoughts into more bracing channels. She had completely forgotten the cat and it was only when she forced herself to strip the bed that she remembered the poor stray, probably by this time escaped from the house through one of the windows she had flung open to admit fresh air.

I never fed it, she thought with compassion, I hope it finds something to eat at a friendly house. The notion recalled to her the fact that there was a glass under the bed, at the far side. She walked round, knelt down and reached under for the tumbler, giving a little start as her fingers encountered the soft touch of fur. She lowered herself flat on the floor and peered into the dimness. The cat was lying stretched out, fast asleep, with the empty tumbler beside it. She edged the tumbler out and then drew the cat towards her.

It didn't wake or even stir. She stood up and cradled the cat in her arms. It was warm and she could feel its heart beating faintly but reassuringly under her fingers. Poor thing, it was probably half dead from the lack of food, perhaps it had fainted—could a cat faint? She could see no reason why not. She shook it gently, murmuring, 'Wake up, come on, wake up and I'll take you down and give you something to eat.'

But it continued to lie unmoving in her arms. At last she laid it down on the stool by the dressing-table, glancing at it from time to time as she whisked about the room tidying and dusting.

When she had finished she returned to the stool and stroked the animal, speaking softly to it, urging it to wakefulness but without success. She thrust her fingers under its body and rather fancied the heartbeat had slackened, she drew back one of its eyelids and met a blind stare. She drew a little sighing breath of sorrow, the poor thing was probably going to die.

I'll take it home, she decided, I'm not going away till the morning, by then it will either be dead or showing signs of recovery—in which case no doubt Ruth could be prevailed on to look after it till she got back from her holiday.

She gathered up the cleaning things and took them down to the kitchen. On a hook near the pantry she found an old straw shopping-bag, possibly some relic of Emily's, overlooked in her abrupt departure; that would do nicely for the cat.

She went back upstairs and closed the windows. In the front bedroom the stray still lay extended on the stool, breathing by now so very faintly that at first she thought it really must have died. She laid it carefully in the bag and clasped the twin handles close together for safety.

Now—the bus home, or rather two buses home, one into the centre of the town and another which would drop her near her own door. She stepped out into the sharp sweet air of the garden and locked the door behind her.

The best part of a pound just to sole and heel a pair of shoes! Emily was appalled at the way prices had gone up. As she made her way up the High Street her eyes suddenly observed her own shopping-bag, the brown and yellow straw one, moving along a few yards ahead, firmly clutched in the fingers of a young lady—who turned her head to glance in at a shop window and revealed herself as Jane Underwood. Emily quickened her pace and caught up with Jane who was now lingering in front of the window display.

'Well now, Miss Jane,' Emily said, causing her quarry to leap back a few startled inches. 'And what may you be doing with my straw bag?'

'Oh, it's you! You took me by surprise. It is your bag, then? I thought perhaps it might be. I've just been up to The Sycamores—' She was about to explain that she'd been clearing things up but thought better of it; she'd heard from her father how Emily had been summarily dismissed and it seemed tactless to mention the subject of domestic chores in the Yorke establishment at this moment. So she told her instead about the cat, opening the bag sufficiently to allow Mrs Bond to peep inside.

'Why, that's my little stray!' Emily said fondly. 'Many's

the time I've given it a saucer of milk and a few scraps up at The Sycamores.' She put in a hand and stroked the animal. 'Did you come looking for old Emily then?' She glanced up at Jane and gave a deep sigh. 'Ever so sorry about your aunt, dear. Poor Mrs Yorke!' She shook her head, sighed again.

'I saw you at the funeral,' Jane said. She thought it best to steer the conversation away from the topic of her aunt's death. Emily Bond was quite capable of bursting into noisy tears in the middle of the High Street. She put a hand on Emily's arm.

'I think perhaps we'd better move aside, we're creating a block on the pavement.' She drew her into the wide doorway of a supermarket and resumed her account of the cat's behaviour while Emily listened with keen attention. 'I'm going away on holiday in the morning,' Jane said, 'but I'm hoping my stepmother won't mind looking after the cat while I'm gone—if it's still alive in the morning, that is.'

'Oh, you can't go bothering your stepmother,' Emily said at once. 'Let me have it; after all, it is really my cat if it's anyone's.'

'Oh, would you take it?' Jane was delighted.

'Of course I will, I'll soon have it fit and well again.' Emily snatched a handkerchief from her pocket and exploded into a series of sneezes. 'Oh, do excuse me, I've gone and got a cold, I shall have to take something for it tonight.'

'I've just thought,' Jane said, 'perhaps I ought to take the cat to a vet.'

'No, you should not,' Emily said stoutly. 'Charge you I don't know how much. And probably want to put the poor creature to sleep. You leave it to me, my dear, I'll look after it better than any vet.'

It occurred to Jane that Mrs Bond no longer had a job and that a cat must be fed and cat-food cost money. Should she offer her a pound note? She had some of her holiday money in her handbag. Would the old woman be offended? She turned her head away, considering, and her gaze fell on a tall pyramid of tinned cat-food perilously erected just inside the door of the supermarket.

'I tell you what!' she cried. 'You hold the cat and I'll just pop into this shop and get a few tins of food for it. You won't have any at home and I do feel responsible for it.'

'Oh well, that's very good of you,' Emily said. 'What about your bus, though?'

Jane glanced at her watch. 'I've plenty of time. I won't be long.' She handed the straw bag to Emily and went quickly into the shop.

Might as well take a turn or two up the street while she's inside, Emily thought, a little weary of being knocked into by resolute shoppers bound for the supermarket door.

Just past the bus-stop, approaching her, she saw two people walking side by side but with an appearance of non-communication, like prisoners in a chain-gang. Sarah Pierson and that brother of hers, what was his name? Arnold, that was it. Often saw him about the streets but not her ladyship, she usually had her little car. Arnold was laden with shopping and had about him something of the air of a mute pack animal; Sarah merely gripped her handbag and a pair of gloves.

'Good morning,' Emily said firmly, not going to let the chance slip by of a little conversation about dear Mrs Yorke and her lamented end. Not a great deal of love lost between herself and Sarah Pierson, in fact Miss Pierson quite used to look down her nose at her, on her occasional business visits to The Sycamores. But I'm not a charwoman any more, Emily thought, I'm retired, the same as she is, we're on the same footing now, so to speak.

'Ever so sorry to learn about poor Mrs Yorke,' she said and plunged into a lively recital of the way she had learned the news and the profound emotions that had immediately assailed her.

Oh yes,' and 'Quite so', and 'Indeed!' Sarah murmured

during brief gaps in the tale. She was unfortunately trapped by the necessity to wait on this particular spot for the bus. After a nod and a word Arnold had removed himself a few yards farther away and stood idly gazing in through the vast glass windows of the supermarket.

'You'll never guess what I've got in here,' Emily said when she had come to the end of her first topic. She opened the bag a little and thrust it out under Miss Pierson's nose.

'Why, it's a cat!' Sarah said, startled.

'It's a poor little stray, from up at The Sycamores.' She began to cough, couldn't get her hand up to cover her mouth on account of being impeded by the cat-basket.

'Have you just come from there?' Sarah asked, looking hopefully up the road for the bus. Really, the way the creature was positively spraying germs about her!

'Been clearing up,' Emily said after a fractional pause. Not exactly a lie, she always liked to stay on nodding terms with the truth as far as humanly possible, she hadn't precisely specified who had been doing the clearing up, but it had dawned on her a little earlier that Miss Pierson didn't know she'd been sacked and she saw no reason now to hand her ladyship that humiliating piece of information on a plate. She began to recount the story of the cat's irruption into The Sycamores, its scurry under the bed—and no less a bed than dear Mrs Yorke's—and its subsequent collapse from starvation, but giving all the time the impression that the principal actor in her dramatic tale had been herself.

'Very interesting,' Sarah said, beginning to feel disagreeably fatigued by the old woman's chatter. And then to her relief she caught sight of young Jane Underwood coming towards them with a smiling look.

'Oh, good morning, Miss Pierson,' Jane said in a friendly fashion, giving Emily a little nod. 'How are you enjoying your retirement?'

'Quite well, so far,' Sarah said. 'Though I hadn't altogether bargained for the fact that there are so many hours in the day.'

'You ought to go away for a holiday,' Jane said. 'I'm sure you deserve one. I'm going away myself tomorrow for a week.'

'As a matter of fact I am going away. It's the first holiday I've had for years.'

'Somewhere nice?' Jane asked.

'Bournemouth. I've booked into a good hotel, it was recommended to me by one of my customers. The Scarsdale Arms. I understand it's in a very pleasant situation. I'm going next week, I may decide to stay for some time.'

'All very well for some,' Emily said loudly, not at all pleased at the way the other two seemed to be excluding her from the chat. Sarah threw her a sharp look and then saw with undisguised pleasure that her bus was at last grinding into view.

'I must go,' she said, moving off. 'So nice to have seen you,' she said to Jane. She gave Emily quite a friendly little nod. 'I hope your cold is better soon.' She glanced round. 'Arnold—the bus,' she called and he turned from the shop window to join her.

'I got three or four tins of several different varieties of cat-food,' Jane said as the bus bore the Piersons away. She held out a large stout paper bag. 'I don't know what kind it likes so I thought it best to have a choice.'

'Strays'll eat anything,' Emily said with conviction.

'Now, can you manage it?' Jane handed her the bulky parcel. 'I think that's my bus coming along.'

'Yes, you hop off, dear, I can manage. And it's very kind of you to go buying all these tins. The poor little thing will fancy it's Christmas. And I hope you enjoy your holiday,' she called as Jane went off. She was beginning to feel an ache in her bones, wouldn't be surprised if she was starting to run a temperature. Only another two or three minutes to wait before she could scramble on board her own bus. She was quite looking forward to getting back to the cottage, now that she had a living creature to fuss over.

Jane had finished her packing; at eight o'clock Kevin was calling to take her out for a couple of hours, then an early night and up in good time in the morning to catch the train to London to join her aunt. Aunt Dorothy had made a brief appearance in Milbourne for Zena's funeral, returning immediately afterwards to her flat in Surrey. She had never been particularly attached to Zena and hadn't been overwhelmed by grief at her death; it had in fact been several years since she had clapped eyes on her.

I'll make a casserole for supper, Jane decided, not used to inactivity during normal working hours. And when I've finished the casserole I'll make a few scones; we can have tea as soon as they come in, supper an hour or two later.

She set about her task cheerfully, smiling a little at her own enthusiasm. I never fancied I'd turn out so domestic, she thought, taking the onions from the larder. It occurred to her suddenly that it might be rather fun to have a small place of her own. After all she was seventeen, lots of girls left home even earlier than that nowadays. She began to ponder the idea as she peeled and sliced the onions.

At a quarter to six Ruth came in. 'Neil not home yet?' she asked as she took off her coat. She sniffed the air. 'Have you been cooking?' She looked surprised and pleased. She followed Jane into the kitchen. 'Goodness, tea all set out on the trolley as well! This is a nice surprise.' She picked up a buttered scone and began to eat it.

'You go into the sitting-room,' Jane said with the firm authority of the one who has prepared a meal. 'I'll wheel the trolley in there. I don't suppose Father will be long.'

'How did you get on at The Sycamores?' Ruth asked a few minutes later as she sipped her tea.

'I think I've left the place looking fairly reasonable and I made sure everything was well locked up before I came away. Oh—a rather odd thing happened—' She recounted the episode of the starving cat and its strange seizure, Emily's offer to nurse it. 'I thought it better to let her take it as I'm going away, there wouldn't have been anyone here during the day to look after it.' She glanced at her step-mother, expecting a reply but Ruth was leaning back in her chair with her eyes closed.

'Oh, I'm sorry.' Ruth sat up and smiled at her. 'I was thinking about something at the office. Yes, I'm sure you were very wise, Emily will take good care of it.' An abstracted look came into her eyes. 'I'll have to go out again later on. Something came up just before I left work. I was going to let it stand over till tomorrow but now I think perhaps I'd better call round and have a word with—' She broke off at the sound of a car. 'Oh, that'll be Neil. Is there some tea left?'

The front door opened and closed, there was a murmur of voices in the hall. Neil came in with Owen. 'I wanted to pick up the keys,' Owen said as he accepted a cup of tea from Jane. 'I had to call in at the town hall on business, so I gave Neil a lift home.'

'But what about your own car?' Ruth asked her husband. 'Where have you left that?'

He sank into a chair. 'It's all right, I've got to go back to the office in a few minutes, Owen's going to run me there. I have some work to finish.'

'Cooking the accounts,' Owen said lightly. 'Best done out of office hours.' He saw the unamused look Neil gave him; working in local government never did much to improve a man's sense of humour. 'Did you manage things all right at the house?' he asked Jane. 'It was very good of you to go round.'

'It was no trouble,' Jane said politely, conscious of a certain tension in the atmosphere. A little to her own irritation she found herself once again embarking on the saga of the cat but no one else seemed anxious to make conversation and it was after all the only thing of interest that had happened to her at The Sycamores. Before she had come to the end of her recital she became aware of a certain bored restlessness in her listeners. She was relieved a moment or two later when her father picked up a scone, allowing her to switch quite naturally to her newly-awakened interest in cooking.

'I made those,' she said gaily. 'Don't you think they're good?'

'Very good,' her father said with unflattering surprise. 'I didn't know you were so domesticated.'

'She's put a casserole in the oven as well,' Ruth said. 'We're going to have it for supper. Won't you stay and have some, Owen?'

He shook his head. 'No, thank you, I can't, I have an appointment.'

'I'll be back again about half past seven,' Neil said to Ruth. 'Don't start on the casserole without me.'

'We learned some cooking at school,' Jane said to Owen, 'but I wasn't very interested then. Now I find I rather like it. In fact I'm beginning to think I wouldn't mind having a little place of my own, running it myself, I'm sure I could manage very well.'

There was a brief silence. They needn't all look at me with such astonishment, Jane thought, other girls leave home.

'Do you mean somewhere locally?' Owen asked. 'Or are you thinking of skipping off to London?' He threw a glance at Ruth. 'You lived there of course, didn't you? I should think rents would be much too high for a youngster like Jane.'

Neil shifted in his chair, he turned his head slightly and looked at his wife. As if—as if he hated her, Jane thought with a thrust of astonishment. But the look vanished; he addressed Jane with an air of casual enquiry. 'Would you like that? Living in London?' She had probably imagined the look, yes, of course she had. 'I suppose you could always share with two or three other girls, that's usual these days, isn't it?'

'I wasn't thinking of London,' Jane said. 'Not yet, anyway.' Her father was only trying to let her feel she could be free and independent if she wished to be, he didn't really want her to go right away, not at seventeen . . . or did he? It occurred to her all at once for the first time that perhaps he did, perhaps he wanted to be alone with Ruth, to be able to steer the course of his second marriage without the perpetual presence in the household of a third person—whoever that person might be.

She felt a strange sense of shock and then, an instant later, a glimmer of understanding. It was after all perfectly natural on her father's part. Suppose—just suppose for the sake of argument that she herself was married, to Kevin, say, would she welcome someone else always about the place? However much she liked that someone else? Even supposing that someone else was her father? No, of course she wouldn't. She looked at Neil as if she was seeing him now as a stranger, not her father at all but a man with his own complicated life to lead.

'In any case,' she said, 'it was just an idea. I don't suppose I'll do anything about it for ages.'

'You might enjoy it,' Ruth said with a smile.

'Yes, I think I might.' Jane returned her smile. It can't have been very easy for Ruth, she thought, the past year must often have been a trial for her, with me mooning about the place, indulging in fits of sulks whenever I felt like it. A little wave of shame rose inside her. How on earth did I ever come to behave like that? she asked herself in wonder.

Owen stood up. 'We'd better be getting along, if you're ready, Neil.'

As Jane gave him back his keys he slipped some folded notes into her hand. 'Just a little something to buy you cream cakes and coffee while you're away,' he said lightly. 'And thank you for being so helpful.' He gave her fingers a friendly squeeze. 'Have a good time. Give my regards to Aunt Dorothy.'

CHAPTER XV

In the wood-panelled lounge of a second-class hotel in Innsbruck Jane sat at a small table opposite her Aunt Dorothy, drinking coffee after a very good dinner.

'Really remarkable value for money, this trip,' Aunt Dorothy said with determined satisfaction. 'There's just one thing—' She sighed. 'I find it almost impossible to sleep. I haven't really done more than doze off for an hour or two ever since we left England.' Too much variety, too much stimulation, too much haste, and the rich food did nothing to assist slumber.

'Couldn't you take a sleeping-pill?' Jane suggested. 'It would be such a pity to spoil the rest of the holiday just because you're over-tired.'

'I don't know,' Aunt Dorothy said dubiously. 'I don't really believe in pills. Though perhaps just for a night or two, I don't suppose it would be habit-forming. The only thing is—where do I get sleeping-pills at this time of the evening?'

'I'll go and ask at the desk.' Jane stood up. 'Some of these hotels have little shops where you can get lots of things.'

'Here you are,' she said triumphantly a few minutes later, setting a small cardboard drum down on the table. 'No difficulty at all.'

'Do you know, I believe I'll take one now.' Aunt Dorothy picked up the silver jug of hot milk which was still half full. 'I can drink some of this with it. Then I'll go up and see if I can get a really good long sleep. Will you be all right on your own?'

'Yes, of course I will.' Once Aunt Dorothy mounted the stairs Jane's feet would carry her swiftly into the dance-room next door to join the other half-dozen youngsters from the coach-party. 'The man said to take two pills, by the way, they're not very strong, one would be no good.'

Aunt Dorothy obediently tipped two pills into her palm and raised the cup of milk to her lips. A few yards away the hotel cat, a sleek black animal, plump and self-contained, uncurled itself from under a table and picked its contemptuous way towards the door. There was a curious kind of click in Jane's brain as if a set of gears had suddenly slipped into motion, she experienced a sort of heightened awareness, everything seemed all at once to assume a vast and deep significance. The pills on her aunt's palm, the cup of milk, the sinuously moving cat—a film unrolled itself clearly and rapidly in her mind, the bedroom at The Sycamores, the overturned tumbler with a white pool forming round it, the lean stray fiercely lapping at the liquid.

She felt a blinding flash of illumination flare across her brain. In that single shattering moment she was totally and monstrously certain that she knew how Aunt Zena had died. She put up a hand to her face.

'Are you all right?' Aunt Dorothy said anxiously. The child looked as if she were about to faint.

'Oh, yes, I'm all right, it's just—it is rather warm in here.' She drew a deep breath and the wave of faintness began to subside. 'I'll go outside and get a breath of fresh air in a minute, as soon as you've gone up.' She smiled. 'It's passed, I feel much better.'

'Well, don't go staying up too late.' Aunt Dorothy pushed back her chair, pleased to see the colour return to the child's cheeks. 'It wouldn't do you any harm to get an early night for once.'

Jane watched her go, then she leaned back in her chair and closed her eyes in order to think more clearly. It wasn't the fact that Aunt Zena had omitted to give herself the insulin injections, she thought; it wasn't that that had killed her, or at least not that alone; it was a combination of forgetting the injections and drinking half a tumblerful of milk powerfully laced with some kind of sedative, a barbiturate or bromide or sleeping-pills, something of that sort, so that she had additionally missed one more injection on the following morning.

Or perhaps the drug in the milk had been strong enough in itself to kill her even if she had taken all her injections at the right time. The way the cat had lain stretched out, so suddenly collapsed, so motionless, barely breathing—how could she have thought it merely the effect of lack of food? She saw now without a trace of doubt that it had been in a state of coma, that it had absorbed a large quantity of sedative along with the milk.

Had Aunt Zena then really intended to kill herself? Had it been suicide after all? Or perhaps a mock suicide that had tragically and unintentionally turned into the real thing? Young as she was, Jane was by no means unaware of the theatrical element in her aunt's make-up. She knew that her father blamed himself for not having gone round to The Sycamores on that fatal Saturday night; had Aunt Zena been relying on his visit, had she made herself a powerful potion in the confidence that her brother would enter the house in time for resuscitation—general alarm and excitement but no actual danger to life?

She had some kind of glimpse into why a woman of her aunt's temperament might do such a thing; she had taken the emotional temperature of the household a long time ago when she began to leave childhood behind, she had a pretty shrewd idea of the way things were between Uncle Owen and his wife.

A new thought suddenly stabbed at her consciousness, causing her for a moment to grip at the edge of the table—could it possibly be, was it even remotely conceivable that it wasn't Aunt Zena but some other person who had mixed that deadly potion? In other words—she forced herself to look the idea steadily in the face—had Aunt Zena's death been murder? But who? And why?

A host of subsidiary notions, alarming, disturbing, rose up in the train of that new thought; her suspicions began to spread out into an area that threatened some deep level of her mind. I'd better stop thinking about it now, she thought with a thrust of panic, I must stop this very moment, before—before her churning brain might throw up some fragment which would compel her by the very force of its recognition to take action that could strike at the roots of her own stability, her own existence.

I know! she decided on a bright wave of relief, I'll put it completely out of my head until I get home and then I'll tell Kevin about it. She almost smiled with pleasure. Kevin stood outside the family circle, he was intelligent, he would be interested, and he was very level-headed. He would be the perfect listener, the ideal person to assess the reasonableness of her prowling conjectures, he would know what she ought to do or if in fact she should do nothing. She exhaled a long breath of relaxation.

'Hello there! Jane!' A head came round the door of the lounge. 'We've been looking for you. Don't you want to dance?'

She sprang to her feet, charged with energy. 'Yes, of course!' she cried. And she walked rapidly and lightly between the tables towards the music and gyrations next door.

Kevin Lang ran the car neatly into position on the forecourt of Milbourne station. He glanced at his watch. Plenty of time, a good ten minutes before Jane's train was due. He stepped out of the car and locked the door, pleased to have such a smart-looking vehicle at his command for the day, particularly convenient as he could drive Jane home with her luggage, take her off somewhere interesting for lunch as well, perhaps. His immediate superior at the firm of estate agents was in bed with flu and Kevin had had to take over some of his appointments, show prospective customers over houses, take down the details of properties and so on.

He bought a newspaper at the bookstall and sat down on a bench to read it till the train came in. At last it came smoothly and powerfully into view and he sprang to his feet; it would be good to see Jane again, he had never known a week go by so slowly. She was standing by an open window, craning out to see if he was there. Her face broke into a delighted smile as soon as she caught sight of him.

When the train halted he swung her down on to the platform and gave her a long kiss. 'I'll run you home,' he said as he picked up her luggage, 'I've got a car for the day.' He explained about the illness of his boss. 'Later on, when I've done one or two jobs, I could pick you up and we can have lunch together.'

She walked beside him on to the forecourt. 'Actually,' she said, 'I'd prefer not to go home right away. There won't be anyone in till lunch-time and there's something I'd like to see to first.' He stowed the bags into the car boot, straightened up and looked at her. A little frown of anxiety creased her brows. 'I'm rather worried,' she said slowly. I want to tell you about it, see what you think. You might say I'm just letting my imagination run away with me.'

'What is it?' he asked. 'Did something happen while you were away?'

She shook her head. 'No, nothing happened, it's something I—look, suppose we get in the car and drive on a bit.' She glanced round at the busy forecourt. 'We can't talk here.'

'Come on then, jump in.' He held the car door open. 'Now,' he said a few minutes later when he had run the car into a deserted spot, 'what's all this about?'

She drew a deep breath and looked up at him with appeal. 'I want you to listen to what I have to say, don't brush it aside, and don't keep interrupting me with questions.' She clasped her hands together. 'You remember the day before I left, I went up to The Sycamores . . .'

At last she came to a full stop and they both sat in silence for several seconds. 'I see,' Kevin said slowly. He put up a hand and scratched his ear. 'What do you want to do now?'

'Oh!' she cried with an odd mixture of relief and apprehension, 'so you don't think it's a lot of nonsense?'

He gave her a long serious look. 'No, I don't. I don't like the sound of it at all.' She felt the tears prickle in her eyes, she realized now that she'd been more than half counting on his dismissing the whole thing with a laugh.

'I thought,' she said at last, 'that we might run out to Mrs Bond's cottage.' She saw his puzzled look. 'I want to see if the cat's better.' She had the feeling that if the cat proved to be all right, she would somehow be able to forget her uneasiness, let her shadowy conjectures drop away into oblivion.

'I can't really see what the cat's going to prove one way or the other,' Kevin said, 'not at this stage. But if it's what you want—' He switched on the engine. 'Do you know where Mrs Bond lives?'

'Oh yes. You fork left at the first junction from here and then I'll show you.'

As they approached the cottage he said, 'There's no smoke coming from the chimneys, she may be out,' and a moment later he added, 'All the curtains are drawn. Could she have gone away?'

'Perhaps she's still in bed,' Jane said. 'She hasn't got a job to get up for now.' Then she suddenly remembered Emily coughing and sneezing in the High Street. 'She might be ill!' she said in an urgent tone. 'She could be lying up there without a soul to look after her, she might have flu, she wasn't at all well the last time I saw her, I'd forgotten that.'

'Now don't get upset,' he said as he switched off the engine. 'If she's ill we can get a doctor for her.' He took her hand and they walked rapidly up to the cottage door. He rapped briskly on the brass knocker and they both stood with their heads tilted, listening for a movement, a step, a voice. He raised the knocker and rapped again, more loudly. Silence settled back into place as the echoes died away.

'Give a shout,' he said. 'She'll know your voice. It might alarm her to hear a stranger calling out.'

Jane looked up at the blind windows. 'Mrs Bond!' she called. 'Are you there? It's me, Jane Underwood!' There was no reply. 'Let's go round the back,' she said. They skirted the side of the house, repeated the knocking and the calling, without success. Kevin tried the back door but it resisted him; they returned to the front of the house and tried that door but it remained unyielding. 'She could simply have gone into town,' Jane said with an attempt at optimism.

'Yes, she could.' Kevin stood considering. 'We passed a little shop back there,' he said at last. 'We could call in, ask if anyone's seen her about recently, they might even tell us they saw her go by this morning.' He put his arm round her shoulders and they went back to the car.

The shop, a small general store, was empty except for a middle-aged woman arranging tins on a shelf. She turned as they came in, gave them a look of keen assessment. 'Mrs Bond?' she said, breaking in before Kevin had come to the end of his first sentence. 'Are you friends of hers?' Scarcely relatives, not a smart young couple with a car.

'I'm a friend,' Jane said at once. 'I've known her for years.'

'Then I'm afraid you're in for a bit of a shock.' The woman's tone was compounded of concern and relish. Jane slipped her hand into Kevin's and gripped his fingers tightly. 'She's dead and buried,' the woman said dramatically. She gave a brisk nod. 'Buried two days ago, inquest the previous day. An open verdict, they said. Do you know what that means? It means they couldn't tell how she died.' Importance rose in her voice. 'We had the police in here, quite a performance, I can tell you. Here—' she added suddenly, coming round the counter and thrusting forward a chair, 'you'd better sit down, you look quite poorly.' Jane dropped into the chair and put her head in her hands. 'Would you like a glass of water, dear? It must have given you a turn, it was very upsetting for us.'

Kevin threw the woman an angry look—blurting it straight out like that, she might have been a little more considerate. He bent down and squeezed Jane's shoulders. 'Don't take it to heart,' he said in a low voice.

The woman came back with a tumbler of water. Jane raised it to her lips and took a long steadying drink, then she looked up at the woman.

'I'm all right now, thanks. What happened?'

'There was this gas-man going round reading the meters. When he couldn't get into the cottage he slipped a card under the door, you know how they do, so you can read the meter yourself, and they call for it next day. Well, he came back next day and the card was still there, sticking out under the door.' She leaned forward, enjoying the drama of her tale. 'And the curtains were drawn—in broad daylight. So he came in here and told my husband about it, asked if we knew anything, if she was ill or away, or what. Well, of course she never went away so in the end my husband phoned the police and they broke in. She was lying in bed, stone dead, been dead a couple of days, it seems. They had a post-mortem and everything.'

'What did she die of?' Kevin asked.

'They said she had the flu and it had turned to pneumonia, very sudden it was, they said it happens like that sometimes. And she'd dosed herself with brandy and a lot of tablets. Sleeping-pills, or something of that sort, she'd taken them with a cup of milk. In the end they couldn't decide whether it was the pneumonia or the brandy and tablets that had finished her off so they brought in an open verdict, meaning they couldn't be sure.'

Jane looked at the woman. 'Was there a cat?' she asked. 'A black cat.'

The woman frowned and shook her head. 'I don't know anything about any cat,' she said. 'Mrs Bond never had no cat. If there had been one I dare say the police would have brought it in here for someone to look after it.'

Jane stood up. 'I'm quite all right now, thank you,' she said firmly to Kevin in response to his anxious look. 'Thank you very much,' she said to the woman. 'It was very good of you to explain everything. I hope we haven't taken up too much of your time.'

'What are you going to do now?' Kevin asked as they walked back to the car. 'Leave things as they are?'

'I suppose so.' Conflicting thoughts whirled through her brain. 'If poor Emily's dead—' She sighed, with an effort she kept back the tears.

He settled her into the passenger seat. 'I have to look over a house,' he said gently. He glanced at his watch. 'It's a furnished letting, I have someone wanting to look over it today, I'm just checking it first. Suppose I run you home, I've got time. Then I can pick you up later for lunch.'

She shook her head. 'I don't think I can have lunch with you. Ruth said she'd come home for a few minutes at lunch-time, just to make sure I got back safely, I can't very well go out. Thanks all the same. If you could just run me home though, I'd be grateful.' In the silence of home she could make herself a strong cup of coffee, sit down and think.

'All right. I tell you what, I'll give you a ring some time this afternoon when I've taken the client over the house, perhaps we can meet for tea. You can see what you feel like then.' Shock might strike her later on, she might be forced to retire to bed for the rest of the day. 'I wouldn't go doing anything very strenuous when you get home,' he said. 'Take it easy.' He decided to switch to a more cheerful subject. 'It's a man from overseas who wants to take a look at Piersons', he's been doing an engineering job—'

'Piersons'?' Jane sat upright. 'Do you mean the house you have to let? Which Piersons is that? Not Sarah and Arnold Pierson?'

'I don't know the exact names,' he said. 'But of course I have the address. Hold on a moment.' He stopped the car, thrust his hand into his pocket and took out a notebook. 'Here you are.' He held an open page in front of her. 'That's the one. To be let for three months in the first instance, with a possibility of renewal.'

'It is their house,' she said, looking up at him with bewildered eyes. 'Why are they letting it? Have they left Milbourne?'

'I'm afraid I don't know anything about that. My boss was handling it, he'd have all the details. Does it matter?'

She tried to marshal her thoughts. 'You'd better drive on again. Don't take me home just yet, I'll come with you to the house while you check it, that will give me a chance to think about it.' He set the car in motion again. 'Don't talk to me for a bit,' she added. 'I just want to work it out.'

She cast her mind rapidly back to her meeting with Sarah Pierson at the bus-stop. Going away for a while, Sarah had said, she didn't know for how long. But surely Arnold would still be living at the house? Had he decided to move into a hotel, take a flat or bedsitter? Why should one or other—or both of them—have suddenly decided to put the house in the hands of an estate agent? Sarah had said nothing about it at the bus-stop but then why should she have done?

There was no reason why she should have disclosed her entire family business to Jane, especially with old Emily standing a couple of feet away . . . Emily, she thought with a horrid feeling beginning to twist the muscles of her stomach. Emily and the little cat. Emily had been chatting to Sarah for some time before she herself joined them. She raised her hand abruptly to her mouth . . . And Arnold had stood a yard or two away, within earshot, looking in through the windows of the supermarket . . . But what possible connection could there be between that encounter and the decision to put the house up for letting? None at all that she could see . . . And yet . . . and yet . . . Emily was dead and no one seemed very sure how she had died . . .

'This is the house,' Kevin said, halting the car. She

jerked herself out of her whirling thoughts and followed him up the path. Inside, everything was clean and neat, bare of personal belongings. Kevin took out his notebook and pencil. 'I have to take a look round just to see everything's in order.'

'Shouldn't be any difficulty about letting the house,' he said a few minutes later. 'Very well maintained, spotlessly clean, and the rent's reasonable. Now, a look round the back, and then we can go.'

Outside by the dustbins there were a couple of cardboard boxes and beside them an ancient wooden gramophone. On top of one of the boxes a message had been boldly inked: For collection by the Scouts.

Kevin removed a lid from a dustbin. Inside was a mass of papers, some crumpled into balls, some torn into thick wedges and a pile of pamphlets and brightly-coloured brochures. 'They had a good clear-out,' he said approvingly. 'You'd be surprised at the way some people go off and leave a house stuffed with all kinds of junk, the tenant has to more or less spring-clean when he takes the place over.'

Jane glanced in at the bin and saw the gay cover of a travel booklet. 'Just a moment,' she said, arresting Kevin's hand as he was about to replace the lid. 'I'd like to take a look at those.' He watched in surprised silence as she removed a handful of the glossy brochures. She sat down on the back doorstep and began to turn the pages.

Cruises, all the leaflets were for cruises, every conceivable kind of cruise. Photographs of ships looked up at her, beautiful liners, views of dining-rooms, cabins, pictures of palm-lined beaches, foreign ports, smiling stewards. Kevin came and sat down beside her.

'Who's going on a cruise?' he asked.

'I don't know,' she said slowly, her heart thumping in her chest. 'Not Sarah, she's in Bournemouth.' She remembered Arnold's eyes looking blindly in at the supermarket and she gave a little shiver. 'Arnold used to come into the library, he was always taking out travel books.' She stopped suddenly at one page; a line had been drawn underneath the details of one particular cruise, an inked circle enclosed a date. 'February the twelfth,' she said, keeping her voice steady. 'That's today.'

He took the brochure from her, ran his eye over the facts and figures. 'It costs a small fortune,' he said. 'It's a round-the-world trip. Is your Arnold Pierson a millionaire?'

She laid a hand on his sleeve, her fingers dug into his arm. 'He's an accountant,' she said. 'He works for Uncle Owen. And he was a friend of Aunt Zena's. He knew her right from the time when they were young.'

'An accountant?' Kevin repeated. 'Do you suppose your Uncle Owen knows about this trip?' He frowned, 'It's one hell of a long holiday.'

She jumped to her feet. 'Let's go back inside. I'm going to ring Uncle Owen at the factory, I'm going to find out if Arnold has gone away, if he knows about it.'

'Be careful,' Kevin warned, taking out the keys again. 'Don't go making a fool of yourself, the cruise might be nothing more than a pipe-dream, just drawing a line round the kind of holiday you dream about.'

'I'll be careful,' she said, 'I'll think of some good reason for asking about him.'

Inside, she dialled the number and spoke to her uncle's secretary, she stood waiting while the girl went to see if he was free.

'Hello, Jane.' Her uncle's voice at last, touched with surprise. 'You're back then. Did you have a good holiday?' A couple of minutes crawled by while she made suitable conversation. Then she said casually, allowing him to think she was speaking from the library, 'I've just called in here to have a chat with the girls and there's a query about a missing book.' It struck her even as she uttered the words that it was rather a frail story but invention threw up nothing more plausible. 'I said I'd look into it, I was dealing with it before I went away. It's Arnold Pierson, he took out the book a month ago—'

'Pierson,' her uncle said in an icy tone.

'Yes, he reported the book as missing—'

'That's not the only thing that's missing,' Owen said. 'Pierson's missing as well.'

'Missing? I thought perhaps I could speak to him—'

'I'd like to speak to him myself. He walked out of here last Friday and he hasn't been back since. Just marched into my office and told my secretary he was going off for a holiday, without so much as a by-your-leave. I wasn't here myself or I'd have had something to say. The audit's coming up in a couple of weeks, a fine time to take himself off.'

With an effort Jane kept her voice level. 'Did he tell your secretary how long he'd be away? Or where he was going?'

'No, he did not. I might have understood if he'd said he felt unwell or produced a doctor's note or given any reasonable kind of explanation. But he did nothing of the kind. And when she tried to argue with him he more or less told her he mightn't come back at all if he didn't feel like it.'

'I suppose,' Jane said hesitantly, 'I mean, the accounts, is there any question of—'

He gave a grim laugh. 'I'd like to know the answer to that one myself but I won't know for certain till the auditors have been in. I've got one of the other fellows working on the books now, he hasn't spotted anything so far. I dare say Pierson got everything well sewn up before he sloped off, it'll probably take a good long time until we unravel it.' Jane screwed up her eyes in concentrated thought. Should she say anything about the brochure? Or the fact that the house was in the hands of an agent? Better not, instinct warned her, say nothing for the present, not till you've had time to consider it.

When at last she replaced the receiver she turned to Kevin and swiftly filled in a few gaps for him; he had caught the general drift of the conversation as he stood at her elbow. 'I'm going to speak to my father about it this evening,' she said firmly. 'He'll know what to do. If he thinks it necessary he can go and see Uncle Owen.'

On the way out of the house she suddenly remembered she had said nothing to her uncle about Emily Bond's death. Did he know of it? Yes, of course he must, it had been reported in the paper.

Kevin turned his head and glanced back at her. 'Come on,' he said. 'I can't hang about much longer, I have another appointment to keep.'

'I'm sorry,' she said urgently, 'but I want to make another phone call. I must, it won't take long. Do let's go back inside.'

He sighed and looked at his watch. 'All right, I suppose I can spare a little longer.' Once again he drew out the keys. 'Who is it this time? I'm going to have a job explaining about these phone calls.'

'I'll pay for them,' she said at once. 'I've got quite a lot of money left over from my holiday. I want to ring up and find out if Arnold actually is going on that cruise. I can't think why it didn't occur to me before. All I have to do is phone the shipping company or the travel agents, the name was stamped on the brochure, the number is sure to be there too. I'll ask if the tickets are ready for Mr Pierson or if they've been collected. If they know nothing about it then it was just a pipe-dream, as you said, and Arnold has simply gone off for a short holiday and he'll turn up again in a week or two and that will be that.'

'Oh, very well,' Kevin said. 'Sounds sensible enough. I'll put through the call myself, I'll keep it pretty short.' Jane stood a few inches away from him as he picked up the receiver.

'Pierson?' said a faint voice a few minutes later at the other end of a crackly line. 'Hold on, I'll just check.' There was a brief pause and then the voice said, 'Yes, tickets already picked up. The *Kyrenia,* sails tonight, midnight, from Southampton, stateroom number twenty-four.'

'He's scarpered all right,' Kevin said as he rang off. 'Your Uncle Owen's going to be disappointed if he thinks Pierson's coming back in time for the audit.' He seemed to have forgotten the urgency of his next appointment, a lively interest entered his tone. 'What do we do next?'

'Ring the hotel in Bournemouth,' Jane said instantly before he had time to protest at the extra delay. 'Wait now till I remember the name—Scar—the Scarsdale Arms, that was it. You'll have to get the number from directory enquiries.' Kevin picked up the phone again.

'And precisely why are we phoning the hotel?' he asked as he waited for the girl to supply the number.

'To see if Sarah has turned up there.'

'Why—where else would she be?'

Jane clasped her hands together. 'That's what I'm wondering,' she said in a low voice. 'If Arnold has been up to something—' A kaleidoscope flashed through her brain, the glass under the bed at The Sycamores, the prostrate cat, Emily talking animatedly to Sarah . . . and Arnold standing a yard or two away . . . Aunt Zena was dead, Emily Bond was dead . . . 'I just want to make sure she's all right, that she got to the hotel, that nothing's happened to her.' A frightful thought struck at her, she sent a horrified glance around, towards the stairs, the upper rooms, then she laid a firm grip on her imagination, resolutely blinking away the vision of locked cupboards, the space under the eaves. No, of course not, Sarah couldn't possibly be—

'Thank you,' Kevin said into the phone. He touched the receiver rest and then dialled again. 'It's ringing at the hotel,' he said a few moments later. 'Hello, is that the Scarsdale Arms? . . . Could I speak to Miss Pierson? Miss Sarah Pierson, from Milbourne.'

Do we actually need to speak to her? Jane asked herself rapidly. Or will it be sufficient to know she's there, that she arrived safe and sound? But perhaps it might be as well to speak to her, they could ask about Arnold—or could they? What could they say? She tried to work something out.

'Not there?' Kevin said. 'Yes, I see, thank you.' He put back the receiver and turned to Jane. 'There is no Miss Sarah Pierson in the Scarsdale Arms. She never showed up.' He became sharply aware of the passage of time. 'For heaven's sake, come on!' he cried. 'I'll get the sack if I don't get a move on. You talk it all over with your stepmother, I'll ring you some time this afternoon.' He urged her through the front door and down the path.

CHAPTER XVI

'I can't stay more than a few minutes,' Ruth said when the greetings, the exclamations, the questions about the trip were over. 'I'm meeting someone for lunch, I slipped away from the office early, just to make sure you'd arrived in one piece.'

'At least have some coffee,' Jane said. 'It's all ready and waiting. There's something I must talk to you about.' Ruth followed her into the kitchen. 'I ought to discuss it with Father but it can't wait till this evening.'

Ruth pulled out a chair and sat down. 'Go on then.' She glanced at her watch. 'Fire away.'

Jane poured out the coffee. 'Do you remember the day before I went away? I tidied up at The Sycamores and there was that odd business about the cat.' Ruth's hand ceased to stir the spoon round in her cup. 'Well, when I was away, I began to think about it, it worried me.' She watched Ruth steadily all the time she talked but Ruth kept her head tilted to one side, listening with a slight frown, her eyes resting on the opposite wall.

Ruth didn't interrupt, didn't ask any questions, and Jane's voice began to falter as she ploughed on. But I will finish it, she thought stubbornly, I'll say what I have to say. If they all think I'm deranged, then they'll have to think it, it can't be helped. She saw the expression on Ruth's face change to one of uneasiness, deepen into anxiety. When Jane finally stopped talking she sat up in her chair and gave her stepdaughter a look of open disquiet.

'I hope you're not going to say anything of all this farrago to Owen? The poor man's upset enough about Zena's death without you going round suggesting she committed suicide.'

Jane's mouth set in a rebellious line. 'I wasn't necessarily implying it was suicide.' She drew a deep breath. 'I've begun to think it might have been murder. And Emily Bond, too. I believe she could have been murdered because she knew about the cat and she was the kind of person who would talk about it to anyone she met.'

Ruth pushed back her chair and stood up. 'I know you've found the last year difficult,' she said, 'and I've done my best to make allowances. But to try to make trouble on this scale—I'm frankly appalled. Emily Bond died from pneumonia, there was an inquest.'

'What about Arnold Pierson?' Jane said obstinately, although a treacherous trembling began to threaten her voice. 'I didn't invent the fact that he walked out of his job.'

'I don't for one moment imagine he's going round the world,' Ruth said with scorn. 'He's just taken himself off for a rest somewhere. There could quite easily be someone else called Pierson sailing on the *Kyrenia*—or someone with a name very like Pierson, I don't suppose you spelled it out for the clerk over the phone. You must remember Arnold's father died only a couple of weeks ago, he was very attached to him—and to Zena—and then Sarah going off for a holiday, leaving him alone, it's quite understandable, he simply felt he had to get away, have a break. He'll be back before long, he'll probably phone Owen in a day or two and apologize for not explaining matters. Owen will understand. You ought to understand too, you're not a child any more, you're old enough to control your imagination, to put it to work in more useful ways.'

Jane got to her feet and stood facing her stepmother. 'But the cat—' she persisted.

Ruth clicked her tongue in irritation. 'The wretched cat had a fit,' she said sharply. 'It could have been suffering from one of a dozen different diseases, it was probably at its last gasp when you let it into the house.' You knew about the cat, Jane thought suddenly, I told you about it. Panic began to wash through her brain. And Uncle Owen knew . . . and Father . . .

Ruth turned and walked to the door, she paused at the threshold. 'I hope this is clearly understood. I absolutely forbid you to mention any of this rubbish to Owen or for that matter to anyone else.' There was a brief pause. 'Have you by any chance considered,' she said in an altered tone, a shade friendlier, more intimate, 'how all this would affect—' She broke off and started again. 'You must think of your father, he would be very upset if he knew what you've been saying.' Again she paused. 'Think about it. You're an intelligent girl, you'll understand.' She went from the room and a moment later Jane heard the front door close behind her.

Jane remained by the table, biting her lip. If I think about it any more, she said to herself, I'll do nothing, it will all fade away. And the *Kyrenia* sails tonight. She had a powerful impression that she must either do something within the next couple of minutes or put the whole thing from her for good. The one question that refused to be silenced danced before her brain; where was Sarah Pierson? She was gripped by the feeling that something terrible had either happened to Sarah or was about to happen to her and that it lay within her own power either to prevent it happening or to bring it to light if it had already taken place.

I can't just forget it, she thought, shaking her head slowly. Whatever motives they'll think I have for persisting, whoever might be involved, I must go on. Now that her mind was made up she felt calmer. She glanced at the clock, detachedly considering the times of buses. If I leave right away, she thought, I can just about catch the next one into town. It stops right outside the main police station. She walked swiftly and resolutely into the hall.

Detective-Inspector Venn put his head round the door of his office and called out to a passing constable. 'Find Sergeant Cottrell, tell him I want to see him right away. He's in one of the interview rooms.' He closed the door and returned to his desk. 'Just one small point.' He gave Jane a fatherly smile. 'Do you by any chance happen to know which hotel it was your uncle stayed at in Seahaven? The week-end he was away, when Mrs Yorke died? We like to have all these little details.'

'Yes, I do know,' Jane said. In his hurry to leave the hotel Owen had left his briefcase behind, he'd rung up to ask them to send it on, he'd used the phone at her father's house, she'd heard him making the call. 'The Cliff View Hotel.'

Venn made a note of the name. A highly-strung girl, he thought, a difficult position at that age, a new and beautiful stepmother in the house, could give rise to heaven knew what complications in a vulnerable personality. He would have liked to give her a friendly pat on the back, tell her to go off and enjoy herself with youngsters of her own age, take to writing short stories if she found everyday life lacking in excitement . . . but professional caution and ineradicable habit stayed his hand.

Just suppose, just for one moment suppose that there was some fragment of truth mixed up somewhere in all this ragbag. Suppose Sarah Pierson never came back from her holiday, suppose later on there were questions asked by adult voices, sharp official voices . . . and it came out that this child had sat in his office and asked him to do something and he'd patted her on the shoulder and told her to run away and play? He sighed. There was a knock at the door and Cottrell came in, flicking a glance from Venn to Jane.

'This is Miss Jane Underwood,' Venn said. 'Sergeant Cottrell.' He tilted his head back and looked at Cottrell. 'Owen Yorke's niece.'

Cottrell nodded. 'Yes, I know your uncle,' he said to Jane.

'She's a little worried about one or two things,' Venn said smoothly. 'She called in to ask my advice.' He smiled at Jane. 'Very sensible of you. I wonder, would you mind waiting outside for a little, while I have a word with Sergeant Cottrell? You'll find a bench out there, I won't keep you waiting very long.'

As soon as Cottrell had closed the door behind her Venn began to talk rapidly, standing up and pacing about the room. 'I don't know what you're going to make of all this, I don't know what I make of it myself. To put it in a nutshell that child has walked in here and more or less told me she believes her aunt—Zena Yorke—and Emily Bond—you remember, the old charwoman who died last week, open verdict—she believes both of them were murdered.' He paused, waiting for Cottrell's laughter.

But Cottrell didn't laugh. He stood motionless, a slight frown on his face, staring up into his own thoughts. Then he said, 'And who does she suggest murdered them?'

Venn flung himself down into his chair. 'You don't just dismiss the whole thing out of hand? You haven't heard a single word of her reasons but you're prepared to consider them?' He sounded vastly incredulous.

'I should be very interested to hear her reasons.'

'Sit down,' Venn said. 'And pin your ears back.' He gave a short laugh. 'It's a trifle complicated.'

Three or four cigarettes later Venn looked up from the transcript of the inquest evidence on Mrs Bond. 'Only Emily's fingerprints on the cup she drank the milk from.' He frowned. 'The suggestion is that Emily was murdered because she knew about the fact that Zena York drank—or is thought to have drunk—heavily doped milk. Now why would Arnold Pierson want to kill Zena Yorke?'

'If he was fiddling the factory accounts,' Cottrell said, 'Zena might have found out about it. But why is the girl so certain it was Arnold? Apparently she related the story of the cat to her parents and Owen Yorke. Any one of them could have had a motive for killing Zena, I could invent you half-a-dozen motives myself, on the spot. And don't forget Pierson saved Mrs Bond's life that time, knocked her out of the way of the car. I can't quite square that with going round to her cottage and murdering her.' The accident, he thought, Owen Yorke's car parked discreetly out of sight, Yorke coming down the steps from Mrs Fleming's house, very anxious to remove himself from the scene. He felt a warning prickle along the back of his neck. 'Where was Yorke the night his wife died?' he asked.

'He was away.' Venn looked down at his notebook. 'At the Cliff View hotel in Seahaven.'

'It wouldn't take long to get from Seahaven to Milbourne and back,' Cottrell said. 'Was he staying at the hotel alone?'

'I did think of that,' Venn said. He laid his hand on the phone. 'And now I propose to find out.' He put through a call to the Seahaven police, asked them to ring him back after they'd despatched a man to the hotel. 'I don't think we need the girl here any longer,' he said when he had replaced the receiver. 'Is there anything you want to ask her before I send her off home?'

Cottrell pondered for a moment and then shook his head. 'I take it she won't go running round the family telling them she's been here?'

'I'll have a word with her. In any case the parents are both out at work, won't be in till this evening. If we're going to do anything about all this we'll be well and truly started by then. Probably have to call round and see them then anyway. Ask her to come in, will you?'

When she was sitting opposite him again he gave her a

warning about the need for discretion. 'Just for the present, you understand. There may or may not be anything in all this but we'll make a few enquiries. Either Sergeant Cottrell or myself will probably call round to your house later on this evening, so it isn't really a question of asking you to keep things from your parents.' He smiled at her. 'Just that it might be better if you said nothing to anyone till we get in touch with you again.'

She nodded. 'Yes, I understand. May I go now?'

'Yes. And try not to worry. You did the right thing in coming to us. Even if it all turns out to be moonshine, you did the right thing, just remember that.'

In the doorway she paused, turned to look back at him. 'Uncle Owen didn't do it,' she said. 'Or—' Then she wheeled round and plunged out of the room.

'She thinks her father did it,' Venn said when the sound of her steps had died away. 'That's why she's so anxious to have it pinned on Pierson.' He rubbed his chin. 'I wonder how Zena left her money. I think I'll have a word with Yorke's solicitor. And Neil Underwood's bank manager.' Only six or seven banks in Milbourne, wouldn't take long to discover which of them handled the account.

The phone rang on his desk, Seahaven with the result of their enquiries at the Cliff View Hotel. 'Mm,' Venn said with interest as he listened. 'That's very useful, I'm much obliged.' When he had rung off he tilted his chair back, linked his hands behind his head. 'Yorke booked into the Cliff View by himself,' he said in a lively tone. 'But our man in Seahaven had the wit to run his eye over a couple of pages in the hotel register. And he observed that another person from Milbourne had registered in the hotel for that same week-end. Mrs Linda Fleming.'

Cottrell raised his eyebrows but said nothing. It's beginning to slot together, he thought, it's starting to jell. 'Wouldn't do any harm,' Venn said almost gaily, 'if I went round and had a word with Mrs Fleming.' He let the legs of his chair bang down on the floor. 'Probe around a little, see what I can discover.' Then his eyes grew wary, he recalled Jane Underwood's look of agitation, the hint of emotional instability. 'Before we really get going,' he said, 'there is just one thing. How do we know there ever was a cat up at The Sycamores? We've only the girl's word for it.' A prominent citizen, Owen Yorke; and his brother-in-law of some account in official circles locally; have to tread very carefully, wouldn't do to go blundering around. Always check your facts, he thought, question the basic assumptions.

'We can get Quigley in,' Cottrell said. 'He was up at Mrs Bond's cottage after she was found, he may have seen the cat.'

Quigley came up from the canteen where he had been snatching a cup of tea before going off duty. 'A cat?' he said in response to Venn's questions, 'no, I don't remember any cat.' He paused, shook his head. 'No, quite definitely, there wasn't any cat.' Then he raised a hand. 'Wait a minute, there was something—yes, that was it. Didn't take much notice of it, but now you ask—there was a pile of tins of cat-food on a shelf. But no cat.' He looked pleased at his own feat of memory.

'All right,' Venn said. 'You can get off home.' The door closed behind the constable. 'At least it looks as if there was a cat,' Venn said. 'Ties in with the girl's story about buying the tins, giving them to Mrs Bond.' He stood up. 'The *Kyrenia* sails at midnight. If we do decide we're going to take a trip down to Southampton then we'd better make a start on a few enquiries. I'm going to have a word with Gethin, he's in hospital with flu but I'm sure he'll see me. I want to ask him why he didn't consider it necessary to hold an inquest on Zena Yorke.'

'And I'd like to have a chat with Turner,' Cottrell said. 'Maurice Turner, he was my captain in the war, and Pierson's captain too. Just a possibility that if Pierson is in any kind of trouble, he might have gone to see Turner.' He saw Venn's doubtful look. 'A bit of a long shot, I know, but I think it's worth a try.'

'Well, if you feel that, go ahead,' Venn said. 'But I don't want any of this to leak out to Yorke. Not just yet.' If we do go aboard the *Kyrenia*, Cottrell thought, and find that Pierson never set foot on the ship or that if he is there he has a perfectly good explanation, if we can just clear Arnold out of the way, then we can get down to the real business—Owen Yorke. And his brother-in-law. And his brother-in-law's wife. But my money's on Yorke, he thought, feeling the exhilarating pulse of the chase. Yorke and Linda Fleming.

'Just a moment,' Venn said abruptly. 'Maurice Turner.' He frowned in concentration, remembering his wife holding forth to him in the car on their way home from the presidential ball. 'My wife witnessed—or overheard—some kind of quarrel between Zena Yorke and a woman from British Foods, what was her name, Gibbs, a Miss Gibbs, at the ball, the Independents' ball. Some fuss about a torn dress, the Gibbs woman had bought it at Underwoods, I don't know all the details and anyway it doesn't matter. What does matter is that Ruth Underwood, Jane's mother—or rather, stepmother—was there too, all this took place in the cloakroom, quite a set-to apparently, and in the course of the general insulting there was some suggestion of a carry-on between Ruth and her boss.'

He raised his eyebrows at Cottrell. 'And Ruth's boss is Maurice Turner. The Gibbs woman implied, if I remember rightly what my wife told me, that Turner was an old flame of Ruth's—or even a current flame—and that that was how she got her promotion.' He shrugged his shoulders. 'May be nothing in it of course. Probably only jealousy, one glass of wine too many all round, but you might just bear it in mind. Ruth Underwood's a very good-looking woman. In fact she's one of the most beautiful blondes I've ever seen outside the movies.'

Cottrell felt a sharp tingle in his hands, the sensation prickled right up over his arms. 'A blonde?' he said casually.

'Yes, she has the loveliest hair you ever saw. Masses of it. And one hundred per cent natural.'

'I had been attending Mrs Yorke just before her death,' Gethin said with a touch of impatience. 'She'd been in a coma more than once in the last few years. I saw no necessity whatever for an inquest.' He knows he'll never practise again, Venn thought, he has no conceivable reason now not to tell the truth.

'If I were you,' Gethin said. 'I'd watch where you are treading. Doesn't always do in a town the size of Milbourne to go round looking under too many stones. I'm a retired man now, you're not.' He felt a vast fatigue sweep over him. All his professional life people had come running to him with their problems, every conceivable kind of problem; it had frequently seemed to him that he practised every profession but medicine.

A nurse looked round the door of the private room. 'Will you be much longer?' She threw a significant glance at Venn. 'Dr Gethin should really get some sleep now.'

Venn stood up. 'I'm just going.' The nurse withdrew her head. 'Do you think you'll enjoy your retirement?' Venn asked Gethin, thinking with yearning of that beacon light ahead of himself.

'I'm going to look for a cottage in Scotland.' Gethin smiled. 'I intend to do some fishing.' He'd been intending to do some fishing for forty years, perhaps at last he might be allowed to get on with it.

'Won't you be lonely?' Venn asked, seeing the solitary figure of the old doctor huddled at the side of a loch, vast acres of heather stretching out under a harsh grey sky.

'I sincerely hope so.' Gethins' eyes looked back at all the faces that had crowded into his surgery over the demanding years. 'I hope to God I'll be lonely. It'll be a welcome change.'

CHAPTER XVII

'No, Pierson hasn't been to see me.' Maurice Turner's fingers played with a pencil on his desk. 'I don't suppose you're going to tell me what this is about?'

Cottrell shook his head. 'I'm afraid I can't.' After all these years he still felt the impulse to address Turner as Sir, but he managed to restrain his tongue. 'I've always been rather baffled,' he said abruptly, 'at the way life in the prison camp affected Pierson, it seemed to alter him completely.' It suddenly struck him that Arnold would never have committed a murder, he would never under any circumstances have run the risk of being shut up again behind bars.

Turner spun the pencil in his fingers. What was it Zena Yorke had said that evening at the ball when Pierson's name had been mentioned? 'A hero!' she'd said with contempt, implying some knowledge of her own. Zena had been beautiful once, Pierson had danced to her tune in those far-off pre-war days. As Turner very well knew, there were things a man would say to a beautiful woman that he would not utter to another living soul . . . and surely Zena had still been beautiful when Pierson had come back to Milbourne after the war, haunted by his prison ghosts. He sat up abruptly.

Ghosts, he thought with a little shiver of recollection. There had been that terrible business of B Company, pretty well wiped out in an ambush. Zena had said something—what was it? He struggled to remember. 'One of your precious companies.' He sat staring down at his hands. Was it possible? The men of B Company—could those have been the ghosts that walked beside Pierson through the Milbourne streets?

'They gave Pierson a pretty severe going-over, if I remember,' he said slowly. 'The Japs, when they questioned him. I seem to recall—' he passed a hand across his mouth—'he was in bad shape for a good time afterwards.' He gave Cottrell a direct look. 'Do you happen to remember exactly when that would be? It wouldn't by any chance have been shortly before that B Company business?'

'Good God,' Cottrell said after a short pause. 'I believe you're right. That would explain everything.' He felt a moment's vast compassion for Pierson, a raw boy, caught up as they all were in that horrifying coil of events. 'He was only a lad,' he said. 'He wasn't made of iron.'

Turner stood up and walked over to the window, he stood looking out at the road, the pavements, the pleasant to-and-fro of secure suburban life.

'The ambush had nothing to do with Pierson. I stayed on in the army for a year or two after the war, I learned one or two things we didn't know in the camp. I know the story behind the B Company slaughter.' He shook his head. 'Pierson may have talked his head off, but he wasn't responsible for the deaths of those men.' He shook his head again, slowly, in useless sorrow at the years of torment that must have crawled by for Pierson. 'When you come across him, tell him to come and see me. If he refuses to come, phone me and let me know where I can get hold of him. I'll talk to him.' A bit late in the day but it was all now that could be done.

Cottrell could have dropped his head into his hands and wept for the boy who had been his friend. 'I'll tell him,' he said. He remembered Arnold at school . . . in the army . . . pushing Emily Bond out of the path of the car . . . A man was all of a piece, he couldn't believe him a murderer, a poisoner, a killer by night. He got to his feet and at the same moment the phone rang on Turner's desk. As Cottrell let himself out he heard Turner say, 'You'd better put this call through to the annexe, Mrs Underwood's working over there this afternoon.'

Even though it was nearly half past five there was still a suggestion of lightness in the air as Cottrell turned his car into the road where the Underwoods lived. A freshness and vitality, a sense of the passing of winter, the first hint of approaching spring. A disturbing season for a man in middle age, Cottrell thought; the spring seemed to threaten him nowadays with a kind of painful beauty that held more melancholy than joy.

From the other end of the street a car came towards him. As it drew nearer he could see the face of a woman, pale and indistinct. She halted the car outside the house, opened the door and stepped out, stood looking at him as he sat behind the wheel. A rather tall woman with a mass of hair the colour of flax, piled up on top of her head; she was wearing an expensive-looking fur coat, almost the same shade as her hair.

He was aware of the ridiculous way his heart was thumping inside his chest, he drew a deep breath and turned the handle of the car door. The blonde goddess, he thought foolishly as he walked towards her, Mrs Neil Underwood, married less than a year. And this is how I meet her at last, with one hand thrust into my pocket, feeling for the warrant card.

'Good evening,' he said in a pleasant, formal tone. 'Detective-Sergeant Cottrell.' He held out his card in the fading light. 'Mrs Underwood?' She nodded, he could read no expression on her face, she appeared totally calm, at ease. 'I wonder if I might come inside and have a word with you and your husband. Your stepdaughter called in at the station at lunch-time—'

She gave a tiny sigh. 'Oh dear, I'm afraid she's rather been letting her imagination run riot. Yes, do come inside.' She glanced at the house, at the lights shining from between the curtains of a downstairs room. 'Jane is probably at home.' She turned her head and looked up the street.

'And I don't think my husband will be long.' A car turned into the end of the road. 'That may be him now.'

As Cottrell followed her up the path a thought suddenly strayed into his mind; why were we all so sure, Jane, Venn and myself—and presumably Owen Yorke as well—that Neil Underwood didn't call in to The Sycamores after all on the night of Mrs Yorke's death—before he came up this very path, opened this door and let himself into this house?

'There has been a certain difficulty with money in recent months.' The bank manager looked discreetly at his watch, Venn had caught him at the end of a busy day, just as he was about to leave for home. 'Underwood is not by nature very careful about his finances.' He spread his hands. 'And a new wife, one is tempted to be extravagant at such times. But I had a little chat with him.' He gave a faint prim smile. 'He's agreed to try and stick to a more realistic budget. We're tiding him over for the present. I understand there's a legacy coming to him from his sister's estate.' A suggestion of enquiry in his tone; he shot a glance at Venn's impassive face. Nothing unpleasant in the wind, I hope, the manager's eyes said, shouldn't care to see an old customer mixed up in police enquiries.

Venn's features remained stolid. 'If I could just see a few figures,' he said. 'And dates. Just to get an idea. I won't keep you long.'

The manager sighed, he stood up and crossed to a filing-cabinet. Not going to get much out of Venn, he thought, I wonder exactly what's going on.

'An absurd little quarrel,' Ruth said lightly. 'Quarrel is really much too strong a word for it. Anthea Gibbs works with me at British Foods. I know her quite well, she's the type that lets people walk over her and then suddenly bursts out into a show of resentment, then it's all forgotten and you hear nothing more about it.' She smiled. 'She's a spinster, lives at home, gets things out of proportion sometimes.'

'And you never heard anything more about the dress?' Cottrell asked casually, aware of the intense concentration with which Neil Underwood was following the conversation, although he said very little.

'Well, as a matter of fact,' Ruth said slowly. 'Anthea did stop me in the corridor at work the other day, she told me with a great deal of emphasis that she'd been in to Underwood's and made a fuss about the dress. She said she'd got her money back, all of it.' She raised her shoulders. 'But quite frankly, I wasn't altogether inclined to believe her. Zena had discussed it with me and she certainly had no intention of refunding the money.' She gestured with her hands. 'Anthea would like me to believe she'd come out top in that little encounter.'

'There is another little matter,' Cottrell said, striving for delicacy, wishing that Underwood would see fit to remove himself from the room for a brief interval but realizing that he had no intention of doing so. 'I understand that Miss Gibbs made some accusation—' he thought better of the word, deciding to substitute another—'some suggestion that your recent promotion—' he caught the way Underwood moved in his chair, the way Ruth's shoulders dropped as if she were consciously relaxing herself—'was not entirely made on merit.' He cleared his throat; Ruth tilted her head back and looked at him levelly. 'Some mention that Mr Turner might have used his influence.'

Neil frowned. 'Precisely what are you insinuating?' he asked coldly.

'I don't know that I'm insinuating anything. I'm merely trying to understand Miss Gibbs's state of mind.'

'I worked with Mr Turner in London, of course,' Ruth said easily. 'I believe he thought well of my work. But my appointment was made by the board in Milbourne, they've always expressed themselves as satisfied with the way I've done my job.'

'I should like to know where all this is leading,' Neil said with a sharp edge to his voice. 'Just because my daughter takes it into her head to go running to you with some hysterical tale—' he threw a look of displeasure at Jane who was sitting with her head lowered, staring down at her clasped hands. He turned an angry glance on Cottrell. 'I could do the same myself if I wanted to engage in nonsensical invention. Emily Bond could have poisoned Zena, then she could have poisoned herself.' He sat upright in his chair, he spoke with fierce contempt. 'That's another hare for you to go chasing after.'

'Mrs Bond certainly didn't leave any kind of suicide note,' Cottrell said calmly.

'Hardly likely she would have done,' Neil flung out. 'The woman could barely write her name. I don't suppose she wrote more than half a dozen letters in her whole life, she'd scarcely start on a literary career in her last moments.' He got to his feet and began to walk about the room. 'It's just as sensible a notion as anything you're implying. Whatever you are implying. God knows, it's all beyond me. But I'll thank you to leave my wife out of it.'

There was a ring at the front door and Jane jumped at once to her feet, her face bright with relief. 'That will be Kevin.' She ran out into the hall. They came into the room a few moments later, the boy with his arm round Jane's shoulders, protective, affectionate.

'This is my boy-friend,' Jane said with an air of loving pride. She smiled as she introduced him to Cottrell, then she sighed. 'He came with me to Emily's cottage.' Cottrell stood up and took a step towards the door. Time was getting on and it didn't look as if he was going to get much more out of Ruth Underwood. Or Neil.

'I'll be in touch again, later on, if anything further crops up,' he said.

'I've no doubt you will,' Neil said provocatively. 'But if you've anything more to say to my daughter, I'd just as soon it was said in front of me. Bear that in mind.'

Cottrell nodded, he turned in the doorway and said something by way of farewell. Kevin Lang was still standing with his arm round Jane, she was smiling up at him, neither of them seemed aware that there was anyone else in the room.

'Mrs Fleming hired a car for her week-end in Seahaven,' Venn said to Cottrell. They were back in his office again, sustaining themselves with coffee and sandwiches. 'She could easily have driven back to Milbourne from the Cliff View Hotel. She maintains, by the way, that she had no idea Yorke was going to be at the hotel for the week-end. She says they had dinner together and that was all.' He frowned. 'I don't altogether know what I make of her. Seems a gentle, charming woman, anxious to be co-operative, made herself out to be mystified at what I was doing there at all, asking questions.' He rubbed his chin. 'But I don't know, I rather got the impression there was a little more to her than appears on the surface, I imagine there's a backbone of steel inside that pretty figure.'

'Did you find out if she's seen anything of Pierson lately?' Cottrell asked. He hadn't forgotten Arnold's presence near Mrs Fleming's house on the evening of Emily Bond's accident. Arnold worked for Underwood's and Mrs Fleming kept a shop in the same line of business, it was quite conceivable that she had been into the factory, had met Arnold there.

'She made no secret of the fact that she knows him.' Venn reached for another sandwich. 'Or that he's interested in her. But she says he hasn't been near her lately, she hasn't heard anything from him for a week or two. She appeared rather concerned when I mentioned him, tried to prise out of me if he was in trouble but of course I didn't enlighten her.' He chewed thoughtfully at his sandwich.

'Is it likely,' he said suddenly, 'that Owen Yorke would do such a damn fool thing as murder his wife? It seems to me a totally fantastic idea. President of the Independents', owner of a thriving business, he's a shrewd, calculating man, he would never take such an insane risk, throw away everything he's always worked for.' He shook his head slowly. 'I just can't see it.'

He felt tired and vaguely angry, more than half inclined to drop the rest of the sandwiches into the waste-basket, go home and eat his hot supper like a sensible man, let the whole ridiculous boiling simmer itself back into oblivion. He heartily wished young Jane Underwood had stayed in Austria and let them all get some peace.

'Yorke could have banked on producing exactly the reaction he has produced—in you at least,' Cottrell said. 'A perfectly sound business reason for his trip to the coast, pure chance that Mrs Fleming decided she needs a little holiday at the same time. And if he makes up his mind to get married again in a year or so, what more natural? But I do ask myself why such a sensible man would go off and leave his sick wife by herself over the week-end.'

Venn drank his coffee. 'He wasn't to know she was as ill as all that, she was fond of crying wolf. And he expected her brother to look in on her, he knew she could get Ruth or Jane Underwood to stay the night if she felt the need. All seems perfectly reasonable to me.'

'That's my point,' Cottrell said with a sigh. 'He could have banked on that, that it would all seem perfectly reasonable to you. Or anyone else that chose to poke about and ask questions.' He scratched his cheek. 'Doesn't it strike you as odd that Neil Underwood didn't call round to see his sister that night? When he was supposed to be so fond of her, always so concerned about her?'

Venn gave a short laugh. 'Easy enough to understand. A man gets home rather late, a beautiful wife waiting for him. Many ways a beautiful wife can detain a man.' He sat up in his chair. 'Yes,' he said on a more lively note, 'many ways a beautiful woman can make sure a man doesn't go round to see his sister.' He frowned. 'I wonder.' He drank the last of his coffee, stood up, yawned, looked at his watch, rubbed a hand across his face, sighed deeply.

'Are we going to Southampton?' Cottrell asked. 'If we don't go right away there's no point in going at all.'

Oh, let the damn ship sail, Venn thought angrily, no one's going to thank me for prodding round, no one wants questions asked. No one except a silly young girl. And she'd probably thought better of it by this time, had probably turned her butterfly attention to other more absorbing matters such as a new dress, a new hairstyle. 'I'm worn out,' he said, 'it's been an irritating day.'

'Sarah Pierson,' Cottrell said. 'If someone comes round asking where Sarah Pierson's got to and it comes out that we just let it all—'

'Oh damn Sarah Pierson,' Venn said with force. 'Who's going to come round asking about her?' He made an irritated sound. 'I suppose there's no help for it, I suppose I'll never hear the end of it from you if I call the whole thing off.' He flung a savage look at the sergeant. 'Well, what are you sitting there for? If we're going, let's go.'

He glanced at the phone. 'I'd better ring my wife, let her know I won't be home till God knows when.' Accustomed to it all by now, Mrs Venn, used to putting plates of dinner in a slow oven, paid no attention nowadays to abrupt phone calls, had paid no attention for years, had made a life of her own, played bridge, organized charity concerts, drank quarts of morning coffee, gallons of afternoon tea, left him businesslike little notes propped up against the clock, arranged her days satisfactorily, or at least without complaint. It occurred to him sometimes that when the day finally came when he turned in his uniform, that he and his wife would find themselves grown into total strangers trying to think of something to say to each other, continuing to pencil little notes out of sheer force of habit. He wondered why any woman was fool enough to marry a policeman.

He laid his hand on the phone. 'We'd better call round and pick up Quigley. He can drive us down.'

Cottrell stood up. Quigley wasn't going to be very pleased to be called out—and doubtless his little bride wasn't going to be very pleased either. He let out a long breath. Quigley might as well get used to the idea now that a copper was never off duty.

'I'll give him a ring,' he said. 'I'll use the phone outside on the desk. Give him time to grab a bite to eat before we pick him up.'

It was raining as Cottrell halted the car outside Quigley's house. Venn glanced out with irritation at the closed front door; Quigley should have been ready and waiting by the gate.

'The trouble with Quigley,' he said, 'is that he's still playing houses with that wife of his.'

Cottrell smiled. 'Give them a year or two and it'll be Fathers and Mothers they'll be playing.'

Venn looked at his watch. 'Well, go in and tell him it's Cops and Robbers just now,' he said sourly. 'We can't sit out here all night.'

Cottrell walked rapidly up the path and pressed the bell. The door was flung open almost at once by Sharon Quigley, a slim young woman with elaborately-dressed yellow hair that looked as if it had been bleached. She didn't speak to Cottrell but jerked her head towards an inner room, indicating that he should come inside.

Quigley was standing by the table with his coat on, he was gobbling down sausage rolls, swallowing scalding coffee, bitterly resigned to the indigestion that would strike him within an hour.

'Get a move on,' Cottrell said. 'His lordship isn't in the best of tempers.' Not the only one, said Quigley's anxious eyes, shafting a glance in the direction of Sharon who was standing with her arms folded in a hostile manner.

'I suppose I've got to kick my heels here until bedtime.' She levelled an unloving look at her husband. 'I shall have to think about finding someone to take me out dancing in the evenings, I can see it's going to be necessary,' she said. The English shrew in embryo, Cottrell thought, aware once again of the undoubted advantages of single blessedness. Pretty enough now, sexy-looking in her way with her rather pouting mouth and slim figure, he saw her suddenly and clearly in fifteen years' time, a fully-developed nag, her face hardened, her curves grown angular, still keeping determinedly abreast of fashion—in the way that the provinces interpreted the modes of London and Paris.

'I'll take you out dancing the very next free evening I get,' Quigley said between mouthfuls, giving her a besotted and placating look, mercifully unaware of the picture of his beloved in the years to come which was forming itself in the sergeant's mind.

'No need actually to choke yourself,' Cottrell said. 'One minute more or less isn't going to make all that difference.' It will take him a long time to fall out of love, he thought, and longer still to admit it to himself—if he ever does get round to admitting it, probably won't, too painful, better all round if he keeps the blinkers on. He saw Quigley in five, ten years' time, shaking his head over the doings of his kids—for he would probably be allowed one child, or two at the most—he saw him in a further twenty years determinedly celebrating his silver wedding, boozily under the impression that what he had experienced deserved the name of happiness.

'You coppers haven't the faintest idea how to treat a wife,' Sharon said.

'I'm not married,' Cottrell said and actually saw a look of patronizing compassion flit across the face of that poor clot Quigley.

The constable banged down his cup and planted a brief but passionate kiss on the lips of his lady. 'I'll stop off somewhere and find you a nice little present,' he said, apparently harbouring the delusion that the inspector was going to sit calmly in the car while his constable pottered around some late-night shops. 'A box of chocolates, you'd like that.' Perhaps it might turn out to be some smashing big case they were going on, he thought hopefully, he might cover himself in glory, Sharon might be able to boast about him all over the neighbourhood.

She followed them to the door. 'If it's as good as the last present you brought me,' she said as they let themselves out, 'don't bother. I don't need any more ten-bob scarves.' Quigley turned with protest on his face but Cottrell put an impatient hand on his arm and pulled him out.

'Oh for heaven's sake,' he said, 'leave your love-life till you get back. Venn'll tear a strip off you if you keep him waiting any longer.'

'I took the scarf back to change it,' Sharon said with needling malice. 'Ten bob it cost, the girl told me.'

'But it was nearly four pounds I gave for that scarf,' Quigley said loudly as the door slammed shut. 'Pure silk it was.' Humiliatingly aware of the fact that he'd had to borrow from the sergeant to pay for it. 'Sometimes Sharon gets a bit browned off.' He sighed and shook his head. 'She says things just to annoy me.' A trace of smugness worked its way back into his tone. 'Can't blame her, I suppose, must be a bit dull without me.'

They reached the car and at once the mantle of the fawning husband fell from him and he was a young constable again, bound for heaven knew what, a stirring evening's work or hours of blank boredom.

'Hope I haven't kept you waiting, sir,' he said deferentially to Venn who had reached a point where he was almost beyond speech. 'But I thought I'd better have something to eat first, never know when we'll get the chance again.' He slid into the driving-seat and Cottrell got into the back, beside the inspector. As Quigley switched on the engine he glanced over his shoulder and saw that Venn was lying back with his eyes closed, like a man who had temporarily decided to take no part whatever in what was going on.

All three of them settled into silence as the car edged its way out of Milbourne, through a stretch of open country, running again into built-up areas, evening crowds, pink-shaded lamps shining out from uncurtained windows, neon strips glittering from the façades of hotels, rain dimpling the puddles, the harsh glare of street lights, the grind of traffic, surges of music, and again the dimly-lit rural roads, a man and a dog keeping close in by the hedge, a solitary cyclist caught in the headlights.

This is a right fool's errand, Venn thought. If Pierson is on the *Kyrenia* he'll have a very good reason for being there. He's a bachelor, no one to consider but himself, why shouldn't he blue his inheritance from his father if he wanted to, walk out of his job, put up his house to let? Plenty of other jobs when he got back, plenty of other houses.

And Sarah Pierson? Might have turned up at the hotel in Bournemouth by now, having stopped to visit a friend somewhere for a day or two. Or, for all they knew, she might simply be in Southampton now, seeing her brother off, with full knowledge and approval of his trip. He visualized the pair of them in a stateroom, Sarah arranging a bunch of flowers in a vase, telling her brother to be sure to send her postcards, looking round in astonishment at the three policemen barging in, the entry of the heavies.

And as to why she hadn't informed the Bournemouth hotel that she wouldn't be turning up for a day or two—she probably had informed them, by first-class mail, which probably meant the hotel would receive the letter a couple of weeks after she'd actually walked into the hotel lounge and signed the register. He had half a mind to stop the car, tell Quigley to turn round and drive them back to Milbourne.

Precisely what was he going to say to Sarah Pierson if she was there in the stateroom fussing over a vase of blooms? 'Do you know anything about a cat, Miss Pierson?' . . . 'A cat, Inspector?' Her eyes, baffled, bewildered . . .

three huge coppers pounding up a gangplank to enquire about a cat . . . He blinked away the distasteful image and conjured up instead his habitual blissful vision of retirement, a cottage by the sea, fuchsias blooming in the hedgerows.

CHAPTER XVIII

Everywhere there was bustle and noise, stewards, passengers, relatives, chattering or tearful, messengers carrying sheaves of blooms encased in Cellophane. The door of stateroom number twenty-four stood ajar. Venn led the way, somewhat refreshed after his doze in the car, his mind clear, geared for action but already more than three-quarters resigned to fruitlessness. Cottrell followed him, ready for anything, but anxious chiefly to be done with it, to get back to Milbourne and start the real work, closing the net round Owen Yorke. Constable Quigley brought up the rear, with only the haziest notion of what was going on but with one hand ready to flash out his notebook.

Venn raised his hand and rapped at the stateroom door, entering at once so that he was already over the threshold before a voice had time to bid them come in. Sarah Pierson was stooping over an open suitcase, she straightened herself and looked at Venn who closed his eyes for a fraction of an instant on the piercing thought : I knew it, all a complete waste of time, then she sent a glance round the elegant room, a calm, contained glance. She looked back at Venn with a faint smile. 'I thought you might come,' she said.

Venn said quietly, 'I'd like a word with your brother. Is he here?' He jerked his head in the direction of the stateroom next door.

'Arnold?' Sarah said on a note of surprise and in that instant Cottrell's brain sprang into motion, thought succeeded thought at immense speed, he saw the whole thing bright and crystal-clear. He turned to Quigley and said in a fierce whisper, 'Where did you buy that silk scarf? For Sharon?'

'At Underwood's,' Quigley said, totally baffled but automatically adopting the same veiled tone.

'I'm afraid Arnold isn't here,' Sarah said. 'Is he in some kind of trouble? I'll do anything I can to help.' She smiled. 'Provided of course it doesn't interfere with my sailing.' Before she had half finished her utterance Cottrell laid a hand on Venn's sleeve, his fingers dug significantly into his arm, he murmured, 'She did it, by herself.' Sarah didn't catch the words, she added, 'I hope it won't take long. As you can see—' she gestured at the cases ranged in the middle of the floor—'I'm rather busy.'

Venn kept his eyes fixed on her, doing his best in the light of Cottrell's murmur to take a massive mental leap, reassess the entire situation. Cottrell was no fool, he must have seen something not immediately apparent to the inspector's seeking brain.

Cottrell moved a step forward. In that first moment when she had glanced round the cabin he had caught the look of farewell in her eyes, the look of a woman who sees a great treasure slip from her grasp.

'An expensive trip,' he said. 'A long and very expensive trip. We know where you found the money for it, we've had a word with Miss Gibbs.' No way she could tell he was trimming the truth. At the mention of the name she inclined her head with a little motion that said as plainly as words, 'So! Anthea Gibbs! Of all people!' The faint smile returned to her lips.

'You sold merchandise at full price,' Cottrell said, aware of Venn listening intently, catching on, making a few deductions of his own. 'You put it through the books at very greatly reduced sale prices. And you pocketed the difference. Only occasionally at first. If you'd found you couldn't get away with it you'd have been able to explain it as a mistake. But when you did get away with it you stepped up the pace. Mrs Yorke took less and less interest in the shop and you grew more and more bold.'

'Don't tell me Arnold went through the books and spotted it,' Sarah said with scorn. 'He has about as much notion of accounts—'

'You got away with a very tidy sum over the years,' Cottrell continued with the same massive certainty.

'They owed it to me,' she said flatly. 'Every penny. I worked for a contemptible wage, they refused me a bonus, I simply took what was mine.'

'And when Zena Yorke took it into her head to deal with Miss Gibbs herself you knew the game was up, you went round to her house and poisoned her.' Sarah drew herself up very straight, she tilted her head back and gave the sergeant a long unwavering look. 'You had a little chat with her,' Cottrell said, visualizing the scene, 'you talked about the shop, about Miss Gibbs, you fussed over her health, you went down to the kitchen and made her a glass of hot milk, you mixed into it a lethal dose of sleeping-pills. Your stepfather's pills,' he added with sudden inspiration, 'the pills left over from his last illness. You added a good stiff dose of alcohol, just to make sure—' he couldn't be certain about the alcohol but Zena had had a reputation for tippling and it was a pretty safe guess. 'And then you watched her drink it.'

'No need for anyone else to put brandy into a glass of milk for Zena,' Sarah said with a trace of amusement. 'She was quite capable of seeing to that for herself.' She gave Cottrell an open smile. 'Very neat, Sergeant, a good imaginative exercise, but I think you may have some difficulty in proving it.'

'But you couldn't stay till she'd finished the milk,' Cottrell said. Outside the stateroom voices laughed and called, people went hurrying by, the cabin seemed a little island of calm in the noise and commotion. 'Perhaps you thought you heard a car, or you were afraid someone might come, or Zena may have made it plain you'd stayed long enough. At all events you didn't see her finish the milk. And she didn't actually finish it, she leaned down after you'd gone and put the glass under the bed, still half full. It stayed there until a week ago when it was knocked over and drunk by a stray cat.'

She raised her eyebrows in an expression of wry acceptance. 'One can't foresee everything,' she said lightly. 'I dare say you've found that out in your line of business.'

'And when you heard about the cat,' the inspector broke in, 'you got into your car and went round to pay a visit to Mrs Bond.' About time he stuck his oar in, he thought, though he couldn't deny Cottrell had done very well. He flicked a look at Quigley and was relieved to see the lad scribbling away in his notebook, getting it all down. 'You repeated the same performance there,' he said. 'She had a bad cold, you showed concern, mixed her a nice little drink of hot milk and brandy, laced with your father's pills.' Should he caution her now? No, better leave it a few minutes longer, give her time to talk, the formal caution had a way of clamping lips tight shut, he'd seen that often enough.

'There was an inquest on Emily Bond.' Sarah gave her attention now to the inspector. 'I read all about it in the paper. She mixed the drink herself, only her own finger-prints on the glass, it said so, everyone was satisfied.'

'Fresh evidence,' Venn said, just as capable as Cottrell of manipulating the facts. 'That's why we're here. We've had a little talk with one or two folk in the district. You were seen leaving Mrs Bond's cottage on the Friday evening.' He held his breath.

'I never went near her cottage on the Friday evening,' Sarah said triumphantly, 'it was the Thursday—' she clapped a hand to her mouth.

Venn released his breath. 'Quite so,' he said apologetically. 'It was the Thursday you went there. Stupid of me, I wasn't thinking for a moment. And of course we have your finger-prints on the glass underneath Zena Yorke's bed.'

No way she could know Jane Underwood had washed up the glass, had returned it to the kitchen. He saw her look down at her hands, the thought ran plainly across her face . . . Surely I wore gloves . . . is it possible I was fool enough to remove my gloves? 'You shouldn't have taken your gloves off,' he said softly.

She raised her eyes. 'I—' But she had already paused too long. And she could think of nothing to say.

She must say something actually and positively incriminating, Venn thought. In the warmth of the cabin he was beginning to sweat, he felt fatigue close in on him again. She still hadn't been charged; if she got hold of a first-class solicitor—they'd be able to pin the embezzlement on her no doubt, but the murders, she might still be able to wriggle free.

Something of the urgency of his thoughts communicated itself to Cottrell who didn't care for the silence that was developing. In silence a person had time to think, to marshal defences. Some indisputable fact, he thought rapidly, something we can get her to tell us that she couldn't possibly know if she was innocent, something that can be checked, produced for a jury, some hard, concrete, material piece of evidence. The cat, he thought, seizing on the notion, surely there must be something connected with the cat. His brain flung up a succession of images.

'What did you do with the cat?' he asked in a friendly, conversational tone, as if he were changing the subject, trying to introduce a less strained note. And to his immense relief, and a little to his surprise, she turned to him and spoke with a more relaxed air, as if pleased to be able to consider some unimportant matter. He was afraid to speak again in case she suddenly realized that what she said now would put her behind bars for all the years that anyone could see.

'I dumped it,' she said. And even Quigley couldn't altogether believe his ears as his pen moved across the page. 'There was the bag, a straw bag.' A look of distaste flickered over her face as she remembered having to pick up the stray—comatose or more probably dead—and stuff it into the carrier. But she might have dumped it anywhere, Cottrell thought with a thrust of dismay, how could they ever find one dead cat in the whole of Milbourne? And the bag was most likely already destroyed, all she had to do was take the bag home and burn it.

'You'd be surprised,' she said with a trace of a smile, 'how difficult it is to dump a dead cat.'

'So in the end,' Cottrell said, scarcely able to frame the words, 'you—'

'I dumped it in the churchyard, bag and all.' She smiled now openly, looking back on that ridiculous moment. 'It seemed a suitable place.' Cottrell closed his eyes and felt a shiver run through him.

Easy enough to find the churchyard, no need to push the matter any further now, don't let her know she's signed and sealed her sentence, only one or two churchyards at most between Mrs Bond's cottage and the Piersons' house. The bag would still be there—who would go poking through a winter churchyard scooping up an old shopping holdall with a dead cat inside—or if a zealous grave-digger had taken it into his head to do a bit of tidying-up, they could run the fellow to earth, he'd remember, his evidence would be as good as the actual objects.

He turned and gave Quigley a significant glance. The constable sighed and nodded, getting the message. Halt the car on the way back—or as soon as he'd dropped them off at the Milbourne station, run round every churchyard in the area. Guess whose job it will be to go stumping between the graves with a flashlight, looking for dead cats and mouldering bags, he thought bleakly. The words ran together in his mind and he smiled briefly to himself. She let the cat out of the bag there all right . . . he smiled again, pleased at his own wit.

'Zena Yorke wasn't a good woman,' Sarah said suddenly

as if all at once seized by the desire to talk.

'And Emily Bond,' Venn said with repugnance. 'Was she a bad woman too?' He recognized her need to release the torrents, he'd seen it all before, sometimes it was as much as they could do to stop the person talking in the end when it had all been said. Something of the impulse of the cornered stag, turning in the final moment and baring its throat to the hounds, a terrible death-wish—he never liked it. Useful as it was professionally, it never failed to turn his stomach. Human beings, after all, the lot of them, coppers and criminals, locked together for one inescapable period of time, the same flesh and bones, the same blood coursing through their veins. It always struck at him with violent nausea to see that doomed eager look, that compliant, relieved, almost joyful leap on to the waiting knives.

'I was sorry about Emily Bond,' Sarah said rapidly, defensively. 'But she was old, she had no job, she wasn't happy. And she'd have talked about the cat. To Owen Yorke, to Neil Underwood, to anyone she met. And she had nothing to live for.' Venn's silence weighed her words, judged them, dismissed them. Did you fancy you were God? he thought of saying, do you imagine you deal in life and death? But what was the use?

'How did you know?' she asked suddenly, frowning. 'About the cat?' She put up a hand to her cheek, she had after all disposed of Emily Bond most particularly in order that no one should ever know about the cat.

'From Jane Underwood,' Cottrell said. 'It wasn't Emily Bond who cleared up at The Sycamores.' Her eyes came wide open at that. 'It was Jane. Emily had been sacked.'

She gave a little nod of comprehension. 'So.' Her eyes met his, tired now, mildly amused, the moment of emotional catharsis past. 'One can't allow for everything.' And a kind of relief also in her look. She had believed that her judgment had betrayed her, had lost something of its sureness because of the unperceived erosion of age, she was pleased now to find it had after all been a chance combination of accidents that had put them on her track.

Cottrell saw with clarity that she would go towards her prison sentence with acceptance, without any further hope and so without disappointment, without fear or despair. He had a fleeting vision of the way she would settle down, adapting herself to the curious life, assuming after a time some little position of authority in the prison, in the library or one of the tailoring workshops.

'If you had known about Jane Underwood,' he said, 'if you had realized that she knew about the cat, what would you have done?'

She turned her head away, he guessed at her thoughts . . . Zena Yorke, that was justifiable: Emily Bond, that was a pity but it couldn't be helped . . . but Jane . . . Jane Underwood! A girl of seventeen!

She drew a long breath, seeing Jane smiling at her across the library counter, Jane with her long shining hair. Other images flicked across her brain, the ship sailing without her to exotic ports, the prison rearing its long grey walls . . . She looked back at Cottrell. 'But I didn't know, you see. As to what I would have done, we shall never know now, shall we? Either of us.'

Venn glanced at his watch. He felt so weary that the action seemed to take place on the fringes of a dream. Better leave the formal charge till they got back to Milbourne. 'Ring for the steward,' he said to Cottrell. 'Get her luggage taken off.'

'There's no need,' Sarah said with a detached air. She took one last look at the smart cases, labelled, luxurious, the elegant new clothes she had spread out on the bed, no longer anything to do with her, part of no life she was ever likely now to lead. She picked up her coat and handbag.

But Cottrell went over and pressed the bell, walked out and met the answering steward, spoke to him in a discreet voice. Not in the least surprised, the steward, not after twenty years at sea on passenger liners. The only thing that ever surprised him now was the fact that a ship ever left at the right time.

Sarah followed Venn from the stateroom, sandwiched between him and Quigley; there was a brief halt while Venn explained matters to the purser, then they moved off again, through the clusters and groups, past the farewells, the tears, the jokes, the men carrying baskets of fruit, armfuls of flowers, gaily-ribboned boxes of chocolates, they came out into the fresh salty air.

When they reached solid ground Sarah turned and looked up at the ship. 'Vigo . . . Lisbon . . . Madeira . . .' she said. 'A pity you couldn't have left it all a little later.' If they'd caught up with her in a week, a fortnight, if men had come aboard at some foreign port and taken her off, she wouldn't really have minded, she'd have had something out of it all. 'They owed it to me,' she said. 'I earned it all, every penny, over more than forty years.'

Cottrell touched her arm and they moved off again towards the car. 'By the way,' Venn roused himself to say when they were settled into the car, waiting while a man stowed the luggage into the boot. 'Where is your brother?' He'd forgotten all about Pierson after the first couple of minutes.

Sarah raised her shoulders with casual indifference. 'I haven't the faintest idea. He threw up his job and took himself off, said he was taking a holiday.'

'Did he know you were going off on this trip?'

She shook her head, smiling. 'No. He didn't tell me where he was going, I saw no need whatever to tell him where I was going.' She seemed with difficulty to restrain herself from laughing aloud.

'Does he know about the house? That it was put up to let?'

Again she shook her head. 'No. That'll be a little surprise

for him when he gets back.'

'He will be back, then?' Cottrell put in.

'I see no reason why not.'

Cottrell stepped out of the car and slipped some coins into the man's hand. It had stopped raining; a cold wind blew in from the sea. He took his seat again and Quigley set the car in motion.

Another hour or two and we'll be back in Milbourne, Venn thought. Another hour or two after that and he would be able to put the key in his own front door. He closed his eyes and saw before him an alluring image of his comfortable bed, warmth and darkness and the indescribable bliss of sleep.

Jane lay curled up under the blankets, dreaming sweetly and peacefully of Kevin Lang. In the room across the landing Ruth stretched out a hand to where Neil lay in rigid silence a good eighteen inches away. 'I won't be working for Maurice Turner any more,' she said. 'I've moved over to the annexe, it's all arranged.' Maurice had taken it very well in the end, she'd made him understand; as soon as was decently possible he was going to get himself moved back to London.

Her fingers met those of Neil, twined round his. One yearned for a straightforward uncomplicated approach to life but all one got—all anyone got—was an intricate weaving of personalities and events, there was nothing to be done after all but accept it, fit into the pattern as best one could, embrace what happiness offered without overmuch puzzling or analysis, without expecting the impossible from those inextricably linked to oneself. For some odd reason a face floated into her mind, baffling her for an instant before she could place it and then she gave a little smile of recognition in the darkness—the sergeant's face, that intent gaze he had levelled at her downstairs in the sitting-room. She closed her eyes and blinked away the image. 'I love you, Neil,' she said. 'You must believe that, you must trust me.'

'I will,' he said. 'I must.' He reached over and took her in his arms.

In his room at the Milbourne Hotel Owen Yorke turned back the covers and got into bed. He must be up early in the morning, the weather was at last turning mild, work could begin on the new site, he must meet the contractor and get things moving, it was going to be a very busy time. He felt overwhelmingly anxious for work, for absorbing activity, he wanted to rear up a busy superstructure on the huge vacuum that had so abruptly arisen in his life. The whole lower level of his being seemed to be caught up in the grip of a vast numbness as if one half of his life had been sheared away. One day would slowly succeed another and in the end some new existence would crystallize; how or what it would be he could in no way visualize but if he waited long enough, if he conscientiously performed the motions of routine living, some meaning would emerge again, some purpose would give sustenance to his remaining time.

For a moment he saw again the graceful slender figure of Linda Fleming coming towards him at the presidential ball. He shook his head slowly and with finality, dismissing the picture from his mind, unable now to credit that he had ever been able to dwell on it with such fevered longing.

He leaned over and switched off the bedside lamp, lay back against the pillows, closed his eyes and waited for oblivion.

In her sitting-room behind the shop Linda Fleming stood up and glanced round, seeing that everything was tidy for the night. She raised her hand in a yawn; it had been a long and tiring day and tomorrow promised to be equally busy. She moved about the room, plumping up the cushions, straightening books. Tomorrow she must phone Underwood's, must arrange for delivery of the surplus stock from the shop. She would speak to a secretary, no need actually to contact Owen Yorke. She had heard nothing of him for some time and she had a strong feeling now that she would hear nothing from him again. The notion presented itself to her without emotion or regret.

As she opened the door of the sitting-room the phone rang suddenly. She frowned as she went to answer it, wondering who it could be at this late hour.

'I hope I didn't disturb you.' Arnold Pierson's voice, firm and clear. 'But I had to speak to you.'

'Arnold!' she cried with surprise and pleasure. 'Where are you speaking from? I've been so worried about you. No one seemed to know where you were.' She wouldn't for the moment mention the visit from the inspector, the delicately probing questions.

'I'm in a hotel,' he said. 'A hundred miles away from Milbourne. I won't go into it all now, I'm coming back to Milbourne in the morning.' To call in at the factory, explain things to Owen Yorke, his unrest, his uncertainties, his need to get away and think. If Yorke wanted to hand him his job back, well and good; if not, there were other, possibly better jobs. Someone else he intended to see, to talk to, Maurice Turner, his old captain. He had come to the end of his walking away from life, he was prepared now at long last to stand and look at it, whatever face it offered to him.

'What I wanted to know,' he said, 'was if I might call in and see you.'

'Of course you may,' she said, smiling and flinging out a hand. 'I'll close the shop—or Iris can look after it. If you tell me what time you're arriving, I'll be down at the station to meet you.'

It was a clear fine night. The car ran between high steep

banks under skeleton trees, along gleaming roads, through towns and hamlets, silent suburbs and sleeping villages, past tall blocks of flats and deserted shopping-centres. Lovers going by with their arms round each other, an old woman scuttling along, youths laughing in jostling groups outside late-night cafés, a man walking with his head down, his collar pulled up round his ears, hands thrust into his pockets, huddling himself along towards comfort or despair.

One day perhaps I might have a home of my own to go to, Cottrell thought; it seemed an improbable notion. He stared out of the car window, looked up at the perpetually astonishing, fathomless depths of the dark blue sky speckled and frosted with stars.

Beside him Sarah Pierson stirred a little. He glanced at her, he had thought her asleep. She gave him a fragmentary smile.

'When I was a child . . .' she said, softly, slowly, remembering the ruby pendant that had turned to red glass on her outstretched palm. But the rest of her sentence died away, it seemed now scarcely worth finishing. She settled herself into her corner, her face relaxed, almost peaceful, she closed her eyes again.

Her words echoed in Cottrell's mind . . . When I was a child . . . He looked out at the narrow blinkered houses bedded down for the night, concealing behind their dark frontages joy or sorrow, love or hatred, dreaming contentment or intolerable pain. We were all children once, he thought, raising his eyes and seeing the beautiful winter sky, the glittering crescent of the moon and the seven perfect, improbable diamonds of the Plough.

The car swung out into a long straight road, went racing over the smooth surface. In the passenger seat Inspector Venn allowed himself to drift in and out of the fringes of slumber. Beside him, Quigley held the wheel in an easy grip, headed towards Milbourne and the police-station, the shadowy churchyards and the decaying cat, towards Sharon and his dried-up supper, his gold-watch years of service and his unborn children, summer holidays and Christmases, festivals and funerals, and his silver wedding coming rushing towards him in the light-punctured darkness from some incredible point of time almost twenty-five years away.